W9-BVJ-229

WITHDRAWN

HOPE BLOOMS

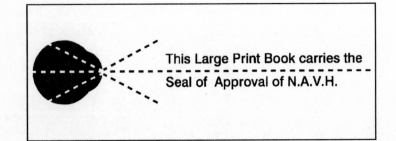

This Large Print Book carries the
Seal of Approval of N.A.V.H.

HOPE BLOOMS

JANICE KAY JOHNSON

THORNDIKE PRESS

A part of Gale, Cengage Learning

Detroit • New York • San Francisco • New Haven, Conn • Waterville, Maine • London

GALE
CENGAGE Learning®

Copyright © 2011 by Janice Kay Johnson.
Originally published as THE NEW MAN copyright © 2003 by Janice Kay Johnson.
Thorndike Press, a part of Gale, Cengage Learning.

ALL RIGHTS RESERVED
This is a work of fiction. Names, characters, places and incidents are either the product of the author's imagination or are used fictitiously, and any resemblance to actual persons, living or dead, business establishments, events or locales is entirely coincidental.
Thorndike Press® Large Print Clean Reads.
The text of this Large Print edition is unabridged.
Other aspects of the book may vary from the original edition.
Set in 16 pt. Plantin.

LIBRARY OF CONGRESS CATALOGING-IN-PUBLICATION DATA

Johnson, Janice (Janice Kay)
  [New man.]
  Hope blooms / by Janice Kay Johnson. — Large print ed.
    p. cm. — (Thorndike Press large print clean reads)
  "Originally published as The New Man in 2003 by Janice Kay Johnson."
  ISBN-13: 978-1-4104-4760-9 (hardcover)
  ISBN-10: 1-4104-4760-X (hardcover)
  1. Large type books. 2. Widows—Fiction. 3. Widowers—Fiction. I. Title.
PS3560.O37913N49 2012
813'.54—dc23   2012004391

Published in 2012 by arrangement with Harlequin Books S.A.

Printed in the United States of America
1 2 3 4 5 6 7 16 15 14 13 12

To my mother, with love

CHAPTER ONE

Helen Schaefer drove the shiny blue pickup truck across the bumpy field and steered down an aisle of gaily colored tents. Strings of flags hung overhead, unmoving in the still air.

Thank you, Logan, for loaning me the pickup! Helen thought. Without it, she would have had to make three or four trips from the house off Roosevelt in Seattle in her old Ford Escort to haul all the goods to set up a booth of Kathleen's Soaps at this craft fair on Queen Anne Hill.

She and her business partner, Kathleen, had a wish list, and a cargo van was at the top of it. They were now doing dozens of fairs and craft shows a year, as well as delivering soap to the stores that sold their brand year-round. Logan, Kathleen's husband, had been generous in letting them use his pickup, but he was a cabinetmaker and often needed it, too.

Helen glanced at the paper on the seat beside her. Number 143. Yes, there it was, printed boldly on a card pinned above the wide entrance of the booth. Number 144 next door was nearly set up, while 142 remained empty. Other exhibitors were working in tents across the aisle.

Helen rolled to a stop in front of her space and turned off the engine. *Made it!* she thought with relief. The pickup was big, and she was so terrified of hitting something, she was always glad to arrive safely.

"Hi," she called, getting out.

The woman rolling a rack of silk-screened dresses into place turned with a smile. "Helen! I saw that you two were going to be my neighbors."

"Let's hope this weekend will be better than last." Helen headed toward the back of the truck and lowered the tailgate.

Lucinda Blick scanned the sky. "No kidding! So far, so good."

"The weathermen claim it's going to be sunny and hot through Sunday."

With practiced ease, Helen slid a pile of folding tables out onto the tailgate, then grabbed the smallest one and carried it into the red-and-white-striped tent. This card table sat at the back and held the cash register and business cards. The others, longer and sturdier, along with half a dozen folding plywood pedestals built by Logan, would display the soaps, shampoos, shower gels and bath oils made by Kathleen.

Helen and Lucinda, an improbably blond amazon who had to be in her sixties, continued to chat as they spread tablecloths and stacked wire bins that held bars of soap in Helen's case and tie-dyed socks and scarves in a variety of hues and sizes in Lucinda's. Other exhibitors wandered by to say hello and commiserate about last week's downpour that had made a disaster of a craft fair in Pierce County.

Helen loved this sense of community she and Kathleen had found among other artists and craftspeople. There was gossip and jealousy, of course, but mostly they had met with generosity and friendship. All for one and one for all, as Kathleen had put it. On a good weekend, everyone profited. On a bad one, they all packed home the goods they had hoped to sell.

"Who's in the next booth?" Helen asked, nodding to the one east of hers.

"Shannon Palmer. Have you met her?" Lucinda shook out a tablecloth. "Stained glass?"

Helen pursed her lips. "I think so. Wasn't she in Anacortes last summer?"

"Probably." Lucinda paused, apparently scanning Commercial Street in Anacortes in her mind's eye. "Wait. Yes!" she exclaimed in triumph. "She was just past what's-his-name with the flying elephants!"

"Oh, right," Helen agreed. "He got mad when her rack collapsed."

"He gets mad if he thinks one of your tables pushes the tent wall two inches into his space. Try not to get stuck next to him if you can help it." Lucinda shook her head. "I never can remember his name," she muttered. Hands on her hips, she contemplated her progress. "I'm starving. Will you keep an eye on my stuff?"

"Of course."

"Can I bring you anything?"

"I packed a sandwich," Helen said, "but thanks."

The other woman picked up a bar of soap and sniffed. "Nice. What is it?"

"Tarragon and geranium."

"You guys use the most peculiar combinations." Lucinda grinned and headed down the grassy aisle. "See you," she called, with a flap of her hand.

Enjoying the warm early-summer evening, Helen continued arranging their wares. Baskets, spray-painted and decorated by her, brimmed with selections of soap and oils and gels. Bars of soap, clear and shimmering with color or milky and dark-flecked, went into labeled bins. Carefully constructed stacks of soap went on pedestals and tables, along with bottles of soapwort shampoo and herbal hair rinses and wintergreen-scented bath oil.

New this year were the pet shampoo, the herbal bath bags and the gritty bars of soap for gardeners or mechanics. Helen expected them all to be successful. She was amazed at Kathleen's creativity. Lucinda was right: the oddest combinations of herbs and essential oils sometimes produced heavenly scents.

She felt incredibly lucky to be Kathleen Carr's partner. It hardly seemed fair that she *should* be an equal partner, considering Kathleen made all the soap. Helen had been the one to suggest that her housemate turn a hobby into a business, however, and she had taken over the task of selling the wonderfully fragrant bars. The packaging was hers — she continually tinkered to improve it — and she was the one who girded herself and approached store owners and buyers to try to persuade them to carry Kathleen's Soaps.

She helped as much as she could when Kathleen went into a frenzy of soap making. Helen did clean-up and stirred and sometimes added pre-measured oils to the bubbling brew when Kathleen told her to. She unmolded bars that had cured with designs imprinted in them and carved into bars glycerine soaps that had been made into long loaves.

But in fact Helen was the business partner, Kathleen the creative one. Extraordinarily, in only their second year Kathleen's Soaps was taking off. Dozens of retailers, from small gift shops to health food stores and co-ops, carried their soap now. And in a good weekend at a big craft show like this one, they would sell most of the stock Helen had hauled down.

Both Helen and Kathleen still held other jobs, but now worked only part-time. Last summer, the craft fairs had involved a nightmarish juggling of schedules, with everyone else they knew called in to help when both had to be at their other, more mundane, jobs. Even Kathleen's teenage daughter, Emma, had manned booths alone.

On a day like this, with the sun shining and plenty of time to set up, Helen felt more relaxed and . . . happier than she had in years. Since before Ben's cancer was diagnosed.

How amazing! she thought, pausing for a

moment. She'd never expected to be happy again.

"Hello," a man said behind her.

Her reverie interrupted, Helen lifted a basket from the tailgate and turned with a pleasant, "Hi."

But the man standing there wasn't one of the craftspeople she knew. In fact, he didn't look like an artist at all, although she wasn't quite sure why. Thick, dark hair cut a bit too short, maybe, and graying at the temples in a way that appeared distinguished rather than scruffy.

He was *very* handsome, with sharply drawn cheekbones and a strong, cleft chin. Despite that hint of gray, she doubted the man was over forty. In jeans and a polo shirt, he was well-built, perhaps six feet tall, with dark blue eyes that appraised her over the bow that decorated the handle of the basket she clutched.

"Alec Fraser." He nodded at the basket. "Can I take that?"

"Oh . . . thank you." Helen held it out. "I'm Helen Schaefer. Just set it anywhere over there." She reached back to grab the next, more to give herself a moment to recover her composure than because she actually needed to keep working. She hadn't felt any romantic reaction at all in so long

13

she was surprised she recognized it. Maybe it wasn't specific to this man, she comforted herself; maybe the brief flutter in her chest was related to the giddy knowledge that she had learned to be happy again.

Waiting inside her tent, Alec Fraser turned slowly to look at the displays she was setting up. He sniffed. "Smells great."

Feeling steadier, she said, "Oh, thank you." She was so used to the fragrance that filled their house and cars and even clung to her clothes that she scarcely noticed it anymore. "When they're browsing, people pick up every soap and sniff it. I love watching their expressions. They'll go from delight to 'yuck' in a heartbeat."

He laughed, turning handsome into devilish and — oh, no! there she went again — sexy.

"You mean, the vanilla fan doesn't like the, uh, avocado-dill soap?" He took an experimental whiff of that one and looked torn.

Helen smiled at his expression. "Exactly. I've wondered whether you could generalize about character type from responses to particular scents, but I'm afraid results aren't consistent."

"What about you?" Alec Fraser asked, nodding toward one of the pyramids of

14

soap, his blue eyes not leaving her face. "What's your favorite?"

She knew she was blushing; her cheeks were warm. "Oh, I'm afraid I'm bland. I like gentle, homey scents. Vanilla and cinnamon and blueberry."

"And yet —" he lifted a hand as if he were going to touch her auburn hair, secured in a ponytail, before he seemed to think better of it and let his arm drop "— you look as if you could be fiery."

Fiery? The idea was laughable. A mouse like her!

"Appearances can be deceptive," she told him, her good mood crumbling at the edges. She made her voice deliberately polite. "Do you have a booth here?"

"No, I'm with the committee putting on the fair. I'm just making the rounds to welcome everyone. I think I forgot to say thanks for coming."

"You're very welcome." She made a business of returning to the truck, only to discover she'd grabbed the last basket or box within reach. Hoisting herself onto the tailgate wasn't the most dignified performance to put on in front of a man Emma would say was "hot — for an older guy."

"Let me," the older guy said, and swung himself up with a fraction of the effort it

15

would have taken her. He then very efficiently moved boxes and the few stray baskets to the tailgate, where she could reach them.

Since he seemed determined to help, Helen ferried goods into the tent as he pushed them within her reach. After a few minutes, he jumped down and helped her, the muscles in his arms flexing nicely as he lifted the heavier boxes.

"You don't have to . . . really I can . . ." she tried to say several times only to be silenced with a glance or a firm "I want to."

Finally Helen let him haul while she unpacked. When he set down a box and said, "Well, that's the last." She tilted her head to be sure she liked the display on the table in front of her, nodded in satisfaction, and turned to him.

"You were a huge help. Thank you. Do you unload for every exhibitor?"

"Ah . . . no. You just looked like you could use some volunteer labor."

In other words, she thought, *I looked helpless. Weak.*

He picked up a bar of soap and took the standard sniff. His expression suggested that he thought raspberry sorbet was interesting but not altogether pleasing. "Is there a Kathleen?"

"Kathleen?" She blinked, realizing she sounded like an idiot. "Oh. Yes. She's my partner. She creates, I market."

"A businesswoman."

"Well . . ." How silly to hesitate. "I suppose I am."

His perceptive gaze noted the uncertainty. "You sound doubtful."

"This is a relatively new venture for us. I'm not used to thinking of myself that way." She didn't like to admit to shaky self-esteem.

He lifted an eyebrow. "We're selective here in Queen Anne. You wouldn't have a booth if you didn't have a great product and you weren't persuasive."

"Kathleen makes the best soap in the world." On impulse, Helen said, "Take one. It's on us."

He gave her a rakish grin. "Bribing me?"

"No, no." She kept her expression innocent. "Just curious what scent appeals to *you.*"

Alec Fraser was already sampling bars, his reactions subtle but visible. "So, I'm a guinea pig."

"Something like that." Helen crossed her arms and watched him. "I need new subjects, you know."

"You're probably a graduate student

working on a dissertation," he muttered. After smelling the watermelon glycerin soap, he looked undecided, then set it down.

Rather than thanking her and grabbing the first bar, to her secret amusement, he took the choosing quite seriously. Maybe he didn't want to smell tropical when he emerged from his morning shower.

Blueberry? His face said maybe. Goat's milk and cucumber? No. Definitely. Vehemently, even. Lemon tart pleased him, but not enough.

The winner, when he turned from the wire bins, was aloe and eucalyptus.

"Good choice."

He smiled. "Most of these were making me hungry."

"You don't want to smell good enough to eat?" Helen couldn't believe she'd said that, especially in such a, well, *flirtatious* way.

His eyes glinted, and his voice seemed to deepen. "I could be persuaded."

Lucinda Blick caroled, "I'm back!" The smell of fish and chips arrived with her. "Thanks for watching . . . oh." She stopped in the entrance to the tent, immediately noticing Alec Fraser. "Hello."

He smiled easily and introduced himself. When Lucinda identified herself as the neighboring vendor, he commented on her

18

beautiful silk scarves with a charm that struck Helen as practiced, or perhaps only rehearsed.

Then he smiled impartially at both women and said, "I'd better get my welcome wagon moving, or I won't make it all the way around. It was good to meet both of you." His gaze lingered on Helen's face. "And thank you for this." He bounced the soap in his hand like a kid with a baseball.

"You're welcome."

A moment later, he was gone. Helen pretended she didn't mind.

"Enjoy your dinner?"

Lucinda peered out. "Lucky him, he's been waylaid by Nancy Pearce. She'll find something to complain about."

"Oh, maybe not."

"You're too charitable," her blond neighbor said dryly. "Our Nancy likes doing the fancy indoor shows. Outside, the ground is *always* bumpy, she never likes her assigned spot, and if it isn't raining it's too hot."

Helen couldn't help chuckling, even though she felt guilty. "She claimed to have twisted her ankle last week, there was such an awful hole right in the middle of her space."

"Conveniently covered by a table skirt, so nobody else could see it."

"Well . . . yes."

Still spying, Lucinda said, "She's laughing! Can you believe it?"

Yes, Helen thought but didn't say. She could.

"Actually —" Lucinda sounded thoughtful "— I'm not totally surprised. He did have a lovely smile. And shoulders." She craned her neck a little farther as Alec Fraser apparently crossed the aisle. "Oh, he's gorgeous." She sighed and turned. "Who could be immune?"

"Not me," Helen admitted. "Especially after he unloaded half my stuff for me."

"I wonder if he's married," Lucinda mused. She pinned her gaze on Helen. "Are *you* married?"

"No, and not looking," Helen said firmly. She lifted a wooden box from a cardboard carton and set it on the table, opening the lid to reveal the soaps packed inside.

Lucinda touched the silky smooth wood. "Those are beauties. I meant to tell you last week."

"Kathleen's husband is a cabinetmaker. This was his idea. Of course, he makes them."

"They'll sell like hotcakes." Lucinda wasn't to be diverted. "Why aren't you looking?"

20

None of your business, trembled on Helen's lips but remained unsaid. Lucinda had been too nice to her.

"I'm a widow." Her words were clipped. "I loved my husband deeply. His illness was . . . terrible. I won't face anything like that ever again."

"How long ago?"

"Nearly three years."

Voice gruff, the older woman said, "I hope you change your mind. My first husband was killed in Vietnam. I couldn't imagine going through that a second time. Now, I can't imagine not having had the past twenty years with Monty."

"I didn't know. . . ."

"That I was married? We have a deal. I do craft shows, he golfs." The grin was unexpected on her weathered face. "The rest of the time, we honeymoon."

Helen couldn't help laughing again. "Who knows? Maybe I'll be lucky enough to meet a Monty someday. But . . . not yet."

"Maybe you're readier than you know." Lucinda waggled her eyebrows as she gave a meaningful glance in Alec Fraser's direction. Then, before Helen could argue, she let out an exasperated sigh. "Listen to my tongue flap. I never give advice, don't believe in it. Anyway, I still have a ton to

21

do." She lifted a hand in farewell and rounded the tent walls into her own space.

A moment later, Helen heard the clank of a rack being assembled and the growl of her neighbor mumbling to herself.

Helen was left feeling unsettled, her sunny sense of contentment clouded by memories and by the unwelcome awareness of a man who wasn't Ben Schaefer.

No, she wasn't ready. She never would be. Once was enough. Ben couldn't be replaced.

She knew even as the thought formed that she was lying to herself. It wasn't that no one would ever measure up to her husband. He'd had his flaws. Just because he had died, she wasn't going to turn him into a fairy-tale prince. There probably *were* men out there with whom she could fall in love.

She just didn't want to.

Having Ben torn from her had hurt too bad. The agony of seeing him lose his hair and his robust color and his muscle tone and finally even the smile in his eyes and the strength in his voice had been unspeakable. Even worse was saying goodbye every day, with every touch and word, for a year and a half.

After the funeral, people had patted her hand and said kindly, "The worst is over. At least this wasn't a surprise. You've had time to grieve in advance, to say goodbye. I know you're grateful for the time you had with him this past year."

Was she? Helen didn't know. She had tried a thousand times to imagine how it would have been if Ben had been late for dinner one night, and a knock came on her door. She could see herself opening it, finding a police officer standing there with compassion written on his face. "I'm sorry," he'd say. "Your husband has been in a car accident. He's dead."

Perhaps they weren't that blunt. She didn't know. Maybe they told you to sit down first, or suggested you call a friend or relative to hold your hand. That wasn't the point.

The point was the suddenness. Ben — the Ben she had married and held the night before and laughed with that morning — would be gone. Poof. His life snuffed out in an instant rather than inch by excruciating inch.

She knew the shock would have been stunning, the grief overwhelming. Grief, she understood. But her last memory would have been of Ben's smile, the warmth of his lips when he kissed her goodbye, as he did every morning. As he *had* every morning, until he became too ill to go to work, and then too ill to get out of bed at all.

Instead she'd had to watch him suffer, his wry humor and intelligence and personality disintegrating until only pain and regret were left. She'd had to believe, for a long time, that each new treatment would work, that he could get better. And then she'd had to pretend that she believed, for his sake and for Ginny's.

And because she was too stubborn, too selfish, to let go. She had made him try hopeless treatments and suffer longer than he had to because she didn't want to lose him.

All she knew was, Ben's death had been so dreadful, she never, ever wanted to love someone else and lose him.

Which meant that these stirrings of romantic interest were unwelcome.

Studying the display with unseeing eyes, Helen decided that it was lucky Alec Fraser wasn't an executive at Nordstrom, where she worked, or a neighbor, or a friend of Logan's, or anyone else she would see on a regular basis. He was a stranger, presumably a resident of Queen Anne, a part of Seattle where she rarely went, and she would very likely never see him again.

Ignoring the sinking sensation she felt at her own pronouncement, she nodded. It was definitely best if she didn't meet Alec Fraser again.

Two hours later, Alec detoured down the first aisle again. Just to see if any of the missing exhibitors had arrived, he told himself.

As a result, he had to waste fifteen minutes explaining to an idiot he remembered from two years ago why he had been assigned a location that was apparently undesirable.

"We weren't aware that any aisle has consistently earned less revenue," he said patiently. "Some fair-goers start at one end, some at the other, some in the middle."

"I've been coming here for five years, and I have a piece in your juried show," the bearded artist said huffily. "I'd have thought I'd earned a spot that wasn't in Siberia."

Alec shrugged. "You made no specific request, and I'm not sure we could have honored it if you had. Our main goal is to have variety from booth to booth. That can get complicated."

"I may not be able to put Queen Anne on my schedule next year," the painter responded.

"That's certainly your privilege." Alec inclined his head. "We have more applicants than we do openings in any case."

If it were solely up to him, he wouldn't have invited this idiot, and not just on grounds of personality. Alec didn't like his grandiose oils, which lacked originality. But they sold well, another member of the screening committee had pointed out. Not everyone had taste, she'd said, adding, "I hope I didn't just deeply offend somebody here who loves his work."

Not a soul had admitted to being so shallow.

Ashamed of his pettiness, which he knew stemmed in part from irritation, Alec moved on.

A jeweler who was a newcomer to this show was laying out wonderful, imaginative pendants and earrings on black velvet trays. Witches and mermaids and fat old ladies in yellow danced from delicate wires. Niobium and glass and sequins had somehow been persuaded to come alive.

He complimented her on her work, fingering one pendant with a fiery-haired enchantress apparently dancing in a tutu. The mere hint was enough to make him glance down the aisle, toward Number 143.

Did Helen Schaefer, businesswoman, ever abandon conventions and let herself feel purely joyful?

Alec frowned. He'd barely met her! She

probably had a Mr. Schaefer at home. He was pretty sure she'd worn a wedding ring. He doubted that she'd meant to flirt, despite that remark about him smelling good enough to eat.

"I'll give you a discount." Smiling, the young, pierced and tattooed jeweler nodded at the pendant in his hand. "You look taken with it."

For a moment, he hesitated, tempted. But what would he do with the thing if . . . No. It wasn't the kind of gift you gave your dark-haired sister for her thirty-fifth birthday. And he wasn't even dating these days.

"Thanks, but I don't think so." With a pang of regret, he laid it back on its spot. "Your jewelry is going to sell like Beanie Babies did in their prime."

He ambled on, nodding and exchanging a few words with vendors he had already met, checking out a booth of framed black-and-white photos of staircases and shadows and faces turned away that stood out from the usual wildlife and scenery fare. The photographer was off somewhere, and Alec made a mental note to stop by the next morning.

He was only a few tents away, engaged in conversation with a candlemaker, when he saw Helen Schaefer come out of hers, close the flaps and climb into her pickup truck without a backward glance. In seconds, the truck maneuevered around the corner, turned into the school playground and was gone.

She'd be back, he reminded himself. Tomorrow he could stop by and say hello, thank her again for the soap. Maybe ask about her family, in the hope that she wore the wedding ring out of sentiment rather than as a label.

As he did. Alec glanced down at the plain gold band on his left hand. It was a part of him. He hadn't taken it off in sixteen years, not since the moment he said, "I do," and kissed his bride.

He wondered how Linda would feel about him taking it off now, maybe putting it in the carved wooden box from Poland she had given him for Christmas many years ago that sat on his dresser. Was she anywhere she *could* know?

What was wrong with him? This wasn't the time to let himself get sucked into an eddy of regret or sorrow. There was no reason to dredge up the past just because he'd met a woman who had fleetingly made him imagine falling in love again.

Still he walked faster and made his last few greetings briefer. It was nine o'clock on Thursday night. Yeah, okay, Devlin was fourteen and therefore old enough to be in charge, but chances were he'd have spent the evening closeted in his bedroom, the door firmly shut, music shaking the timbers of the house. If his sister was being abducted, he wouldn't hear her bloodcurdling screams.

Not that Lily wasn't responsible, too. She knew better than to answer the door without being sure she knew who was on the other side. But she was only eleven, teetering between childhood and adolescence, her body dragging her along despite any protests her father occasionally uttered to himself. Lately she'd taken to hunching her shoulders and wearing sacky sweatshirts stolen from her brother's closet. Alec guessed it was time to tackle buying her first bra. Not the kind of purchase he had ever envisioned having any part in.

There weren't any police cars parked in front of his house, and he didn't feel a bass thumping through his bones when he got out of his Mercedes in the garage. Alec frowned. Dev wouldn't have taken off and left his sister alone, would he?

But upstairs he found unusual harmony, the two slouched at opposite ends of the couch as they watched a movie that wasn't familiar to Alec. The coffee table was littered with plates, empty pop cans and candy wrappers.

"Hey, guys." He leaned against the back of the couch. "I'm home."

"We noticed," his son said disagreeably.

"Hi, Daddy." Lily didn't tear her eyes from the big-screen TV.

"What are you watching?"

His son gave him an impatient glance. "Don't worry. It's PG13. We rented it. Last night. Remember?"

Alec did vaguely recall paying for a couple of DVD rentals while they were grocery shopping. He'd glanced to see what they had chosen. He hadn't recognized either title, but neither had appeared inappropriately gory or racy for an eleven-year-old.

"Good enough," he said. "I take it you had dinner."

"We ordered pizza. There's some left in the fridge," Devlin added begrudgingly.

"Thanks." Obviously not needed in the family room, Alec retreated to the kitchen, where he put a couple of slices of pizza in the microwave. He shouldn't eat crap like that, but he didn't have the energy to hunt for something more nutritious.

While the microwave hummed, he checked his voice mail and glanced through the day's snail mail. Neither produced anything interesting or urgent to distract him from his restlessness.

Setup for the annual arts and craft fair, which he and Linda had been involved in starting, was going smoothly. The quality of work for sale was better than ever, publicity had gone like clockwork, and the weather was cooperating. His kids were getting along.

So what was wrong with him?

Of course he knew. Something about Helen Schaefer's big brown eyes had gotten to him. He'd loved her smile, her gurgle of a laugh, her puckered forehead when she concentrated on laying out the soap. His hand had itched to touch her hair, a shade of auburn that could be subtle or brash depending on the light.

He was pretty sure she'd worn no makeup to enhance her creamy skin. Her hair had been scraped back in a ponytail so tight it looked painful. Her gray T-shirt and faded blue jeans sure hadn't been worn to entice. But something about her had punched him in the gut.

He scowled at the microwave, which beeped obediently as if he'd terrified it into finishing. About time. He didn't like hanging around the kitchen.

Carrying a soda and his plate of pizza, he

stopped in his tracks. Funny, it hadn't occurred to him until this minute how uncomfortable he was out here.

He turned around and looked at the room
he and Linda had redone when the kids
were little. Small-paned windows framed a
view over roof-tops of Puget Sound. Mexi-
can tiles covered the floor, their warm rus-
set color echoed in the smaller hand-painted
tiles that formed the countertop and backs-
plash. They'd eaten most of their meals at
the antique table in the center of the room.
In those days, he had paid bills at the desk
in a nook that had once been the pantry. A
refinished armoire had held toys and games,
and the kids played on rag rugs Linda wove
on crude looms. She had always kept several
vases filled with flowers in here. They'd
loved the kitchen when they were done
remodeling it. They had lived in here.

The kids still ate at the kitchen table when
they gobbled breakfast or lunch, but when
the three of them sat down for a meal
together, it was in the dining room. He
didn't even remember what excuse he'd
used to initiate the change. They were all
probably too numb to notice.

He couldn't stand the kitchen because it
reminded him of his wife. As if he'd con-
jured her, he saw Linda turning from the

stove, smiling at him. She had been a tall woman, only a couple of inches shorter than Alec, her Swedish blond beauty flawed only by a nose she claimed was too big, and by a tendency to be clumsy. The first time they met, she fell into his arms. Literally. Given her size, he'd barely kept her from crashing to the ground.

"Linda," he whispered, and she faded, taking with her the clear memory of her face.

Turning abruptly, he fled the kitchen for his office. There, the photograph of his wife was too familiar to bring her to life.

Looking away from it, he had a flash of memory in which he saw another woman's face, another woman's smile.

And the glint of gold and diamonds on the other woman's left hand.

As he lifted the can of soda to take a swallow, he eyed his own wedding ring.

There was undoubtedly a Mr. Schaefer, but it wouldn't hurt to ask, would it? There was something about Helen, who confessed to loving scents redolent of kitchen and home, that had given him hope he might love again.

A smile tugged at the corner of his mouth, and he remembered the bar of soap still sitting on the seat in the car. He'd have to go

33

get it. Start his day tomorrow with the pungent scent of eucalyptus.

CHAPTER TWO

"Do you have the cash box?" eight-year-old Ginny asked, with the air of someone who constantly has to remind her mother how to drive, cook and tie her shoelaces.

"In my bag," Helen confirmed, hiding her smile. She locked her car, parked on the gravel shoulder of a side street. "Ready?"

"Of course," her daughter said with preternatural composure. A small, slight figure, she adjusted her day pack on her shoulder. "We'd better hurry."

It was true, Helen saw with a glance at her watch. A minor accident on Aurora had slowed traffic to a crawl.

She and Ginny walked as fast as they could the few blocks to the elementary school field where the arts and craft fair had sprouted like a peculiar mushroom after a rainfall. Even first thing on Friday morning, tantalizing aromas drifted from the food booths that had sprung up around the periphery. Colorful flags fluttered above the red-and-white-striped tents. The juried art show was in the gymnasium, and another displaying children's art filled the halls of the school. Banners were slung along chain-link fences.

Helen had just enough time to tie back the front flaps of her tent, say hi to her neighboring exhibitors and put money in the cash register before the first shoppers, a pair of women, wandered in.

"Ooh!" one exclaimed, lifting a bar of soap. "Smell this one."

Ginny gave her mother a satisfied smile.

Kathleen was working at her day job today, but, with her daughter Emma, could handle the booth tomorrow. Jo, who had roomed with the two women until she married Kathleen's brother, Ryan, had promised to spend a few hours here this afternoon to give Helen a break.

By ten-thirty in the morning, the grassy aisles between the rows of tents were clogged with mothers pushing strollers, fathers bouncing toddlers on their shoulders and grandmothers outfitted with walkers and flowery hats. Overshirts were vanishing into tote bags. Spaghetti straps and straw hats abounded. The day promised to be the hottest yet in July, which meant the mercury would top eighty. Given the humidity, Helen was glad to be in the shade most of the time.

Ginny's shyness vanished at craft fairs. She gravely answered questions, helped people find particular soaps and assured them that the shampoo was "the best."

"My hair is really clean." She tilted her head so these particular women could see. "Some of the stuff from stores makes me itch. Mom says my skin is sensitive."

One of the women hid her smile. "Really. Mine is, too. I'll give it a try."

"So's Buster's skin." Her companion reached for a bottle of the pet shampoo. "That dog is allergic to everything!"

Ginny smiled her approval. "Auntie Kathleen doesn't put anything artificial in her shampoos or soaps."

Both women laughed. Ginny looked puzzled. Her solemnity and adult speech came naturally to her. Somehow, after her father's death, she'd quit being a child. Once she came out of her shell, she was a miniature adult. She could never understand why real grown-ups found her amusing.

"What a doll!" The woman with the pet shampoo took bills from her wallet. "Is she yours?"

"Yes." Helen smiled as she made change.

"She's eight going on forty."

"And what a saleswoman."

Helen laughed, too, although she worried about Ginny. An eight-year-old should be playing with Barbies or jumping rope with friends, not going to work with her mom. But this was almost always Ginny's preference. She did have a few friends, which was an improvement over two years ago, but she would politely turn down offers to go to one of their houses if her mother was working a craft fair that day. Helen could never decide whether Ginny loved selling soap so much, or whether this was another manifestation of the way she'd clung after Ben died.

But if Helen argued, Ginny would gaze up at her with wounded eyes and say, "But aren't I a help? You always say I am."

What could Helen do but throw up her hands. "Of course you are! I just don't want you to feel you have to come."

"I *want* to."

So here Ginny was, a skinny little girl with mouse-brown hair in two braids, a thin face and great big eyes, patrolling their booth with the relaxed efficiency of an experienced saleswoman.

Jo showed up at noon on the nose. Despite the heat of the day, she managed to look cool in khaki shorts, sandals and a white tank top, her short dark hair shining and bouncy. In contrast, Helen kept pushing escaping strands off her sweaty forehead.

Jo made a face. "I had to park about a mile away. This place is jammed!"

"Business is really good." Helen turned from her and smiled at a customer who was holding one of Logan's beautifully made wooden boxes packed with Kathleen's products. "Oh, you'll enjoy this," she said, ringing up the purchase. "The mint is wonderful."

"Actually, I'm going to tuck it away for Christmas. This —" she set down a citrus bar on the card table "— is for me."

"Ah. Well, I'll put a card in your bag in case you decide you want more after you use this one up. A number of stores in Seattle stock our soaps." She glanced at the total. "That'll be $68.73."

"You do take checks?"

"You bet."

Another satisfied customer. In the lull that followed her departure, Jo asked, "Do you want to grab a lunch break?"

Helen looked around. "I'd better make it a quick one. I don't know if you can keep up by yourself."

"I'm Wonder Woman." Jo flexed what biceps she had. "Of course I can."

Helen laughed. "Well, Ginny is itching to see the children's art. I wish her teacher had known how to enter her students' work."

"Wouldn't she love that?" Jo flapped her hands. "Go, go! I'll be fine. Get something to eat while you're at it."

"Thank you." Helen was starting toward Ginny when the sight of a man entering the tent made her heart give a funny bump.

Alec Fraser, of course.

He looked directly at her, as if half a dozen other people didn't crowd the tent. "Hi."

"Hi." She returned his smile.

He sidestepped so a young woman pushing a stroller could maneuver between him and a pyramid of soap bars. "Looks like business is good."

"It's amazing. If it stays this busy all weekend, we'll sell everything."

"That's the way we want it." He paused. "Can I get you anything? I can bring you lunch, if you tell me what you like."

She almost asked if he was offering this service, too, to all exhibitors, but refrained. She wasn't sure she wanted to know.

"Oh, thank you, but I have help. In fact, I was just about to take my daughter to look at the children's art."

"Really?" His gaze followed hers to Ginny,

40

who was getting a bar of soap from a bin and handing it to an elderly woman with a cane. "I'm heading that way."

Helen's heart gave another lurch. She knew a lie when she heard one. He wanted to spend time with her. She didn't understand why. As handsome as he was, he must be fending off women with considerably more style — not to mention looks — than she had. But he stood there with his hands in the pockets of his chinos, smiling warmly at her and waiting as if in sublime confidence that she would say "How nice. I'd love your company."

Blinking, she realized she'd actually said it, not just thought it. Out of the corner of her eye, she saw Jo wink and give her a surreptitious thumbs-up. Helen blushed.

She raised her voice. "Um . . . Ginny? Jo's here. Let's go look at the art inside."

Ginny pointed the elderly woman toward Jo and joined her mother. "Okay. Can we get lunch after?"

"Of course." Helen put a hand on her shoulder and steered her out of the tent. "Ginny, meet Mr. Fraser. He's on the committee putting on this fair. Alec, this is my daughter, Ginny."

"Nice to meet you." He smiled at her. "I have a daughter not much older than you.

41

Lily is eleven."

"Lily is a nice name."

"Thank you."

Her brow furrowed. "Are you coming with us?"

"I thought I would, if you don't mind."

The furrows deepened.

Helen squeezed her shoulder meaningfully.

"Okay," Ginny mumbled.

"Thank you." Looking over the eight-year-old's head, Alec met Helen's gaze. His eyes were very blue.

She felt sure she was blushing again, and hoped he'd attribute it to the heat.

They made their way through the crowd toward the school, Ginny lingering at food booths to check out the choices, before they entered the cool building.

A few people wandered about, looking at the children's artwork and talking in low voices, but there were nowhere near as many as were outside. Helen had a long drink from the fountain beside the rest rooms. Ginny was already twenty feet ahead, crouching in that effortless way children have to examine a brightly colored picture that hung low on the wall.

Alec looked at Helen's mouth, then back to her eyes. "Feel better?"

"Lots," she admitted. "Crowds get to me."

"Claustrophobic?"

She wrinkled her nose. "Maybe a little. Oh, I don't know. I really enjoy selling, which is weird since I don't exactly have the right personality. I work at Nordstrom, too." *As if he cared,* she chided herself. But he looked as if he did, her shy glance told her. "But when it's crowded like today, I can hardly take a breath between helping people. Not," she added, "that I'm complaining."

"I didn't think you were." He stayed at her side as she slowed to look — oh, admit it! she was *pretending* to look — at some charcoal drawings.

When she glanced at him again, she saw that he was watching Ginny, who had her head tilted like a bird as she examined something with intense concentration.

"Is she artistic?"

"Yes, actually she is." Helen watched her daughter, too. "I think her drawing is really extraordinary for an eight-year-old. She takes it seriously. I wish . . ." She stopped.

"You wish?" Alec Fraser's focus, as intense as Ginny's, was on her face.

"Oh, just that I could give her more opportunities."

"I wonder," he said thoughtfully, "if expensive art classes really are valuable. Your

Ginny may learn more sketching on her own, without any pressure, than she would if she had lessons."

"I wish I could be sure."

Ginny had moved on to a case of what appeared to be ceramics. Her nose nearly touched the glass.

"What parent is ever sure?" Alec's tone was dry.

"You said you have an eleven-year-old?"

"And a fourteen-year-old son, who is in a sullen phase. I'm hoping Lily doesn't decide to imitate her brother." His smile wasn't quite a smile. "My wife died two years ago. It's been tough on the kids."

Helen's chest felt squeezed and her voice came out sounding thin, not her own. "And on you. I know, because I'm a widow."

They had both stopped walking and stood facing each other. His eyes narrowed. "When?"

"Three years ago."

"What happened?"

"Ben had a brain tumor. It was . . . drawn out." Those few words barely began to hint at the agony of the two years that followed his diagnosis. "Your wife?"

"Leukemia. She started feeling tired, went to the doctor, and six weeks later she was dead. That quick."

"You were very, very lucky then," Helen said simply.

His mouth twisted. "It . . . didn't feel that way. But I know you're right. If she couldn't get better . . ."

Her voice hardened. "Watching a person you love suffer is a living hell." *Especially when you knew you were the one responsible. The one who insisted one more treatment be tried, that — however irrationally — hope not be abandoned.*

"Yes." That was all he said; all he had to say.

Together they turned and started down the hall again, shoulder to shoulder.

"You haven't remarried?" he asked after a minute.

"No." She thought of all the things she could say, but chose not to. "You?"

"No. I've barely dated. Helping the kids through this has consumed me. Linda and I were involved in starting up this arts and craft fair and administering the scholarships we give with the proceeds, but I didn't even come last year. I just . . . couldn't."

Hearing the anguish in his voice, Helen asked, "Did Linda come the year before?"

Looking straight ahead, he talked. "Sick and shaking, she insisted. We both knew she was dying, but we pretended. She bought a

45

hat to cover her bald head. She wouldn't wear a wig." He was silent for a moment. "She died eight days later."

"I am so sorry," Helen whispered, reaching for his hand in an instinctive need to comfort.

He glanced down in surprise, then turned his hand in hers to return her grip. The smile he gave her — tried to give her — was flavored with grief and lacked the charm of his earlier ones. "Thanks."

They were gaining on Ginny, who was spending long minutes in deep concentration on works of art that interested her. Helen gave his hand a gentle squeeze before letting go. The last thing she needed was to have to explain to her daughter why she was being so friendly with a man she barely knew.

"Hey, kiddo. See anything you like?"

"This one." Ginny turned her head several ways, as if to change the perspective. "I wish I could draw like that."

In the colored pencil work that had attracted her attention, a boy and a puppy wrestled on a shaggy lawn, scattering fluffy dandelion heads. The detail, shading and lifelike quality were extraordinary. Especially for an artist who was only . . .

"Seventeen," Helen said. "The girl who

drew this has nine years on you, Ginny. Imagine what you can learn in nine years."

"I don't know if I can learn this much." Ginny sighed and said abruptly, "I'm hungry. Can we go eat?"

"Sure. Did you decide what you want?"

Ginny, of course, was a connoisseur of fair-type food. "I think I'll have a gyro today. A chicken one. With feta cheese."

"Sounds good." Helen bent to kiss the top of her head. "I'll have the same."

"It's one of my favorites," Alec said. "Do you ladies mind if I join you?"

Ginny eyed him but remembered her manners. "No, that's okay."

Alec did know how to talk to kids well enough to get her chatting about what things she especially liked that were for sale outside.

"There's pretty jewelry," she conceded, "but I don't like jewelry. I'm not old enough. I like some of the paintings, but some of them aren't very good. The stained glass right next to Mom's tent is especially beautiful. I wish I knew how to make stained glass."

"More expensive lessons," Alec murmured out of the corner of his mouth to Helen.

"Lots of the stuff looks kind of alike," Ginny continued. "If I had the money

47

today, I'd buy —" she frowned in thought "— one of those mosaic mirrors." Pushing out her lower lip, she gave a decisive nod. "Have you seen them? You can stand them on your chest of drawers, or hang them on the wall. The lady had one last week with green and blue tiles mixed with silvery ones. It was like a swimming pool. Somebody bought it, though."

As they emerged into sunlight to the noise of a band tuning guitars in the pavilion set up behind the gym, Alec asked, "Have you seen the porcelain dolls a couple of rows over?"

Ginny gave him a look that spoke louder than words. Why would she have any interest in a doll? But, very politely, she said, "No, I haven't."

Alec hid a grin.

"Does your Lily collect dolls?" Helen asked.

"Actually, she does. She doesn't play with them, but she still seems interested. I thought of picking one out for her birthday."

They joined the short line to order at the Greek gyro booth.

"When is her birthday?" Helen asked.

"August thirtieth."

The person ahead of her stepped away and Helen ordered for herself and Ginny.

"Lemonade?" she asked her daughter, then confirmed their order with the teenager inside the trailer, "Two lemonades."

Alec tried to persuade her to let him pay for all three lunches, but she was already handing over bills. Ginny gave him a suspicious look. Helen poked her under the guise of moving her to the next window where they waited for their gyros.

"He was just being nice," she whispered.

"*Why* is he being so nice?" Ginny asked, her voice carrying.

"Because he's a nice man!" Helen hissed, then gave him a bright smile when he joined them. "Your kids here?"

He shook his head. "Lily went swimming with friends, and Devlin . . . well, in theory he's mowing our lawn and several of the neighbors' lawns today. He's set himself up in business."

"Enterprising."

Alec grunted. "Honestly, I think he just wants to buy more CDs and go to more movies with his friends than I'm willing to pay for."

"But at least he's willing to work for them."

"True enough."

His frown hadn't entirely cleared, though, telling her that he worried about his son.

Helen thought perhaps she was lucky that Ginny had been so young when her father died. The two awful years of Ben's illness had changed Ginny forever, of course. Helen hadn't had the time and energy for her the way she once had, and, at four and five years old, Ginny just hadn't understood what was happening. She became scared of her daddy near the end, and Helen had feared that she would be haunted because she hadn't said a proper farewell. But so far Ginny hadn't asked questions and hadn't expressed regrets.

Maybe it was worse when children *did* understand what was happening. Alec's son would have been twelve, a transitional age anyway. Helen remembered how confused she'd been at twelve and thirteen. What if she'd had to say goodbye to her dying mother? She shuddered at the idea. Did the boy blame himself somehow, as kids so often did, for his mother's illness? Was he mad at her for leaving him? Did he fear that his father would die or desert him, too?

The dreadful thing was, Helen hadn't been able to afford counseling for Ginny, and she had no idea whether her own daughter harbored anger or fear or guilt. By the time Helen had crawled out of her own grief enough to worry about Ginny, she didn't want to talk about the past. She claimed she didn't remember her father that well. Maybe she didn't. She'd only been three when he was diagnosed, and by her fifth birthday he was a skeleton with tubes going into his veins and nose, the hiss of the respirator enough to drown out his feeble voice. By then all she knew was that her mother cried constantly and spent hours of the day at the scary man's side. He wasn't Daddy; couldn't even pretend to be.

Alec, Helen and Ginny found a shady spot at one end of a picnic table. Despite the crowds, Helen was grateful to sit for a few minutes, and she drained her lemonade even before she finished the gyro. They chatted about past craft fairs and how this one compared to others in the region.

When Ginny lost interest in the remnants of her gyro and asked if she could go closer to the band, Helen nodded. "But stay where I can see you." Once her daughter was out of earshot, Helen asked, "Have your kids been in counseling?"

"We've tried it." His expression still didn't clear. "Lily seems okay, although I keep wondering what'll happen when puberty hits. Dev just talks in monosyllables to the counselor. He tells me it's stupid. He doesn't want to talk about his mother." Alec sighed. "We're taking a break from it this summer." He looked at her. "How about you? Have you seen anyone, or taken Ginny?"

She shook her head. "My health insurance, such as it is, doesn't cover stuff like that. I just couldn't afford it. I'm not sure I'd have wanted to go anyway. I'm afraid I'd have felt a little like your son does."

She'd earned a shadow of a grin. "Don't like spilling your guts to a stranger, huh?"

"It's not at the top of my list," Helen confessed. Besides, there were things she didn't want to talk about, didn't want to tell anyone, not even a counselor. With a sigh of her own, she wadded up her wrappings. "I'd better get back. It must be wall-to-wall in our booth. Nice as it is to sit here . . ."

"Duty calls." He gathered his own garbage. "For me, too. I've enjoyed the break, though."

"So have I." More than she liked to admit even to herself. How long had it been since an attractive man had wanted to spend time with her? Maybe she'd never see him again, but she appreciated the boost to her ego.

She swung her legs over the bench and stood. "Maybe I'll see you another day."

"I hope so." His gaze held hers over the

table. "Would you have dinner with me some night, Helen?"

She shouldn't have been so shocked, but . . . oh, dear. It *had* been a long time.

"Dinner?" she squeaked, then felt gauche.

He raised a brow. "Maybe a movie."

Dinner? A date. That's what he meant. Did she *want* to go out with a man? Helen wondered.

"Tough decision?" Alec's tone was light, but he couldn't be enjoying having a woman he'd asked out stare as if he'd suggested she start singing at the top of her lungs.

"No, I . . . I'm so sorry! You just took me by surprise. I haven't . . ." She flushed. "It's been a long time, you see, and . . ." Better and better. "Yes," she finished in a rush. "I think I'd like that."

He didn't puff up with indignation and say, You *think*? Instead, he nodded in an undemanding way. "I picked up one of your business cards. Is that your home phone number?"

"No, but I check that voice mail daily. Or, if you have a pen, I can give you my home number."

She scribbled it on one of her business cards and watched as he tucked it carefully into his wallet. Then he smiled at her. "I'll call," he promised, and left.

53

She looked after him until he disappeared into the crowd, then went to fetch Ginny.

"Where's that man?" her daughter asked, peering around as if he was going to leap out and say, *Boo!*

"He's busy making sure the fair runs smoothly." Helen steered Ginny ahead of her. "I hope Jo managed without us."

The going was slow, with the crowd shuffling along, exclaiming over new delights and abruptly veering into booths, bumping into each other, apologizing, maneuvering strollers. Her friend looked like a drowning woman when Helen and Ginny squeezed into their tent.

"Did you have a good break?" Jo asked in a low voice as she rang up a sale.

"Wonderful. Thank you!"

"Excuse me," a woman said right behind her.

Helen turned with a practiced smile. "May I help you?"

As the afternoon wore on, she didn't have much time to think about Alec Fraser or the fact that he'd asked for her phone number, but it was always at the back of her mind. In brief pauses, she would picture his smile, or his face as he told her his wife had died.

We both knew she was dying, but we pretended.

Oh, how well she knew what that was like! The smiles, the way you avoided meeting each other's eyes, the chatter to cover the sick dread, the wondering. *Had* Ben really thought he could get better, or had he known, too, that he was dying? Or she would ask herself, *Am I being a coward in pretending to believe? In* insisting *on believing?* Would it have been better for Ben to talk about his impending death than to keep up the front? Would she have been able to work through her own grief sooner if they had talked more frankly early on, when he still could? She didn't know.

She hadn't joined a support group for widows, but she'd thought about it. There were so many things she'd never say even to Jo and Kathleen because they hadn't gone through that kind of loss. And her friends from before had disappeared from her life after the funeral and brief sympathy calls. Death made them uncomfortable. Or perhaps her ties with them had already eroded during the two years she'd been so occupied nursing Ben. She wasn't sure. All she did know was that within a week or two of the funeral, the doorbell and phone had quit ringing. Maybe she'd ask Alec if it was the same for him.

It wasn't very romantic of her to be excited about going on a date because he was a widower and they could talk about illness and death and grieving. But still . . . She knew he, too, had felt the connection. He might have regrets and guilt of his own he'd want to talk about.

Yes, she decided with new confidence, dating would be good for her. It didn't have to be the first step to love, commitment and loss.

CHAPTER THREE

"You have a date?" Kathleen exclaimed in delight. "Good for you!"

"With a hottie," Jo told her, grinning at Helen.

The three women sat at the kitchen table in the big brick house in Seattle's Ravenna district where Helen and Kathleen still lived. Of the original three housemates, only Jo, now married, had moved out. She had just finished getting her master's degree in librarianship at the University of Washington and had accepted a job with the Seattle Public Library.

Feeling pleasantly reminiscent as she sipped her orange spice tea, Helen thought of the huge changes in all their lives since that September when they came together under one roof. Three women used to living independent lives, they had rubbed along together with some difficulty at first. Jo had been sure she didn't like children, and was appalled to discover that Helen had a six-year-old. Kathleen, the perfectionist — or the "princess," as Jo had dubbed her — had made all her housemates uncomfortable with her insistence on a perfectly ordered and spotless home. Once upon a time, she'd alphabetized the soup cans! Blond and elegantly beautiful, she had seemed out of place without a housekeeper and gardener.

And Helen . . . Well, she'd lived in such a daze of grief and forgetfulness, she could have stepped on their toes until they were black and blue, and never noticed. Neither she nor Ginny had been good company for a long time.

Helen was intensely grateful that Kathleen had let her move in, and that both women had been kind but not pitying. They had let her mourn, but also dragged her along with them on their journey of self-discovery as they began new lives.

They had both found love along the way, Jo with Kathleen's brother Ryan and Kathleen with Logan, the cabinetmaker who had built the gorgeous cabinets that gave this old high-ceilinged kitchen such warmth. Unfortunately, that meant the other two women thought Helen should also be seeking true love. She could see the gleam in their eyes now.

"I thought," she said sedately, "Alec and I could talk about what it's like losing someone you love. And helping kids through it, and so on."

Jo's merriment faded.

Kathleen cleared her throat. "I suppose that *is* part of getting to know each other, but . . . as conversation goes, it sounds pretty grim. Surely the fact that he's a widower isn't the only reason you're having dinner with him!"

Helen laughed at their shock. "No, of course not! Having that in common is an attraction for me, though. Honestly, I'm not very interested in dating. But I liked him, and he sounds like he's going through a tough time with his son, and . . . I did think it might be good for me to be able to talk to someone who'd understand."

They knew how she felt, and only shook their heads.

"Someday . . ." Kathleen muttered.

Jo set down her cup. "When I was falling in love with Ryan, and was all confused, I asked you one night whether it was worth it. Do you remember? You'd been crying, and I wanted to know whether you would have taken it all back if you could. If you'd foreseen how Ben would die, would you have said no when he asked you to marry him?"

Helen was already shaking her head.

"That night, you told me it *was* all worth it. So . . . how can you refuse to think about being happy again?"

"You don't believe in once-in-a-lifetime love?" Helen asked them. "Would I face the agony of losing him again, if I could have him back for a while?" She tried to smile. "Yes. Of course I would. Do I want to face it so I can have a companion in middle age?" She shook her head. "I'd say I'm okay on my own, except that, thanks to you two, I'm not exactly on my own."

"And isn't that nice?" Jo said with satisfaction.

Kathleen said nothing, only watched Helen. She knew what was coming.

"I've been looking for a small place for Ginny and me," Helen told them. "Maybe just an apartment."

Jo's mug clunked to the table. *"What?"*

"I think it's time Kathleen and Logan and Emma had the house to themselves. They're a family. They've been very nice about letting Ginny and me stay, but none of us intended it to be forever."

"Logan and I did." Kathleen's jaw squared. "You *are* part of the family."

"He may not feel the same."

"He does. When he asked me to marry him, we talked about my moving in with him and renting this house to you. But . . . all of us together makes this home. He wanted that, too."

"It's not as though I won't be over here half the time anyway," Helen said mildly. Her sidelong glance was aimed at Jo. "Like someone we know and love."

Jo tilted her head. In the year since her wedding, she had made a habit of dropping by and even studying here on evenings when Ryan's kids had friends over.

Looking straight at Kathleen, Helen continued, "When you told me you were getting married, I was terrified at the idea of having to find a place for Ginny and myself. I'd come to *depend* on the two of you. I wasn't ready then." She paused a beat. "Now I am."

"I don't like it." Kathleen scowled at her. "I'd miss you!"

"No, you won't. Like I said, I'll be over here all the time anyway. What with the business, I'll have to be, won't I?"

"Then why move?" Kathleen asked, clearly believing the question was unanswerable.

"I suppose . . ." Helen groped to explain. "I suppose because I need to know I *can* take care of myself and Ginny. Because you and Logan ought to be able to have privacy when you want it. And because, honestly, I feel a little like a houseguest, now that you don't need my rent money."

Kathleen let out an impatient huff. "This argument isn't over."

"I know it isn't."

"Did you find some place?" Jo interjected.

"Not yet," she admitted. So far, everything she'd looked at had either been beyond her means or so crummy she hadn't been able to contemplate moving in. She didn't want to live in a place where she'd lie awake at night expecting a break-in, or have to battle cockroaches, or walk from her parking spot to her front door past half a dozen men who seemed to spend their days leaning on their cars eyeing passing women. But sooner or later she'd get lucky. She wanted Kathleen to know that she was serious.

"Business has really taken off, hasn't it?" Jo sipped tea.

"Um." Kathleen still watched Helen with a brooding expression, but she went on, "I'm having trouble keeping up with demand."

"Are you thinking of quitting your job at the chiropractor's?"

"Actually, yes."

This was news to Helen. "Really?"

"You know how much I hate it. Logan has been getting really annoyed at me. He makes good money and likes what he's doing. He wants me to ditch the job and concentrate on making soap, which I enjoy. If I don't pay half the bills for a while, so what?"

"I think we're at the point where you need to do that anyway," Helen said thoughtfully. "I've been worrying about it. If we add even a couple more outlets where the soap sells well, we won't be able to keep up *and* continue the craft fairs."

"*I* was thinking," Kathleen said, "that if I quit my job, you should, too. We need to expand to other markets. Portland is a natural. Spokane, Boise, even the smaller towns like Walla Walla, Yakima and Bend. As things stand, you can't travel. I can't make soap and try to sell it, too."

Helen didn't like to be suspicious, but . . . "Is this an excuse to keep me from moving out?"

Kathleen tried to look wounded but wasn't a good enough actress. "What do the two things have to do with each other?"

"You know I can't afford to pay for my own place on what I make from Kathleen's Soaps."

Kathleen leaned forward. "But you can if we expand. And we can't expand if we don't both commit ourselves full-time."

Catch-22. Helen, too, had dreams of Kathleen's Soaps expanding throughout the Pacific Northwest and even farther. The idea of making Kathleen's hobby a business had been hers in the first place! They needed a better website, to run ads in national magazines and perhaps create a catalog. Kathleen had been making some soaps lately with patterns and even pictures embedded in them. Now was the time to be aggressive.

But Helen also knew the time had come for her and Ginny to have their own home.

"I'll think about it."

Kathleen nodded.

"Logan's boxes seemed to sell well," Jo remarked.

"We sold out this weekend," Helen said. "In fact, I've been thinking that we should be selling soap dishes, too. I saw a wire one with curlicue feet in an antique store the other day. It had been painted white and was really distinctive. I wonder if we could find someone to copy it?"

Kathleen got up to pour herself another cup of tea. "Do you think we could make them ourselves?"

Helen mulled it over and finally nodded. "I'll try."

They continued chatting about upcoming craft shows, a change in packaging, and Jo's plans for the branch library she'd be taking over in a few weeks.

Eventually, inevitably, Kathleen asked again about Alec. "What's he do for a living?"

"I have no idea," Helen admitted. "I didn't think to ask."

"He must live on Queen Anne or he wouldn't be involved in something like the fair."

"I guess so."

Her friends gazed at her in exasperation. "Don't you know anything about the man?" Jo asked.

"He has an eleven-year-old daughter and a fourteen-year-old son. His wife died of leukemia. He said she felt tired one day, and six weeks later she was dead."

"Okay, okay. It's a start." Jo studied Helen critically. "What are you planning to wear?"

"Nothing fancy. It's supposed to be casual."

"You won't wear your hair up." Kathleen sounded as if she were announcing an undisputed fact.

"Why not?" Feeling defensive, Helen

touched her ponytail. "It doesn't look that bad."

"You have glorious hair," Kathleen said. "The way you yank it back looks . . ."

"Repressed," Jo finished for her.

As sulky as a teenager, Helen just about snapped, *If I want to be repressed, I will be!*

Instead she muttered, "I don't like hair in my face."

The way Kathleen scrutinized her, Helen felt like a mannequin in a store window waiting to be posed and dressed.

"If you won't wear it loose, we can do something to it that's still softer."

"Maybe." And they wondered why she was ready to move out! Deliberately she changed the subject. "You're sure you don't mind watching Ginny?"

"She lives here. It hardly qualifies as babysitting."

"No, but it does mean you and Logan can't go out."

"Unless Emma is home." But they both knew that wasn't likely. Emma, between her junior and senior years in high school and nearly eighteen, was dating a freshman at Seattle U. She was almost never home on Friday or Saturday nights anymore. "Besides —" Kathleen had a gleam in her eye "— I have every intention of being here when he

66

picks you up."

"So you can quiz him about his intentions?" Helen asked with deceptive tranquility.

Kathleen flashed a grin. "So I can satisfy my curiosity."

Helen had to laugh. So, okay, they were busybodies. They irritated her sometimes. But the two women were her closest friends. No, they were family. Way more important to her than Alec Fraser ever could be.

Alec parked his Mercedes on the street a few driveways down from Helen's place. It was a nice brick house dating from the 1920s, if he was any judge. Big leafy maples and sycamores overhung the street, buckling sidewalks, while flowers tumbled over retaining walls. The flower bed above Helen's wall looked new, the earth dark and the rosebushes spindly.

At six in the evening, the sun still baked the unshaded pavement and the small, dry lawns. At midsummer in Seattle, night didn't fall until nearly ten o'clock.

It was irrational but Alec felt better leaving the kids alone with the sun still shining. As if teenage boys only did stupid things in the dark.

He rang the doorbell. A woman he didn't

know answered. Beautiful and assured, she had honey-blond hair worn in a loose French braid.

"Hi. You must be Alec Fraser?"

"That's right. I'm here for Helen."

"I'm Kathleen Carr." Smiling, she held out her hand. "Her housemate."

He shook. "*The* Kathleen."

"Of Kathleen's Soaps, you mean? The same." She stepped back. "Come on in."

As he followed her, a slender teenage girl with an unmistakable resemblance to Kathleen came down the stairs. Her ponytailed hair was a shade lighter, and she had the impossibly delicate build of a ballerina, but her inquisitive blue eyes could have been her mother's.

"Oh, Emma. This is Alec Fraser. Alec, my daughter."

"Nice to meet you."

He could see through an archway into the living room, where a dark-haired young man slouched on the sofa with a laptop computer open on his knees. From the other direction came music; Alec recognized the voice of a singer who recorded CDs for children. A man called for Kathleen from some other part of the house.

Who *were* all these people?

"In a minute, Logan," Kathleen called

back. "Helen, Alec's here!"

He was reassured to hear her voice float from above, "I'll be right down."

A moment later, she appeared, coming down the stairs as lightly as the teenage girl had. Something squeezed in his chest at the sight of her in linen slacks and a rust-colored, sleeveless top that he thought must be made of silk. Her hair was drawn up in two tortoiseshell clips and then flowed, like rivers of dark molten lava, over her shoulders. She was . . . not beautiful, but something better. Not so artificial. Her eyes were a warm, smiling brown, her skin the creamy pale of a true redhead — although her cheeks and shoulders were rather pink — but she lacked the freckles. Instead, her nose was peeling.

"You got sunburned." *Way to go,* he congratulated himself. Surely he could have thought of a greeting that was slightly more suave. Out of the corner of his eye, he could see Kathleen and Emma agreed.

But Helen only smiled. "Yup. I *always* get sunburned. I'm incapable of tanning. If I don't put enough suntan lotion on, I burn, over and over, all summer long."

"It's not good for you." Oh, better and better.

"I know." She wrinkled her nose, then

winced. "Truly. I try."

"Sorry. I bug my kids to wear suntan lotion, and . . ." He smiled crookedly. "It's that parent thing. There's an administrative assistant at work always having to brush her bangs away from her eyes. I want to clip them back with barrettes in the worst way."

Helen laughed. "Oh, dear. I know the feeling." She started down the hall. "Let me go say good-night to Ginny."

Ah. Well, at least there wasn't yet another child in the house.

Alec turned to Kathleen. "I'm going to have to buy more of your soap. My son stole the bar Helen gave me. He's at that stage where he showers three times a day. You wouldn't know it from his hair or choice of clothes, but he really likes to be clean."

"Helen said he's fourteen?"

Alec nodded.

"Trouble with acne?"

He pictured his son's face. "Uh . . . some."

"I have just the thing for him." She'd gone into saleswoman mode. "We're not selling it yet because I haven't made enough, but this soap has eucalyptus, aloe and peppermint. It's really good for oily complexions."

"I'd love to buy a bar."

"Don't be silly. I'll get you one." She flapped a hand and headed into what he presumed was the kitchen.

Emma looked at him. "It really works."

Her delicate porcelain skin didn't look as if anything as unsightly as a pimple would dare mar it.

"Devlin will appreciate it." Alec had pretended to be irritated but had actually been amused when his soap disappeared and he found it in the kids' bathroom. So, his son had taken to browsing Dad's bathroom for personal hygiene products.

"The soap in our shower smells girly," Dev had groused, when Alec mentioned the case of the missing bar.

"That's good stuff, isn't it?" Alec had asked, and gotten a surprisingly enthusiastic response.

"Yeah, it lathered great and it smells really cool."

Maybe, Alec thought, he should suggest the boy star in a TV ad for Kathleen's soaps. He could see it, Devlin scrubbing his underarms and grinning disarmingly at the camera.

"Smells cool and lathers great. Any guy my age would love it."

Right. Nice picture, except Dev didn't smile very often these days. He'd apparently forgotten how.

The two women returned from the

kitchen, Kathleen with a grocery sack in her hand.

"Here's several bars." She handed it to him. "Compliments of the house."

"Hey, thanks."

"The green one is for your son."

"He'll appreciate it."

"Shall we go?" Helen asked.

The heat hit them the minute they stepped outside.

"Doesn't that feel good?" She raised her face to the sun. "I swear, I'm cold most of the time."

"Maybe you should move to Arizona."

"I've thought about it, but then I'd be freezing all the time because everyone cranks the air-conditioning up so high. Besides . . . I like a green landscape. So let me enjoy this rare summer heat wave."

"And get sunburned," he added.

Reaching the sidewalk ahead of him, she looked back with a guilty face. "I can't resist basking just a little. Why can't I have a skin that likes to brown?"

"Because —" he flipped one of her curls "— it wouldn't go with this."

"You know, there are no redheads in my family?" She sounded outraged at the genetic betrayal. "Not one. Dad still teases my mother about having a changeling. But, she insists his great-grandmother looks like her hair is auburn, too, in a couple of old pictures."

"Which are black-and-white." Alec stopped beside his car, unlocked the passenger door and opened it for her.

"Mm-hmm. And if my great-great was a redhead, she didn't have freckles either."

Helen was buckled up by the time he got in.

"This is nice." Helen stroked the leather seat. "I've never been in a Mercedes before."

"I felt like I'd arrived when I could afford one." She could see the boyish pleasure he felt owning the luxury sedan. "I'm not a car guy, but growing up, I used to look at them and think, now, *that's* status."

Her big brown eyes held curiosity. "I didn't think to ask what you do for a living."

"I manage a small company working on wind turbines."

"Wind?" She sounded as mystified as if he'd said he made thingamajigs.

He'd gotten the same reaction often enough to have a practiced explanation. "Same concept as windmills. Have you been to eastern Washington lately? Seen the rows of turbines on ridges?"

"No."

"I'll have to take you," he said absently, backing out of the parking spot. "They're quite a sight. Some people think they're ugly. I don't. In that barren country along the Columbia River, they seem to belong. There's something spare and clean about them, like the landscape."

"I vaguely knew that the utility companies were buying some wind power. I guess I hadn't thought about how it was generated." Her brow furrowed. "And your company builds them?"

"We don't actually install them. Or manufacture the tower. What we've done is to design a turbine with flexible, hinged blades that reduce fatigue, so the turbine can be quite a bit lighter and therefore cheaper."

"Are you an engineer, then?"

He shook his head. "Financial management. I have degrees in economics. I'm a C.P.A."

"Oh, dear." She cast him an embarrassed look. "Our little business must seem like awfully small potatoes to you."

"All businesses start small."

"Did your wind company?"

"We had big financial backing, but we faced a lot of the same challenges. We needed to manufacture our turbine and then prove it worked as well if not better

74

than existing ones. It was several years after start-up before we actually had any commercial success."

"You mean, before you sold one?" Helen sounded horrified. "Several *years?*"

Alec laughed. "That's normal, believe it or not. The investors were gambling. We could have spent all that money and never made a sale."

"Oh, my." She gazed at him in awe. "How terrifying."

"It was a little scary," he admitted, merging onto the freeway. "But I've worked in the wind industry before, so I recognized the brilliance of my partner's concept. I thought it could help bring wind energy into the mainstream by reducing costs. Think about it."

No matter how many times he'd given this speech, genuine passion still infused his voice. "We're running out of fossil fuels. Dams cause ecological damage. But wind . . . it has all the power of a great river like the Columbia, and we can't use it up. We borrow it, then let it whip on its way, unharmed by having spun the blades. It's a nonpolluting source of electricity, it's indigenous . . ." He glanced at her. "We don't have to buy it from foreign nations. What's the down side?"

She smiled at his fervor. "You tell me."

He grimaced. "Well, the wind does die down sometimes, so it's not a steady flow like a river. Better storage could solve that, though. The turbines do make some noise, and they can kill birds."

"And they're ugly," she finished.

"Alien, maybe," he conceded. "The beauty of it is, the land where the wind blows hardest is the least populated. Yeah, if we had a row of turbines climbing Capitol Hill or Queen Anne in Seattle, people would protest. But on a bare lava ridge beyond Vantage . . . why not?"

"The person who lives there might not agree," she argued.

"That's true. But what are the alternatives? More dams? Atomic power plants? They'd look awful rearing above the Columbia River."

Helen nodded thoughtfully. "That's true, of course."

He'd chosen a Greek restaurant right off Broadway on Capitol Hill, near the Harvard Exit Theater, which showed foreign and independent films. He and Linda had come here often, before they'd had children and started going to Disney movies at the multiplex instead.

Parking was always tricky here, but he got

lucky and found a spot only a couple of blocks away. Walking the short distance, he asked Helen what movies she enjoyed, and found her tastes were similar to his.

"Actually," she admitted with a sigh, "I don't see very many rated much above PG. Sometimes, Kathleen or Jo rent something for us to watch after Ginny has gone to bed. They both like blockbusters. You know, lots of special effects, big-name actors. I've always preferred *small* movies." She said it almost timidly, as if embarrassed by her tastes. "The kind where nothing huge happens, but you're left feeling good. Like, a while ago we rented *Italian for Beginners.* It's actually Danish. Have you seen it?"

He shook his head.

"It was . . . sweet." She laughed. "Okay. Now you can tell me you love Jerry Bruckheimer extravaganzas. Or you're a James Bond fanatic."

Alec grinned and took her arm as they crossed the street. "Not me. Hey, I already admitted I was never a car guy, didn't I? I like numbers and computers. I was a geek."

She gave him a look that raised his spirits considerably. "I can't believe you were ever a geek." Then she blushed as if realizing what she'd given away and added hastily, "Besides, some of them probably live vicariously by watching *Terminator* and what have you. After all, if Clark Kent can turn into Superman . . ."

"They, too, can jump from a helicopter onto the roof of a speeding car to rescue the damsel in distress?" He laid a hand on her lower back and steered her into the doorway of the restaurant.

Her chuckle was a delicious gurgle. "Something like that." Then she looked around. "Oh, this is nice. I don't go out often."

"Single parents don't."

The hostess approached them with a smile. "Two for dinner?"

They followed her to a corner table in a room with dark beams, murals on plaster walls and tile floors. He liked the atmosphere here as much as the food.

Helen opened her menu. "I suppose you wine and dine customers and investors all the time."

"Sometimes. But these days, we do most of our business by email or conference call. Why waste hours to get together face-to-face when you can make decisions or discuss a problem in a few minutes?"

They glanced through the menu and ordered in between snatches of conversation. Alec watched her sip mineral water, her fingers slender on the glass, her hair shimmering as she tilted her head back to swallow. Her neck was long and slim, her throat white. He imagined kissing her in the hollow at the base, perhaps tasting that pale creamy skin. He would tangle his fingers in her riot of hair as he worked his way to her delicate chin and soft, full mouth. Perhaps by then her cheeks would flush the color of wild roses.

Captivated by the sight of her across the table from him as well as by his parallel fantasy, he took a moment to realize she seemed to be waiting for an answer.

"You're so pretty." His voice came out husky.

Her cheeks did turn pink. "Why, thank you."

He cleared his throat. "Your household seems unusual. Do all those people live there?"

She laughed, her gaze still shy, her cheeks flushed. "I didn't tell you, did I?"

"Tell me?"

"I only rent a room from Kathleen. It's actually her house. And, yes, we all live there, except for Raoul, Emma's boyfriend. He was the one studying in the living room."

Alec nodded.

She explained that Kathleen had bought

the house after her divorce and, to help pay the mortgage, had taken in two housemates, herself and Jo Dubray.

"She was the friend who took care of the booth while I went to lunch that day," Helen explained. "Kathleen got married, and Logan moved *in*." She laughed again at his expression. "He sold his house, which was smaller, and moved his workshop — he's a cabinetmaker — into the basement, which we weren't using anyway. He and Kathleen insisted that they wanted Ginny and me to stay. But I'm looking for a place to rent now. Kathleen and Logan have been great, and Ginny loves Emma, but . . ." She hesitated.

"You want a home of your own."

She nodded. "Exactly. And also I suppose I want to prove to myself that I can take care of us. That's probably silly, considering how easy I have it. Do you know how nice it is not to have to make dinner every single night, for example? Right now, we rotate, Logan, Kathleen, Emma and I. So I only cook once or twice a week. That's pure luxury!"

"So it would be," he said, amused. And — face it — a little jealous. Linda had loved to cook, so he'd been spoiled. Coming in the door after work every day to the smell of dinner in the oven, the kids running to meet him, his wife smiling and waiting for him to hug them and kiss her.

In one day, that had changed. He'd arrived home only to have Lily put her finger to her mouth and say, "Mommy's napping 'cuz she's tired. So we're supposed to be specially quiet." But even before that first warning, he had sometimes felt so lucky it scared him. He and his family had stepped from the canvas of a Norman Rockwell painting.

Amid the grief and shock of Linda's death, putting dinner on the table every night had become an onerous chore. The kids helped as much as they could, but he still had to do the planning, the shopping, and about seventy-five percent of the cooking.

"Maybe you don't want to move out," he said, only half kidding. "Do you know what I'd give to have someone else make dinner some nights?"

"But would you give up having privacy? I do have my own bedroom, but sometimes I'd like to watch what *I* want on TV, or pig out on ice cream in the kitchen without having to share, or cry without having to explain. Or wander around without a bathrobe, or hear about Ginny's day at school without at least a couple of other people commenting, too, or contradicting me if I'm trying to be stern." She let out a gusty sigh. "And, oh, I feel so petty and ungrateful even saying that!"

Alec found there was so much he wanted to know about her, he ate without tasting his dinner, and didn't notice when the waitress cleared their table. The one subject he avoided was her marriage and her husband's death. He wanted to hear about her husband — eventually. But not tonight.

And he didn't want to talk about Linda yet, either.

So he heard about Helen's parents, her dad a mechanic, her mother a nurse, devoted to their only child, and told her in turn about his own upbringing with well-educated, financially successful parents who didn't have much time for their two offspring.

They each talked a little about their children, and about grandparents and pets and coworkers. Two, then three hours flowed by. Entranced by her every expression, the purse of her lips or brief thoughtful frown or amusement that quivered at the corners of her mouth, he scarcely took his eyes from Helen's face the entire evening.

He was startled when she suddenly gave a

cry and said, "Oh, it's ten o'clock! How did it get to be so late?"

"That's not exactly the wee hours," he teased.

She made a face at him. "No, but I have to work in the morning, believe it or not. Some of us don't rest on Sundays."

Alec was surprised himself to realize how reluctant he was for the evening to end. They'd hardly scratched the surface of each other's lives!

Glancing at the check, he tossed bills on the table and stood. "Then we'd better get you home."

Night had fallen now. The walk back to the car felt curiously intimate, only the two of them on the dark sidewalk. In the car he was even more conscious of being alone with her. He couldn't remember the last time he'd been so eager and awkward and nervous.

How would she feel about him kissing her? He hadn't dated much; she hadn't at all, apparently. Maybe she'd thought this was just a friendly dinner. Had he imagined the sparkle in her eyes or the warmth of her smile or the way she'd looked at him when she said, "I can't believe you were ever a geek." Maybe her apparent fascination with his life had been mere politeness.

She was quiet during the drive, responding with only a few words to his comments or questions. In the light of a streetlamp he saw that her fingers were knotted on her lap and she sat with her knees primly together and her back very straight.

Was she nervous, too?

Scowling ahead, he couldn't decide if he was glad or sorry. He hated the idea that he scared her. But if she wasn't nervous at all, then that would mean she didn't feel the anticipation he did.

He pulled in right in front of her driveway, then turned off the engine. In the sudden silence, Helen gave him the look of a wild creature, cornered.

"I enjoyed tonight," he said quietly.

"I, um, did too."

"Can we do it again?"

Her look gave him hope. "That would be nice."

He wanted to reach for her, and was terrified she'd shrink away. "I'll walk you up."

"You don't have to."

"I want to."

The night was still warm. A motion light above the garage came on, showing the way up the steps to the porch. Alec was grateful that the drapes were drawn, and even more grateful when she didn't reach immediately for the door knob, instead turning to face him.

"Thank you, Alec. It was a lovely dinner."

He couldn't help himself. He reached out and slid one hand beneath the heavy silk of her hair. A quiver ran through her, but she stood her ground.

He bent his head slowly, slowly, giving her time to withdraw. She only waited, eyes huge and unreadable, lips slightly parted, until he feathered a kiss across them. They felt plump and warm and satiny, and he tasted the mint she had eaten after dinner.

He kissed her again, still gently, a brush of mouth to mouth, a mingling of breath.

She sighed and swayed toward him.

Finally he made himself let her go. "Good night, Helen. I'll call you tomorrow."

She blinked, as if dazed, and took a step back, until she bumped the door. "Thank you again for dinner." She said it as if by rote, a child taught to recite the proper thing.

He nodded and backed away, but he didn't turn until she opened the door and slipped inside.

On the way down to the street, Alec counted the hours until he could talk to her again.

Chapter Four

Sunday at work began quietly. Before the store opened, Helen set up a new display of back-to-school clothes. In the midst of a July heat wave, it was difficult to feel enthusiastic about a Shetland wool sweater and brown corduroy flare jeans, but when she stood back to study the ensemble, she was pleased with the effect. The curly-haired mannequin wore a forest-green crocheted cap and scarf over the green, brown and rust sweater. The book bag at her feet bulged convincingly, and she combined preteen chic with schoolgirl innocence. The autumn colors were a nice contrast to summer brights.

Perfect, Helen decided with a small nod.

When Nordstrom's customers failed to pour into the children's department at ten o'clock, she straightened tables of turtlenecks, poor-boys and embroidered jeans, all miniature versions of the clothes sold downstairs in the teen department. Once the half-yearly sale was advertised next week, they'd be too busy to tidy up.

She wished she was too busy today. She was brooding. About Kathleen's proposal that they both concentrate full-time on their business, about postponing her plan to make a home just for her and Ginny, about Alec and last night — and about the kiss.

After checking sizes on a rack of toddler dresses to be sure all were hung where they should be, she looked hopefully toward the escalator. A woman with a small child stepped off but walked briskly toward Linens.

Helen wandered through the department, straightening a pile here, reorganizing a rack there.

How would she feel about quitting this job? She loved the store and the quality of the merchandise, and took pride in her own department. As she'd told Alec, she enjoyed helping customers find just what they wanted.

On the other hand, her feet did hurt every night. And she wasn't making enough money to give Ginny the luxuries other children seemed to take for granted or to even feel she had financial security.

Maybe, just maybe, Kathleen's Soaps

could change that. *If* she resigned herself to continuing as a guest under Kathleen and Logan's roof. Which was not so terrible, of course, but lately she had become fixated on the idea of having her own place, however small.

She'd long held the suspicion that some of her terror of losing Ben had been fear that she wouldn't be able to manage on her own. She had never had to earn a living. What if she couldn't? What if she had to beg her parents for help, or she and Ginny ended up in a homeless shelter, or . . . Well, those were the worries that had tumbled through her mind at night, along with the schedule for Ben's next treatment, the symptoms to expect or when his next appointment was; with the awareness that Ben had looked weaker today, or that he had said "I love you" as if it might be for the last time. She'd forgotten how to sleep during that last year before his death. She was always listening for him, always worrying. It had taken over a year after his death before she awakened one morning in shock to find that she had slept for nine uninterrupted hours.

Even though he'd been dead for almost three years, she still wasn't sure she could really cope. She'd had so much help!

Helen frowned at an innocuous display of fleecy infant sleepers in angelic pastels. The very fact that Kathleen *wanted* her to commit fully to the business meant that she believed Helen was not just capable but a real businesswoman, didn't it?

Unless it was only an excuse to keep her from moving out, because Kathleen didn't think she could cope and wanted to shield her.

She let out a gusty sigh, turned and saw with relief that a tiny, bent, white-haired woman with a cane was shuffling into her department on the arm of a middle-aged man who was taking patient half steps to match her pace.

Helen greeted them. "May I help you find something?"

In a voice as wispy as her hair, the old woman said, "I need a baby present." She straightened her hunched back. "For my first great-granddaughter."

"A great-granddaughter! Wow. That's something to celebrate."

Her face crinkled in pleasure. "I didn't think I'd see the day. Now that I have, I'm crocheting her a blanket, but I also wanted to buy something practical to wear. Maybe —" she peered around "— one of those fuzzy little suits with feet."

89

"We have some very cute sleepers," Helen assured her.

They discussed whether she ought to buy a size for a newborn, which the infant girl might wear for only a few weeks, or a larger size that could be tucked away until the baby grew into it.

Helen wasn't surprised when her elderly customer chose the latter — and several sleepers rather than just one. Helen wrapped them carefully in tissue paper and put a gift box in the bag while the woman slowly rooted through her purse, came up with a wallet and, with trembling hands, counted out bills.

"I don't believe in credit cards," she told Helen. "Spending money you don't have . . . that's just foolish."

The son — or was he a grandson? — smiled but didn't argue. Nor did Helen, who was inclined to agree. Credit was for those who didn't need it except as a convenience, and for the truly desperate.

She stayed busy enough after that and was able to think about Alec and last night only in snatches, alternating with worries, which seemed to have become chronic. Keep looking for a rental, or be dependent on Kathleen and Logan for a while longer? Would she be able to find a job as good as this one, if Kathleen's Soaps didn't take off? She remembered with new astonishment Alec's matter-of-fact comment that his company had taken several *years* to make a first sale of their turbines. Perhaps she didn't have the nerve to be successful at business.

She wondered if he really would call. Did she want him to? It scared her a little, how much she'd enjoyed last night. The hours had slipped by so fast. He was entertaining, intelligent and seemingly as interested in her stories as she was in his. The part that amazed her was how much they *hadn't* yet talked about. She wasn't sure that in all those hours she'd even mentioned Ben's name, or heard his wife's. Having experienced the tragedy of losing a loved one to a terrible illness was what they had in common. And then what did they do but not even talk about it!

During her lunch break, Helen opened the newspaper and began her daily search for new rental listings. While she absently ate a bagel with cream cheese, she read the ads in the *Seattle Times,* the tip of her pen pausing at possibles.

One bd w/ lrg closets. Well, the price was within her range, but she read the meager text again dubiously. Were large closets the only good thing to say about the apartment?

Would Ginny have to sleep on a pullout sofa in the living room? Or would she? Nonetheless, she circled the ad, and several others.

Lg 2 bd, all applcs, fenced yd & gar. The price made her wince, especially with the insistence on first and last month's rent as well as a deposit. She could never come up with that much money. Nonetheless, she thought wistfully of having a house with a real yard, a garage — maybe even with an electronic garage door opener so she could drive straight in — and two bedrooms, so she and Ginny could each have their own. Ginny probably wouldn't mind a sofa sleeper or a futon, but still . . . ! Ginny was used to having the privacy of her own room since Jo got married and moved out.

Helen sighed but didn't circle that ad.

Cute cabinlike 1 bd, fresh paint inside & out. Oh, dear. She could interpret *that.* Forget large closets; this rental *was* a closet.

Ginny loved having the extended family. With no siblings, she had declared Emma her big sister. She called the original two housemates Aunt Kathleen and Aunt Jo. Teasing her last week, Logan had asked if he didn't deserve to be an uncle.

Helen hadn't heard her daughter's reply. Perhaps his status was elevated to family now, too.

Would she be doing Ginny a disservice by removing her to a small apartment and maybe even after-school care instead of Emma's company?

She hadn't really asked Ginny what *she* wanted, only told her what she, the adult, planned. Ginny had nodded in her usual grave way and said, "That would be nice."

Ginny never truly argued with her mother. She was too compliant, too anxious to please. While Ben was ill and in the months after his death, Helen had cried sometimes in front of her young daughter. She was haunted as much by the fear in Ginny's big eyes as she was by the sight of his waxen face. For at least the year after his death, Ginny had stuck close to her mother's side, her hand often creeping out to squeeze her mother's as she whispered, "Are you sad, Mommy?"

Helen tried never to give Ginny reason to ask any more. As she found her way out of the thick fog of grief and saw how desperately her daughter needed her, Helen had marshaled the self-control to cry only at night, in the dark kitchen after others went to sleep, or in the privacy of her bedroom, her sobs muffled by her pillow.

She would ask Ginny what she preferred, Helen decided as she tucked the folded newspaper into her tote bag. Helen didn't want to treat her solemn daughter like another adult, but she was mature for eight and deserved to have her wants heard.

The day remained slow. July was too early for serious back-to-school shopping, and Seattleites were taking advantage of the rare eighty-degree weather to hike, go to the beach or windsurf on Green Lake rather than wandering the mall.

It was nearly six o'clock when she got home, grateful to smell dinner cooking.

"Hi, I'm home," she called.

Ginny exploded out of her bedroom and raced downstairs to hug her mom. "Guess what we did today?"

Her cheeks were flushed from the sun, her nose pink.

"Went swimming?" Helen ventured.

"Rollerblading!" her daughter announced with deep satisfaction. "I went with Emma and Uncle Ryan and Aunt Jo and 'Lissa. I kept up and everything! We went all the way around the lake!"

"Cool." Helen smiled down at her daughter. "That's at least three miles! I'm not sure I'd have made it."

"It was fun." Ginny wriggled with satisfaction. "And I helped make dinner, too. Guess what we're having?"

This was Ginny's favorite game. *Guess!* she always insisted.

Helen sniffed again. "It smells good. Spaghetti?"

"Close."

"Ravioli?"

"Tortellini! And garlic bread and cauliflower."

"That sounds wonderful." She kissed the top of Ginny's head. "Just let me change. I'm starved."

In the kitchen, Logan began to sing something vaguely operatic as he often did when he was cooking. Ginny danced into the kitchen while Helen trudged upstairs, her feet pinched in her pumps.

Who had she been kidding? she thought. If she and Ginny lived on their own, would Ginny have been able to spend the day with a bunch of people who loved her?

Well, maybe. Helen suspected they would go fetch Ginny, wherever she lived. Sometimes. But maybe she wouldn't be included as often. She was glowing today, an extraordinary contrast to the pinched, clingy child she'd been when she and her mother first moved into this house. She was still too serious, but Jo and Ryan and his children, together with Kathleen, Emma and amiable, down-to-earth Logan, wouldn't let the

95

youngest child in their midst stand shyly on the sidelines. As Helen paused at her bedroom door, she heard Ginny's thin, childish soprano join Logan's deep tenor.

In the bedroom, Helen pulled the folded newspaper from her bag. She weighed "lrg closets" and "fresh paint" against the wonderful aromas from the kitchen, the enthusiastic impromptu concert and her daughter's delight in keeping up "and everything."

It was no contest.

She dropped the newspaper into her trash basket, kicked off her pumps and squirmed out of her panty hose.

She had lived timidly until she got the idea of marketing Kathleen's soap. What was the good of going into business at all if they didn't take the risks required to achieve real success?

And she'd tried. It was Kathleen's own fault if she and Logan were stuck with housemates!

Comfortable in jeans, fuzzy slippers and a sweatshirt, she went downstairs to have dinner with her family.

In a particularly good mood, Alec got up later than usual Sunday morning and didn't, for once, think about the empty side of the bed or the fact that, not so long ago, he would have smelled coffee brewing and wandered downstairs to discover Linda, always an early riser, putting pancakes on the griddle. Instead, his first waking thought was of last night. He saw Helen's face, heard her laugh, remembered her soft, trembling mouth against his.

This morning, Dev's bedroom door remained closed — the kid could sleep fifteen hours at a stretch, Alec swore — but tinny laughter came from the family room. Smiling, Alec stopped in the doorway.

"Good morning, Sunshine."

Lily, who had her father's dark hair and blue eyes, sat cross-legged on the floor with her back to the couch, her cereal bowl on the coffee table in front of her. She still wore her pajamas.

She turned her head, although her gaze lingered on the television screen. "Morning, Daddy."

"We should do something fun today."

Her gaze finally left the TV to pin hopefully on him. "Really?"

He had a pang of guilt. What with work, keeping the house up, grocery shopping and chauffeuring the kids to swim lessons, soccer practices and counseling, he must seem like a drill sergeant to them. Alec was very much afraid that his most frequent words to them were "Aren't you ready?"

"I can't think of anything that needs doing today. Let me eat breakfast, and then we can rouse your brother and see what he wants to do."

She made a horrible face. "*He* won't want to do anything with us. He never does."

Alec was afraid she was right. "Then we'll make him," he said heartlessly.

"Do we have to?"

Alec was optimistic enough this morning to believe that, away from his friends, Dev could be persuaded to be the funny, sweet kid he'd once been, protective of his little sister and certain his dad was the coolest guy ever.

Alec grimaced. He'd settle for funny and protective. A few carefree hours away from home were not going to be enough to make his sullen teenage son think Dad was even remotely cool.

To Lily, he said only, "He's your brother."

He made coffee, fetched the Sunday paper from the front porch and popped some whole wheat bread in the toaster. He ate in the dining room, newspaper spread out before him. As always, he read with an eye to how world and national events and economic trends would affect his business.

The perpetual tensions in the Middle East

98

made him shake his head. Why didn't the administration concentrate on developing alternative sources of energy rather than plunge the nation billions more in debt by using military might to protect its ability to buy oil?

Unemployment had risen yet again in the state of Washington, hardly a surprise with the airlines still in trouble and Boeing laying workers off. Not good. Consumers were more likely to pay a little extra for renewable energy in good times.

Before he reached the sports page, Lily bounced into the dining room.

"Can we go to Alki? We could eat fish and chips, and play on the beach."

He had the fleeting wish that Helen was free and he could ask her and her daughter to come.

But she wasn't, and his own kids deserved his undivided attention for once.

"Works for me," he said. "I'll go get Devlin up."

His first knock on the boy's door brought only silence; the second, a snarled "I'm sleeping!"

"Not anymore," Alec said through the door. "We're having a family day. Up and at 'em. We're going to Alki."

"I don't want to go! I'm sleeping in."

"It's almost eleven o'clock. You've already slept in. I'll expect you downstairs in ten minutes."

Way to win his son's heart, Alec thought, as he walked down the hall ignoring the bellow of outrage behind him. But nothing else was working, either. About all he had going for him was the fact that Dev did still obey direct orders.

Devlin grumbled while he ate breakfast and sulked the whole way to West Seattle and Alki Beach, but at least he reserved his glares for his father. Maybe he thought their evil Dad had made Lily go, too.

Once he sneered at his father. "So, did you have a hot date last night?"

Alec's jaw muscles tightened, but he ungritted his teeth to say, in an even tone, "If you mean, did I have a good time, yes I did."

"Is she nice?" Lily asked timidly.

They were crossing the West Seattle bridge, the industrial south of the city spread beneath them.

"Very nice. Helen has an eight-year-old daughter who helps out at the craft fairs."

"What is she, divorced or something?"

Devlin was trying for disagreeable. Alec suspected he was more curious than he wanted to let on. His father hadn't dated much.

"Her husband died three years ago. He had a brain tumor."

Lily let out a gasp. Dev turned his head away quickly and didn't say another word until they had parked and were walking to the shore.

Because of their late breakfast, they agreed to put off lunch. After wandering on the rocky beach with the kids, Alec finally found a comfortable spot where he could sit with his back to a driftwood log. He thought about reading the paperback he'd set down beside their towels and kite, but instead savored the scent of the salt air, the sound of seagulls calling and children playing, and small waves whooshing against the shore. Seattle sprawled before him on the other side of the sound. Green-and-white Washington State ferries left Seattle for Bainbridge Island and Bremerton at regular intervals, their horns blasting deep goodbyes, the arriving ferries crossing their wakes.

Lily brought a crab for him to inspect, then took it back to the water's edge. Dev's mood seemed to improve when a gaggle of teenage girls settled nearby on a blanket, where they spread suntan lotion on each other's shoulders and giggled, casting sidelong glances at the other boys on the beach.

His son was a good-looking kid, Alec thought, trying to be objective. He had his mother's blond hair and height and classic Scandinavian features. He'd be starting his freshman year in high school this fall, and the basketball coach had already made his acquaintance. Right now, he was gawky, with big feet that occasionally tripped over each other, but he was also a natural athlete, quick, smart and intense. Alec was praying that sports would be Devlin's salvation. His grades had dropped since his mother's death, he'd been involved in a couple of fights in middle school, and he resented just about everything his father asked of him.

Maybe Dev's teenage years would have been tempestuous even if his mother hadn't died. A counselor ventured the opinion that Devlin was "testing" his father. He was so afraid of losing both parents that he had to make sure his father loved him and would stick by him no matter what.

It all seemed pretty convoluted to Alec. He could see it if Linda had walked out. But she hadn't. Dev had been old enough to understand her illness and the fact that she hadn't wanted to die.

As far as Alec was concerned, that had

been the worst part: her fear and wrenching grief. Helen had expressed the belief that a quicker death was better, but he still wasn't so sure. Given more time, Linda might have achieved acceptance. She might have been able to gather precious moments with her children that would have given them all peace. Sure there would have been more time to regret and to suffer. But Linda would have also had more time to think of what she needed her children to know and remember about her, to put photos into albums, write notes and to help *them* let go.

But the astonishing, horrifying speed of Linda's illness had swept them all up as if it were the rare big wave that snatched un-lucky beach-goers from a rock. The first week had been spent finding out what was wrong with her. The next deciding on treat-ment, and too many of the ones after that believing she'd get better. There was so little time left once Alec and Linda realized she was going to die, much had gone unspoken. They had barely said goodbye. Maybe he'd been too stubborn in refusing to believe modern medicine couldn't save her. Maybe he'd communicated his misplaced faith and baffled rage to the children.

Alec didn't know. After the funeral, he, Lily and Devlin had clung together, trying to figure out how to function without their linchpin. How would days begin? Who would do the tasks that had magically been done before? Who would fill this silence, tuck in that child?

He tried; they all did. At first they were grateful when Alec donned any of their mother's roles, and forgiving when he fouled up or forgot to do something. After he had the minor heart attack, they'd even tried to take care of *him.* He couldn't seem to convince them that he'd just had a plumbing problem. An artery was clogged, the cardiologist had reamed it out, and Dad was fine.

It was several months later he started noticing that, as far as Dev was concerned, everything he did was wrong.

"You're late," he'd snap, throwing himself into the car after basketball practice.

Or he'd push his plate away at dinner. "This doesn't taste like Mom's."

"*Mom* would have let me" became his favorite, sulky refrain.

A few times Alec had cracked and said, "I'm not your mother."

The return was always a snotty, "Yeah, you're not."

Lily had been very, very quiet for months. Sometimes her eyes would unexpectedly fill with tears and she'd bolt to her bedroom. But she remained cooperative, and she was just as apt to bury her face against her dad when sadness overcame her.

Alec had been patient with his older child. Maybe too patient. He'd tell himself that this was a tough time for Dev. He was at a bad age to lose a parent. He was mad at fate. He'd get over it.

Only, he hadn't. In two years, he'd gone from being a skinny kid who cried when he thought of his mother to a six-foot tall teenager who spoke to his father as little as possible and then with a sneer in his voice.

But today, despite his awareness of the teenage girls on the beach, Dev stuck close to his little sister. Taking up his book, Alec would read a few pages then glance up to see them crouched side by side examining a tide pool or trying to get their kite up despite the still air. Once Devlin's shout of laughter rang out, a sound that brought Alec's head up and a lump to his throat. When was the last time he'd heard his son laugh?

Midafternoon they left to have fish and chips. At a small outdoor table, knees touching, they concentrated hungrily on their food.

Alec finally sighed. "Boy, this tastes good."

Even Devlin mumbled an agreement.

Devlin slouched in the front seat on the drive home, but his expression was more peaceful than usual. He looked younger, his hair tousled and his posture relaxed instead of rebellious.

Maybe there was hope.

In the garage at home, Alec turned off the engine. He turned to his son and said quietly, "Thank you for coming."

Under other circumstances, it might have been funny watching half a dozen emotions and unspoken responses chase each other across the boy's face. As it was, Alec braced himself and sensed Lily, in the backseat, doing the same.

But after a minute Dev shrugged. Grudgingly he said, "It was okay."

Praise of the highest order.

"We need to do things as a family more often."

Back to form, the fourteen-year-old curled his lip. "I'm not a little kid."

"If I can make time, maybe you can, too." Alec grabbed the keys and opened his door before Devlin had time to think of a comeback.

In the house, Lily wrapped her arms around his waist and gave a quick squeeze. "I had fun, Daddy," she whispered, then

106

darted off.

Smiling, Alec headed for his den. Let's hope his daughter didn't wake up one morning transformed into a pouty teenager wanting to get her belly button pierced.

The teenage part couldn't be held back. Today, she'd been a little girl. But he had a bad feeling that back-to-school shopping was going to be different this year. Lily was going into sixth grade. He'd seen signs of her noticing boys. One of her friends was already "going out" with a guy, a relationship which seemed to consist of no more than the announcement.

"And they I.M. each other," his daughter had told him. "They talk *a lot.*" Clearly she was impressed. Now *that,* her tone told him, was a real relationship. Even if it was taking place online.

Alec had hidden his amusement — and dismay. His daughter was a little girl!

Nonetheless, Lily was going to want jeans barely more decent than Christina Aguilera's, tops that exposed her midriff and knee-high boots instead of canvas tennis shoes.

He was going to be seriously out of his depth. Mothers were supposed to shepherd their daughters through the travails of becoming women. Not fathers.

Upstairs, the heavy throb of Dev's music vibrated the floor. From the family room came canned voices from the television.

Alec wondered what time Helen got off work.

Helen pretended that she wasn't waiting for Alec to call.

Tomorrow, he'd said, but he might not have meant that literally. Anyway, weren't men famous for saying "I'll call" and not meaning it?

But, secretly, she knew he was going to. He'd seemed as startled as she to discover how many hours they'd spent together. He had found her as easy to talk to as she had found him. She had seen it in his eyes, felt the reluctance with which he broke away.

When the phone rang at 8:05 p.m., Emma jumped to answer it. But Helen, reading at one end of the couch while Ginny sketched at the other, felt a shiver of excitement run through her.

"Helen?" Emma said with surprise. "Oh. Yes. Just a minute." Face alive with curiosity, she handed the cordless over and then plopped onto the arm of the couch to eavesdrop.

Conscious of her audience, which included Logan slouched with the newspaper

108

in an easy chair across the room, Helen said, "Hello?"

"Hi, this is Alec. I hope I caught you at a good time."

"Um . . ." She eyed her audience. "This is fine. I'll just take the phone into the other room."

Logan barely glanced at her. He might genuinely not have been paying attention. But Ginny watched her mother rise and leave the room with narrowed eyes, while Emma said loudly, "Cool! Helen has a boyfriend."

Kathleen was in the kitchen — no privacy there. Helen climbed the stairs.

"I'm going to have to hide out in my bedroom," she told Alec. "There are too many people in this house."

He laughed. "Sort of like a college dorm?"

"A little bit," she admitted. "Although nobody has loud parties spilling into the hall."

"My son would like to."

"So would Emma, I suspect. Kathleen does try to be relaxed, but she's a little too uptight to endure music at full volume."

"I'm beginning to realize that your attitude changes when it's *your* teenager."

It was Helen's turn to laugh. "I wouldn't know yet."

"I was looking at Lily today and realizing we need to buy her a bra." If his dismay hadn't been so real, it would have been comical. "Not a task my experience prepares me for. And she was chattering earlier about one of her friends who is 'going out' with some guy named Shane. Realizing it could be her scared me."

Going into her room and shutting her door, Helen said, "She's eleven, huh?"

"Almost twelve."

"I had a boyfriend when I was twelve," she remembered. "His friends asked my friends if I'd go with him, and I sent word back that, yes, I would. But I've got to tell you, I don't remember that we even talked, and we sure didn't kiss or anything. We danced together, and that was about it. Honestly, I think he was terrified of me."

She loved his laugh, a low, rusty rumble.

"Yeah, girls scared me at that age. They're a lot more mature than the boys are."

"And the girls know it. Sadly, the high school boys aren't much interested in sixth-or seventh-graders."

He laughed again, but with a wry note. "Good thing," he muttered.

Helen sat on the bed, one leg tucked under her. "So, did you enjoy the sunshine today?"

He told her about taking his kids to Alki and his son's slight softening.

"He's not a bad kid. He's just mad. He gets in fights, irritates his teachers, and defies me at every turn."

"Have you talked to his friends' parents? Maybe they're all like that."

"Oh, they can all be snotty, but you can feel him seething all the time. That can't be normal."

"No-o," she said hesitantly. "But you've tried counseling."

"For what it's worth."

"Have you actually, um, confronted him about it? Asked him to think about why he's mad at you?"

He was quiet. "No. We're more likely to fight."

She must sound preachy. "As if I'm any expert. Ginny just . . . withdrew. And clung to me. The opposite, I guess."

"Yeah, Lily got real quiet," Alec said. "And eager to be helpful and cooperative. Sometimes I thought she was trying to step into her mother's shoes. I don't know. It was great to have her want to cook dinner once in a while. That kind of thing. But the kid was only nine years old. She acted like an adult. My guess was that Lily was trying to fill a vacuum. Things were wrong. She thought somehow she could make them right."

They talked more about their kids, and why each reacted in such an individual way to the same tragedy. He told her some of what the counselor had tried to make him understand, and Helen quoted books she'd read.

"I keep thinking that there must be some secret, some bit of wisdom out there. If I can just find it, I can make sure Ginny isn't left with scars from losing her dad the way she did."

"Maybe that isn't the right way to look at it," Alec said thoughtfully. "We're each a product of our genes and our childhood, right? All of our experiences, good and bad, shape us. Does the death of a parent 'scar' you, or is it just one of those life experiences — good or bad — that alters who you'll be? Maybe Lily will be more responsible than she would have been otherwise. Maybe Ginny will focus more intensely on her goals."

Helen liked the idea, which wove Ben's death into a tapestry of life: Moments small or large that shaped and colored Ginny's life. Perhaps Ben's illness was a striking pattern or a strong color that darkened the whole, but it was not a flaw, only part of the whole.

"And Devlin?" she asked.

Alec made a sound in his throat. "I think that, more than either of our daughters, Dev isn't finished with his grieving. I have no idea how he'll come out at the other end."

"But he had his mother for twelve years, and he still has you. Those influences have to be stronger than grief."

Alec didn't say anything for a moment; when he did, his voice was a little thick, as if she had moved him in some way. "I hope you're right."

Helen didn't quite know what to say after that. For the first time in the conversation, the silence felt awkward.

"I actually called," he said, "to find out your schedule and see if we can get together this week. I spent a good part of the day thinking about last night. Things I said, didn't say, wanted to ask you or tell you."

"Me, too," she admitted, just above a whisper.

"I want to see you."

Her chest felt tight. "That would be nice."

"Good," he said, in a deep, quiet voice.

They settled on lunch Tuesday. Helen worked the afternoon and evening; he said he could leave the office for a couple of hours.

When she hung up, Helen grabbed a pillow and hugged it. She wanted to believe she'd just enjoyed his company and was looking forward to seeing him again the way she might any friend. But she wasn't good at lying to herself.

Alec made her feel things she'd sworn she would never feel again. But that wasn't what scared Helen. What she did not dare feel was this deep sense of connection, this hunger to know another person, to open her own heart and soul to him.

She could not — ever — be so vulnerable again, or burden another person with love so needy, she couldn't let him go when she should.

And yet she was too weak to call him back and say, *I'm sorry, I can't do this.*

In a panic she wondered how, without her noticing, it had become too late.

CHAPTER FIVE

Alec was waiting in the restaurant's foyer. Dressed in a well-cut charcoal suit that emphasized his broad shoulders and athletic build, his shirt crisp and white, the tie a muted red, he was so handsome Helen had an immediate attack of shyness. He was the kind of man she had noticed from afar in the past. He couldn't be waiting for *her*.

But the moment he saw her, his expression warmed, and it was as if the two of them were alone in the restaurant. "You look beautiful today," he said huskily.

She'd known this morning when she stood in front of her mirror that she looked good. *Beautiful* was never a word she thought in reference to herself. *Prettier than usual* was more like it.

But, thanks to her Nordstrom discount and the need to look stylish for work, she'd built up a wardrobe of clothes she really liked. Today she wore an unstructured silk suit in a warm brown with matching pumps and a peach silk tank top. Simple and elegant. She'd had a meeting this morning with the owner of a fancy new day spa in Kirkland, and had assured herself she was dressing for that, not for Alec.

Lies. All lies. The depth of her pleasure at the compliment and at the expression in his eyes exposed her self-deception.

She answered with dignity. "Thank you."

The host seated them by a window looking over Lake Union and left them with menus.

Alec didn't reach for his. "I meant it, you know. I always think I can picture you, then when I see you I realize I've forgotten how exquisite your skin is, or how your smile lights up your face."

"I'm not . . ."

"You are." He grinned at her discomfort. "Trust me."

Did she? Helen didn't quite know. She did believe he thought she was pretty. Why would he pretend? When Alec looked at her, she knew he wasn't seeing anybody else. That kind of focus was seductive.

"Sometime, I should show you a picture of me when I was a kid." She made her tone light. "I was incredibly scrawny, with this wild bush of hair I *hated* to let my mother

116

brush. We had wars over it. She so wanted to send me off to school with neat pigtails like the other girls instead of my rat's nest."

His gaze lingered on her smooth chignon. "She'd approve of the way you wear it now, then."

Unlike Jo and Kathleen.

"It has a will of its own. I like to keep it confined."

"I have this picture," he said softly, "of your hair flowing around your shoulders."

Helen flushed at the way his eyes darkened. "Someday I'll surprise you." Then her cheeks heated even more at the assumption in her words: they would continue seeing each other.

"I'll look forward to it," he murmured, then reached for a menu. "I suppose we'd better figure out what to order."

Flustered, Helen opened her own. "Yes, I can't be late for work. The half-yearly sale starts this week."

"I suppose I should take advantage of it and drag the kids in to buy for school."

"You sound so enthusiastic."

"Devlin likes the skater look. Baggy clothes, a couple of faded T-shirts on top of each other, hair never brushed." Alec grimaced. "Lily has taken to borrowing his shirts, presumably because she needs a bra."

Helen's amusement faded in a rush of sympathy. "You know, the clerk would help her."

"She's embarrassed. What if some clerk should want to measure her bust?"

Helen couldn't help laughing. "I love the way you say 'bust.' As if it were a hideous thing."

He growled something about Lily being his little girl.

Taking pity, Helen said, "Would you like me to help her? Maybe we could make it kind of casual. I have to buy a few things for Ginny, too. I'll steer them to the lingerie department and shoo you away."

Alec looked like a shelter puppy who'd heard the word "home." "Would you?"

Helen laughed again. "Yes, I would. And I suspect you were angling for the offer."

"It never crossed my mind." With a smile in his eyes, he sketched a salute. "Scout's honor."

"I won't ask whether you were a Boy Scout." Out of the corner of her eye she saw the waiter approaching, and quickly scanned the menu.

After they ordered, Helen told him about her morning.

"Most salons and day spas carry big-name products, but this owner is going to try our soaps as well."

"Good for you," he said warmly.

Helen took a deep breath. "I've decided to quit my job at Nordstrom."

His brows rose. "You're serious?"

"I think so. Yes," she said more positively. "I know so. It'll mean putting off my plan for Ginny and me to have our own place, but Kathleen and I both think we can make the business grow beyond local markets. She'll need to invest more time in making soap — and maybe even hire some help — and I'll have to travel more. Right now, we're both limited by our jobs."

"Good for you," he said again. "It's scary, though, isn't it?"

She recognized the question she'd once asked him and made a face. "You know it is. Plus, in my case . . ." She hesitated. Helen's personal finances weren't something she usually talked about with anyone but her parents, Kathleen or Jo, and only guardedly with them.

"Plus?" he nudged.

This time she *couldn't* talk to Kathleen, and she tried to avoid worrying her parents during their weekly phone calls.

"In essence," she admitted, "I'll be financially dependent on Kathleen's husband. This wasn't a step we could consider until she married. Now we have another income. We've decided I won't pay rent for the time being, I'll just pay a share of the grocery bill. But, I feel funny about that."

Alec frowned. "You don't think he'll want some kind of payback."

Shocked, she exclaimed, "No! No, it's not like that."

His frown relaxed. "You sound as if you're all pretty close."

"We are." *Family.*

"Do you think *he* resents supporting you?"

"No."

The idea was laughable. Logan, one of the most easygoing men she'd ever met, had been nagging the two of them to quit their day jobs since he first carried Kathleen over her own threshold. He had faith in them, he repeated often, adding with a grin, "I expect to be a man of leisure once Kathleen's Soaps is a household name."

"No," she said again to Alec, slowly. "I'm being silly, aren't I? I was just raised to believe I should stand on my own two feet." How sad, then, that she never really had.

Their lunches arrived and Alec didn't comment until the waiter had gone.

"If you were unemployed and not trying very hard to find a job, that would be one thing. But you're working to make the business a success. I think you can toss your scruples."

"Really?" His opinion meant more than it should.

Alec smiled. "Really."

Helen's sigh released some of the strain she had been feeling. "Okay. You've made me feel better. I can be a kept woman."

"You know," he said, picking up his club sandwich, "you may find the business expands so fast that you can handle the bills again in no time."

Helen reached for her fork. "That's the spirit."

They talked idly then, about wind and water and where they'd grown up. Out the window they could see a windsurfer hopelessly waiting for a breeze to billow the scarlet sail of his board. Rows of white boats were moored at a nearby marina, masts like pickup sticks. That was one of the things she loved about Seattle: from almost anywhere you could see mountains, the lakes or Puget Sound. Seattle had a setting like no other city she knew.

Alec had grown up in San Francisco, in an elegant pink town house not far from the Presidio and the Golden Gate Bridge. He talked about watching the fog roll in from the Pacific like a steamroller, inexorable and predictable, about the deep blasts of fog-horns and the clang of cable cars.

"Maybe that's why I chose Queen Anne," he said. "I'm used to steep hills."

"We do have that in common with San Francisco, don't we?"

Helen's parents had retired to San Diego, but she had grown up in a suburb of Portland. "I met Ben in college," she said, "and when he got a job up here, I never looked back. By the time he died, my parents had moved. It never occurred to me to return to Portland. I pretend I'm a native now."

Alec laughed. "At least you're not a hated Californian, like I am."

"True," she agreed, only half kidding. "We Oregonians know what rain is like, too."

"It's supposed to be dry next weekend," said Alec, motioning to the waiter for the check. "Any plans?"

"There's a small fair up in Snohomish County but we're skipping it. We did it last year, but didn't make that much, so this summer we've decided to take a few down days."

Helen told him about last summer's crazy juggling act, when family members and friends helped keep the balls in the air. "It was awful. We'd suddenly realize that, thanks to a snow day back in February,

Emma really had two more days of school and wouldn't be available to work the fairs. Jo's dad had a heart attack so she had to fly to California. Kathleen's one of the most honest people I've ever met, but she told work she needed time off for a family emergency. Well, I suppose it was." She laughed. "Each time we did a show last summer, we had to be sure to pack food and not drink too much pop, because we hardly ever had backup. No wandering the fair for us, or even galloping to the bathroom, unless a day was really slow."

"So, are you busy this weekend?" he repeated, producing his wallet.

"No. Do you want to take the kids shopping?"

"If you can, I'll fall at your feet in gratitude."

She looked around at the elegant dining room. "In here?"

He grinned. "I was speaking metaphorically."

As they walked out, he put his hand on the small of her back. For some obscure and utterly feminine reason, she loved the feeling. Of course, his hand was warm and solid, but she thought it was more. Some innate response to a man being proprietory, probably. Ridiculous, but nice nonetheless.

In the parking lot, Alec waited until she unlocked her car, then said, "Helen?"

When she turned to him, he wrapped that same hand around her nape, tilted her face up and kissed her. An instinctive zing of panic mingled with her body's response to the kiss. His confidence scared her.

Alec released her with the same reluctance he'd shown the other night. He stroked his fingers down her cheek, said roughly, "I'll call," then got in his car and drove away.

She all but fell into her car, exhilaration and anxiety flip-flopping in her stomach. The first date had felt like just that — a tentative, getting-to-know-someone outing. Harmless, except perhaps for the kiss at the end. But lunch today had felt different. People made time in their day to meet someone for lunch because they were having a relationship. They kissed goodbye in the parking lot, in broad daylight, when they were a couple. She was very much afraid she'd given him the impression that they were. Or at least, could be.

Gripping the steering wheel, she closed her eyes. She liked him! She didn't want to say, *Forget it.* She wanted . . .

Helen didn't know what she wanted. To have her cake and eat it, she supposed. To enjoy his company and his kisses without

124

fearing either of them would fall in love.

It was funny, when she thought about it. The single women at work grumbled incessantly about commitment-phobic men, how they all had no interest in helping wash the dishes or chauffeuring a kid to soccer practice. The very idea of a wedding ring and the promise of forever was enough to send the average bachelor running, if her coworkers were to be believed.

But she, Kathleen and Jo had all been uninterested in finding husbands. When Jo met Ryan, *she* was the one terrified of permanence, not him. Kathleen had had her qualms about Logan.

And now, Helen thought, here she was, dreadfully afraid she'd met a wonderful, marrying kind of man. Instinct told her Alec Fraser wasn't a playboy.

In the beginning, all she'd wanted was to have a chance to talk to someone else who'd experienced the loss of the person they loved most in the world. She had kept so much of her tangle of sorrow and guilt and longing to herself, she didn't know how much of what she felt was normal.

With a sigh, she backed out of the parking spot. How had it happened that she'd had a second date with the man, and they *still* hadn't talked about the deaths of their spouses or the painful aftermath?

Worse yet, how was it that she didn't even think of talking about Ben while she was with Alec?

"Back-to-school shopping Saturday," Alec announced at dinner on Wednesday evening.

They both gaped at him with identical expressions of dismay.

"I don't need anything," Devlin said. Then, "Can't I go with Evan or Kyle?"

"The way you're growing, nothing from last year will fit. And what about basketball shoes?"

"I don't need you there."

"But you do need my money." He paused. "Unless you want to buy clothes with the money from your summer job?"

He could see from his son's face that the answer was, *No.*

"Can't you just give me money?"

"You know," Alec said conversationally, "I feel terribly parental, but I'd like to see what my money is buying."

Glowering, the teenager said, "Anyway, it's July! Why do we need to go shopping now?"

"Because there are sales on, and I want to take advantage of them."

"Kyle and me were doing something Saturday."

Alec raised his brow. "Something?"

Dev muttered, "Hanging out."

Alec thought. "Here's the deal. You can bring Kyle with you —" He held up a hand to forestall argument. "We'll buy the shoes, check out a few other things, then I'll give you some money and you two can go off on your own. On the condition that you show me what you've bought later."

Devlin grumbled a little more but finally agreed.

Alec turned to Lily. "Helen and her daughter, Ginny, are coming with us. I know you'll be shopping in the junior department, but I hope you can be patient while Ginny and Helen look at clothes, too."

Dev shoved back his chair and got to his feet. "You're bringing *her?*"

Alec felt familiar tension grip his shoulders and neck. "And that would be a problem . . . why?"

The fourteen-year-old's face was twisted in rage. "I don't want to meet your girl-friends!"

"I have never asked you to meet any woman I've dated before. In fact, I have hardly dated. Your mother has been dead for two years now."

"Don't talk about Mom!" he yelled.

Alec pushed back his chair and stood, too. Voice rough, he asked, "Why not?"

Devlin flung the chair to one side, where it crashed to the floor. "You've forgotten her!"

"I have not and will never forget your . . ."

Not listening, the teenager stomped from the room.

Torn between anger and a sick sense of failure, Alec stared after him. Finally he remembered Lily was in the room, too. He turned his head to see her sitting completely still, her head drawn in as if she were a turtle. She looked petrified.

He muttered under his breath, righted the chair Devlin had thrown down and sat beside his daughter, massaging the back of her neck gently.

"Hey, it's okay. He was just throwing a temper tantrum."

Tears ran down her cheeks. "He scared me," she whispered.

"You know he'd never hurt you. Dev may be a big, tough teenage boy, but he loves you. You're not the one he's mad at."

Lily lifted her head for the first time, her eyes huge and wet. "But why is he mad at you?"

Question of the day. Or the year.

"I have no idea," Alec admitted. "Maybe he isn't really. Teenagers rebel against their parents. Maybe he's mad at fate for taking your mom, and now he's got these hormones racing around in his body letting him know he should become a man and why is his father still giving him orders."

She gave a tiny giggle. "He doesn't like it very much when you leave us notes. You know. Telling us what chores to do."

"I'll bet he doesn't." Alec wiped her tears and smiled. "Better?"

Lily nodded. "Will you ground him?"

Should he? His instinct said no.

"You know, he was just telling me what he felt. I don't think he deserves grounding for that."

Her mouth pursed. "He threw the chair."

"We'll pretend he knocked it over accidentally, okay?"

Looking disappointed, his daughter nodded. "He's lucky," she pronounced.

"Not so lucky. This means he still gets to go shopping with us on Saturday."

She thought about that. "He might not be nice."

"If he's not, *then* he'll be grounded."

"Oh." Her forehead creased. "Do you really like Helen?"

"As a friend, I know I do. You will, too."

He hesitated. "I told you her husband died?"

Lily nodded.

"Maybe that's something you and Ginny could talk about sometime. She may not know anyone else who had a mom or dad who died."

"But what would I *say?*"

Alec shrugged. "Just tell her you know what it feels like. She may want to talk, she may not."

His daughter digested the idea, then squared her shoulders. "Okay."

"Good girl." He kissed the top of her head, then pushed back the chair. "What say we have some ice cream?"

"Yeah!"

Terrific, Alec thought later, getting ready for bed. The very idea of meeting a woman his dad was dating had set Devlin off like a firecracker. What if he refused to go Saturday morning? Or — worse — went and was rude to Helen? Disciplining was easy when you could sit a five-year-old in the corner. It was another story when your kid stood six feet tall and simmered with rage.

Up till now, Devlin usually did what his father told him to do. Sullenly, slowly, defying him in small ways, he did ultimately obey. What, Alec wondered, would happen the day that changed?

■ ■ ■ ■

Helen parked as close as she could get to the Nordstrom at Northgate Mall. Although she worked in the downtown store, she and Alec had decided to shop here, so his son and the friend coming with him had a mall to prowl afterward.

"We can have lunch and wander ourselves," he'd said.

He hadn't been able to pick up Helen and Ginny because, with his son's friend, there wasn't room in his car.

"That's okay," she'd assured him. "Also . . ." She didn't finish, and he didn't ask her to. They both knew what she'd been going to say: *Also, if your son can't stand me, we won't be stuck.*

Alec had told her, in a tone constrained enough to make Helen guess she was hearing only part of the story, that Devlin wasn't crazy about him dating.

"Nobody is supposed to replace his mother in any way."

"Isn't that natural?" she'd asked.

"Probably." After a small silence she heard the effort he made to sound upbeat when he changed the subject.

Now she was going to meet his son. *Oh,*

goody, she thought.

Ginny scuffed her feet as they crossed the parking lot. "Why do we have to shop with *them?*" she muttered.

Unseen by her daughter, Helen rolled her eyes. Not Ginny, too!

"I thought you might like to meet Lily."

"She likes *dolls.*"

"She collects them. You know, doll makers are considered artists."

Her daughter snorted.

"It's also possible," Helen pointed out, "that Lily isn't very interested in dolls at all, but thanks her father so nicely every time he gives her one that he keeps buying them, and doesn't realize she's outgrown them."

Ginny frowned. "I guess."

"Give her the benefit of the doubt."

Her daughter waited while her mother opened the door to the store. "What does that mean?"

"It means, don't make up your mind ahead of time. You might even like her."

"She's older than me."

They were passing Menswear. Helen looked down at her daughter. "So?"

Ginny marched on, expression a cross between matter-of-fact and belligerent. "She won't be interested in me."

132

Giving up, Helen said, "Maybe not, but I trust you'll both be polite."

Ginny just had to have the last word. "We don't even shop in the same department."

Feeling this whole expedition was doomed to failure, Helen resolutely led the way to the shoe department, where they'd agreed to meet — and start their shopping.

Helen saw Alec right away. Even in corduroy pants and T-shirt, he stood out, handsome enough to be modeling Nordstrom clothes. *A suggestion which would no doubt appall him,* she thought in amusement.

He was studying athletic shoes with two teenage boys, both nearly his height but skinny. She had no idea which was his son. Both wore sacky pants hanging low on their hips and faded T-shirts with, in the case of the blond boy, a tear across the back. Both also had enormous feet, she saw as she and Ginny neared.

Taking a deep breath for courage, she called cheerfully, "Hi. Find anything yet?"

The moment they turned, she knew which of the two was Alec's son. The brown-haired kid barely glanced back, his indifference obvious. It was the boy with the shaggy blond hair who swung around, his blue eyes hostile. He didn't look much like his father, Helen thought.

133

"Helen." As if unaware of his son's mood, Alec kissed her cheek. "Let me introduce my son, Devlin, and this is his friend, Kyle."

Kyle glanced over again and gave an awkward nod. Devlin glared.

"Dev," his father said steadily, "this is Helen Schaefer and her daughter, Ginny."

"*Ms.* Schaefer." The boy managed to make her name sound like an insult. He hardly looked at Ginny.

Alec opened his mouth to say something; but as she said hello, Helen gave the tiniest shake of her head. After a moment, jaw muscles still knotted, he said, "Lily is looking at shoes. Let's find her."

"I'm sorry," he said in a low voice as they left the boys looking at athletic shoes. "He's sure he's going to hate you —"

"It's okay," she interrupted. "My feelings aren't hurt." She smiled again at the dark-haired girl who turned, her arms full of shoes. "Lily, I presume?"

"I look like Dad," the girl said resignedly.

Alec went through introductions again, then said, "You already have quite a pile."

"I want to try everything on at once, so I can get it over with."

Helen felt Ginny's hand relax in hers.

"That's Ginny's attitude, too," Helen said. "In fact, while you're trying them on, we'll find shoes for her."

Ginny hated everything except sneakers. Lily was more enthusiastic and chose a pair of knee-high boots, clunky lace-up shoes and some brand-name leather sneakers. Helen insisted that Ginny choose something she could wear with a dress.

She gave a long-suffering sigh. "I don't like dresses."

"But you occasionally have to wear one, and I know you've outgrown those patent-leather shoes."

"Good."

Lily stood up. "Come on. I'll go look with you. We can find something that'll be cool."

Ginny, who was not very interested in being "cool," nonetheless jumped up and went with the older girl to look at more shoes.

Alec dropped into the chair beside Helen. "Why did we have children?"

She laughed. "We were young and foolish and carried along by societal expectations. At least, that's my story."

"Mine, too," he said gloomily.

"They do have their moments, don't they?"

"In Dev's case, years."

She gave his hand a squeeze. "They outgrow it. Or so I'm told."

Gazing at his son, Alec asked, "When?"

Helen laughed again. "Come on. Remember when you were that age."

"I thought my father was an idiot, but I didn't dare talk back."

"You were afraid of him?"

Sounding plaintive, he said, "Is a little healthy fear such a bad thing?" He slumped lower in the chair. "Yeah, yeah, you're right. I don't want my kids afraid of me."

His daughter hung over the back of the seat. "Why would we be afraid of you?"

Alec jumped. "You scared me!"

"Why," she repeated persistently.

"Wishful thinking," he told her. "That way, if I just snapped my fingers, you'd hop."

Lily giggled.

Eventually Ginny reappeared with a couple of shoes dangling from her hands.

Once Helen had approved the styles — and prices — the clerk whisked them away to find her size.

Devlin approached with two shoe boxes stacked in his arms. Not looking at Helen, he said, "These are the ones I want."

"Good. We'll be done here in a few minutes."

Looking dismayed, Dev said, "We don't have to wait, do we?"

"No, why don't you boys go look at

clothes? I'll find you in a few minutes."

Devlin set the two boxes beside his father, turned and walked away without a word. Helen felt the rigidity in Alec's arm.

"Too cool to be seen with us, huh?" she said lightly.

"He always walks ahead of us when we go places," Lily said. "So nobody knows he's with his dad and his sister."

"Ah."

Alec sighed. "I did promise that he and Kyle could go their own way."

"We don't need them hanging around while we pick out clothes, anyway, do we, girls?" asked Helen.

Lily made an awful face. Watching her, Ginny did the same.

The second pair of dress shoes, Ginny conceded, were "okay."

"Great." Helen nodded at the clerk. "We'll take them and the sneakers."

Alec and his daughter took their pile of purchases out to the car while Helen and Ginny went to the children's department. Ginny chose a few shirts and jeans but they decided to leave more shopping for another day. By the time Alec and Lily returned, Helen was already paying.

"If you want to check on Devlin —" she turned to Alec "— we can take care of lingerie while you're gone. Lily, do you need anything? If not, can you be patient?"

Lily's eyes widened.

Alec said hastily, "Sounds great. I'll meet you in the junior section in a bit?"

Helen chatted all the way up the escalator. Only when they were well away from other shoppers and were among the racks of bras and nightgowns did she ask, "Do you need bras, Lily? I thought you might rather shop with me than with your dad. If I'm wrong . . ."

"No!" Lily swallowed and looked around. "I do need . . . I mean, I guess . . ."

"Do you know what size you wear?"

She hunched her shoulders. "No. How do I find out?"

"Let's just grab some and you can try them on," Helen suggested. "You can find out yourself what's comfortable."

Ginny was surprisingly patient as they picked out some dainty bras in pretty colors. She and her mother waited outside the dressing room while Lily tried them on, Helen doing her best to interpret success from Lily's, "Um, I don't, um, quite fill this one."

At length the eleven-year-old was satisfied and they bought three. Helen paid for them so that they could disappear discreetly in a bag. Lily would die of humiliation if they had to carry them around the store.

"Three ought to do for a while. Your size will probably change soon," Helen told her.

"I don't want boobs," Ginny grumbled. "I don't have to have them, do I?"

"Unfortunately, you have no say. Sorry, kiddo. Short of plastic surgery, you're stuck with what nature gives you."

"It's not so bad," Lily said, sounding far more worldly than she had half an hour before. "Clothes look cooler when you're not shaped like a board."

"Who cares?"

Lily grinned at her. "You will. In a couple of years."

Ginny gagged.

"When you like *boys*."

"I will never . . . !"

"You will."

"Never!"

They ended up giggling and poking each other and whispering all the way to the junior department.

The girls were picking out jeans for Lily to try on when Alec returned. He looked harried, but his face lightened at the sight of Helen.

"Mission accomplished?" he asked quietly.

"Yup." She handed him the bag.

He frowned. "You paid?"

"Are you kidding?"

Looking at his daughter, he grinned. "I guess she wouldn't want to carry them around, would she?"

"Toilet paper dragging from her waistband would be preferable."

His eyes met hers. "Thank you."

His expression, serious but warm, made her heart do a tap dance.

"You're welcome."

"Now," he murmured in her ear, "how do we ditch the kids?"

CHAPTER SIX

She'd done it. Helen walked out of the office with her hands shaking and her legs unsteady.

She had quit her job and given two weeks' notice. The personnel manager had been nice about it, wishing her luck.

Luck. Helen hated to think her future was dependent on something so unpredictable.

A picture of composure, she started the first of her remaining days of work, but, inside, panic sent adrenaline shooting through her body.

But she'd just slashed her income in half. And was gambling that she — timid Helen — could persuade retailers across the Pacific Northwest to carry Kathleen's Soaps. She had become even *more* dependent on Kathleen, Logan and Emma, because she'd have to leave Ginny with them while she traveled.

It was Sunday, and she was having dinner

with Alec tonight. She should have said no; after all, they'd been shopping just yesterday. But they'd hardly had a minute to talk, and when they were saying goodbye in the parking lot and he murmured, "Dinner tomorrow night?" she'd nodded vigorously.

Dizziness swept over her. Her arms were full of clothes she was carrying out of the dressing room. She dumped them on the counter beside the cash register and took several deep breaths. How had her life spun so out of control, and so quickly?

Just a few weeks ago, Helen had been content with no man in her life, sure that was the way she wanted to keep it. She'd been on the verge of moving herself and Ginny to their own place. She'd felt confident — good about Kathleen's Soaps, about her ability to juggle two jobs, about reaching a point in her life where financially and emotionally she could support herself and her child.

She laughed, then stole a hasty look around to be sure no one had heard her. She sounded like a lunatic, cackling at her own jokes!

Why was she having dinner tonight with a man she didn't dare fall in love with? Wasn't it bad enough that she was planning a cross-state trip in her old car to visit retailers who would no doubt gaze at her in bemusement when she asked, "Hi, wanna carry our soap?"

Gradually her pulse slowed and her head cleared. What other choice could she have made about her job? She couldn't be a store clerk forever. And the owners of shops in Yakima and Spokane wouldn't be any more intimidating than the ones she'd already faced in Seattle.

As far as Alec went . . . they were having fun. That was all. He was probably no more interested in a trip down the aisle than she was. After all, like her, Alec was barely dipping his toe in the dating waters. She would, well, *warn* him, when she got the chance, that she had no intention of ever remarrying. She'd just laugh lightly and say, "Once around was enough." He'd probably be relieved.

Equanimity restored, Helen picked up the clothes again, hung them on a rack and began fastening buttons.

That evening, she barely had time to change when she got home. Ginny sat on her bed watching her and looking glum.

"What do you think?" Helen asked, turning from the closet mirror. *She* was pleased with how she looked in a batik-print broomstick skirt and simple white cotton shirt.

As if reluctant to admit it, Ginny mumbled, "You look pretty."

Helen sat next to her daughter on the bed. "Is that bad?"

"No." Ginny's thin shoulders slumped. "I just wish you were staying home."

"Why? Didn't you rent a movie?"

"Yeah, but you could have watched it with me."

"I heard Emma say something about being bored. I'll bet she . . ."

"Maybe." The eight-year-old straightened. "I guess I can ask."

"You do that." Helen gave her a hug. "I don't go out *that* often."

"You didn't used to." Ginny slid off the bed and plodded toward the door. "Before you met *him.*"

Scooping up her purse, Helen followed. "Don't you like Alec?"

Shrug. "He's okay."

"I know you liked Lily."

"She was better than I expected. Considering she has dolls."

Helen laughed at her daughter's disdain. "Did you ask her about them?"

Halfway down the stairs, Ginny shook her head. "You told me not to be rude."

"You could have asked nicely. As in, 'Your dad says you collect dolls.' "

The doorbell rang before they could pursue the subject. Ignoring the front door, Ginny continued into the living room. For once, Helen answered it herself.

Even though she expected Alec, her heart took a leap. "Hi," she said a little shyly.

"Hi yourself." He stepped over the doorstep and kissed her. "Where is everyone?"

"You mean, why didn't half the household trample each other to answer the door?"

He laughed. "Well, yeah."

"Because Emma knows that Raoul is working tonight, and she's therefore indifferent to who comes or goes. Kathleen is deep into some nineteenth-century book on soap making that apparently contains cryptic recipes, and Logan is in his workshop sawing, sanding or measuring."

"Ah. Shall we flee, then?"

She laughed, tucked her hand in his arm, called, "I won't be late," and let him escort her out.

Tonight they tried a French bistro in Ballard. Rough-plastered walls, cream-colored crockery, warm woods and pretty flowered linens gave the place a country feel.

"Mmm," she decided, looking over the menu, "the beef burgundy crepe sounds good." She smiled at the waiter. "That's what I'll have."

After he'd ordered, Alec leaned back and looked around with pleasure. "Linda would have liked this place." He stopped. "I'm sorry. That was tactless, wasn't it? No woman wants to hear something like that."

Helen shook her head. "Don't be silly. Of course you think of her. How can you not? Ben's on my mind. Constantly."

"Still . . ."

She didn't let him go on. "I mean it," she said firmly. "Was Linda a good cook?"

His frown eased. "Yes. She enjoyed it, unlike me."

"You must miss that." Helen flushed. "I mean, of course you do."

"I do." He told a few funny stories about his own attempts to take his wife's place in the kitchen, then asked, "What about you? Sounds like you have no urge to create glorious meals."

"I'm afraid not. I never rise above the mundane in the kitchen. Everyone agrees that my best dinner is homemade macaroni and cheese. A far cry from gourmet cuisine."

"Beats my specialty — frozen pizza."

"You haven't talked much about Linda. Did she work?"

"She owned a travel agency when we met. She kept working until she got pregnant with Devlin, then sold the agency." He seemed to be looking into the past, the lines on his face deepening. "I used to ask her if she missed it, but she said no. As far as I could tell, she was genuinely delighted to sit on the floor and do puzzles with the kids, take them to the playground or help them make cookies. Linda was a natural mother. She was talking about going back to school herself and getting a teaching certificate when the kids got older."

"Do you have a picture of her?" Helen asked softly.

He nodded and reached for his wallet, unfanning a fold of photos that seemed mainly to be his kids' school pictures. Helen caught glimpses of a blond boy grinning at the camera, of Lily minus her two front teeth, of her older and in a plumper stage, of a more recognizable Devlin gazing expressionlessly at the photographer.

"Here," Alec said, and pulled out a photo of a beautiful blond woman laughing over her shoulder.

Helen had an immediate, sinking feeling of inadequacy, of which she was ashamed. She'd asked to see the picture. She could not, would not, compare herself to Alec's dead wife.

"She's gorgeous," Helen said. "And Devlin looks just like her, doesn't he?"

"Well, he wouldn't want to be called gorgeous." He grinned at her expression. "They were especially close, too, which made losing her even harder for him. I think they had more than looks in common. She was the one who played basketball in high school, for example, not me. He's quite an athlete," Alec added. "I don't know if I've said. She and he were the extroverts in our family, while Lily and I would just as soon stay home."

As the waiter put salads in front of them, Helen continued to study the picture. This was the woman Alec had loved so much. Linda Fraser wasn't quite model-beautiful, when you looked closely. Her nose was possibly a little big with a distinct bump on the bridge, and fine lines fanned from her eyes and her laughing mouth. Yet those eyes sparkled with delight and the smile was infectious. In the photo her ash-blond hair was in a ponytail, and she wore a loose-fitting cotton dress with tiny sprigs of flowers sprinkled on a slate-blue background.

Helen couldn't help thinking she would have liked this woman. She couldn't decide how that made her feel about the fact that she was having dinner with her husband and would undoubtedly kiss him good-night.

"She's lovely," Helen said, handing the

photo back.

"Yes, she was." He looked himself, as if needing to see his wife's face, before he carefully tucked the picture back into its plastic sleeve and returned the wallet to his pocket. "Turnabout is fair play, right? Do you have one of Ben?"

"Yes." It felt odd, showing her husband's picture to this man across the table. As if, oh, Ben would be judged in some way. Which was silly — Alec was just curious, as she'd been. Wordlessly she handed over the photo.

He looked in silence, then said, "Ginny takes after him."

"She does, doesn't she?" Helen took the picture back, looking down at it herself. Ben had been a pleasant but not extraordinarily handsome man, with a wiry build and a laugh that could make total strangers smile. A less self-absorbed individual Helen had never met. Ben was *comfortable* with himself. He wasn't awfully ambitious; he seemed only to want a decent living, his wife and a house full of children. They'd been planning for Helen to get pregnant again when he said one day, "You know, my fingers have been feeling weird. The little one on my left hand is numb."

They had both thought of carpal tunnel,

149

although as a middle-level manager in an insurance office he didn't spend that much time on the computer. He'd wanted to shrug the symptom off. Helen was the one to insist he get it checked out. "You don't want it to get worse," she said firmly.

Watching her put the picture away, Alec asked, "Do you miss him much, even now? I mean, day to day? Do you still think, 'Wait till I tell Ben'?"

The question took her by surprise, and she hesitated, thinking about the past few days, trying to remember the last time she had forgotten Ben was dead, even fleetingly.

"It used to be a constant ache." Without thinking about it, she pressed her hand to her chest, as if quelling the pain. "But after a while it did diminish. You know. I'd go a few minutes without thinking about him, then a few hours. Now a few days. And when I do, it's . . . different. Not immediate, as if he might be waiting at home." She focused finally on Alec's face. "I had so long to watch him die, you see. You must have woken up every morning thinking it couldn't possibly have happened, it must just have been a nightmare, while I had over two years to see death taking him. To know that it was real."

His face haggard, Alec nodded. "You hit

the nail on the head. I felt . . . stunned disbelief. I guess that's the best way to describe it. I must have spent the first year enveloped in a haze of unreality. This was happening to someone else. Not us. Linda would be there when I got home. When I opened my eyes and rolled over in bed, she'd be there." He shook his head. "I know the kids felt that way, too. One of them would start to say, 'When Mom . . .', then look stricken."

"But that wasn't the worst part, was it?" Helen felt as if she had a frog in her throat. Remembrance, or compassion, had made her voice husky. "The worst was when reality hit."

"Yeah." He tried to smile but gave up. "Yeah, I woke one morning and lay there *knowing* she was gone. I almost didn't get up. I'm not sure I would have, if I hadn't heard the kids downstairs."

Helen nodded. "That happened to me, too, only it was before Ben died. I really, really believed he wouldn't. He couldn't. The doctors sounded so optimistic — although now I know they weren't. I heard what I wanted to hear. But he had a bad night, and when he finally slept I curled up in the chair with an afghan. And then I just knew. It was like diving into icy water. I felt myself falling, and suddenly my teeth were chattering and I huddled there in shock, hoping he wouldn't wake up and see me."

Somewhere during this speech Alec had reached across the table and taken her hand. His was warm and strong and comforting. She returned his grasp, giving as much as she took.

"After that," she said simply, "I pretended, but I know Ben could see I was lying. Sometimes he tried to get me to admit . . ." Eyes burning, she swallowed. "Oh, dear." She sniffed, gave a sad laugh, then said, "Our salads are sitting here untouched. The waiter is giving us worried looks."

Alec gave her hand a last squeeze. "Eat," he ordered, and reached for his own fork.

But Helen couldn't help asking, a minute later, "Do you still . . ."

He read her mind. "Miss Linda? In some ways, yeah. But not with the same urgency. Just regret."

Helen nodded. "That's it exactly. Regret."

"Especially when one of the kids does something special."

Helen nodded. "Ben so wanted children."

"Linda, too. So it makes me angry that she was cheated." His voice cracked and Alec pinched the bridge of his nose, briefly closing his eyes.

"I tell myself," Helen said quietly, "that either they can see the children growing up and rejoice in their triumphs, or they can't, and they're beyond sorrow. Either way, we're the ones grieving, not them."

He thought about that, then nodded, the pain on his face easing. "Yeah. You're right."

They talked about other things, then, the finality of giving notice on a job, the retail environment in eastern Washington, the wind turbines she would see during her drive.

"I'll watch for them," she promised.

"You can't miss 'em." Alec pushed his dinner plate away and nodded when the waiter offered coffee. "What's your itinerary?" he asked, when they were alone again.

"Ellensburg, Yakima and Walla Walla, then up to Spokane. After that, I'll see what I can manage on the drive back. Maybe Moses Lake and Wenatchee. This *is* my first venture."

"You'll be great. You've been successful in the Puget Sound area, obviously."

"We have." She told him about her dream of producing a catalog, and he commented from his experience. They discussed the problems of volume sales. Did she and Kathleen really want to hire people to make and package the soap? In other words, did they want to be executives or craftswomen?

"I don't know," she conceded. "Sometimes we dream, but mostly we focus on next month and the one after that. This step — quitting our jobs — is the first real leap of faith we've taken."

"You can always get another job," he said comfortably. "But I'm betting you won't have to. I never did tell you how thrilled Dev is with his bar of anti-acne soap, did I? He doesn't like to talk to me, but he sidled into my home office the other day to ask if I could get him some more. Seems to me you're appealing to just about everyone — pet owners, teenagers, people who work with their hands, not to mention women looking to treat themselves."

Helen took his words home with her, still savoring them when they kissed good-night.

It occurred to Helen, just as she was on the edge of sleep, that somehow she had failed to slip in her little warning. With them talking about Linda and Ben, it would have been the perfect time to say, *I don't know about you, but I've vowed not to remarry. Hurting that much once is enough, thank you.*

Only, she hadn't. And he might assume . . . She fell asleep without completing the thought.

The minute Alec pulled into the garage, he could *feel* the music. If you could call it music. He'd never imagined as a parent that he'd have a problem with anything his kids listened to, but he hadn't counted on the obscene and violent crap he heard coming from Devlin's bedroom.

Oh, no! he thought, getting out and slamming the car door. One of these days a neighbor would call the cops to complain, and Alec wouldn't blame them.

His mood wasn't improved by finding the kitchen trashed. The kids must have had dinner, then a dozen snacks. Or Devlin had had friends over, which wasn't expressly forbidden when his father wasn't home, but . . . If Kyle or one of the other guys came and didn't mind hanging out with Lily, fine. A bunch of them holed up in Dev's room, ignoring his little sister, was not fine. Either way, the rule around here was that if you made a mess, you cleaned it up.

Upstairs, the music pounded. Alec was heading straight to Devlin's room when he saw that Lily's bedroom door was ajar. Her bedside lamp was still on, creating a soft

155

pool of light that kept night at bay. She was in bed, covers drawn up high, her back to the door.

Alec gently pushed open the door and stepped in, his footfall quiet on the carpet, but she turned sharply, her eyes wide and dark.

"Oh!" she gasped with relief. "Daddy!"

"Hey, sweetheart." He went to the bed and sat beside her, smoothing her dark hair back from her forehead. Only then did he see the tracks of tears on her face. "You've been crying. What's wrong?"

"Nothing," she said, too quickly. Lily didn't like to rat on her brother. "I was feeling scared."

"Scared?" Alec kept his voice gentle. "Of what?"

"Dumb stuff," Lily whispered. "I watched a movie that scared me. I know it isn't real. But I keep thinking . . ."

"What movie?"

"*Signs*. You know, with Mel Gibson. And there's aliens. There's this scene where the little kid is standing there, and you see one behind him." She shuddered.

Alec drew her into a hug. "Hey, it *was* fake."

"I know." Her tears wet his shirtfront.

"You shouldn't have watched a movie that scary."

She sniffed and mumbled against his chest, "I didn't know it was."

"I suppose Dev chose it."

She went still, warning Alec that he wasn't going to like what was coming. Or that she intended to lie.

In a small voice, the eleven-year-old said, "He didn't watch it."

"What?"

She drew back and eyed him warily. "Kyle came over, and they decided to do something else, so I watched it by myself."

Steamed now, Alec said, "And where were they, while the movie was on?"

"Oh . . . around. You know."

"Eating, obviously," he muttered. Then they'd shut themselves in Devlin's bedroom with the stereo blasting.

"It's not *his* fault I'm scared."

"Sounds to me like he abandoned you this evening. He knows better."

Fresh tears started in her eyes. "He'll be mad at me if he knows I told you!"

"I'll be careful what I say," Alec promised. "Do you think you can sleep?"

She nodded, eyes puffy. "Now that you're home."

"Okay. I'll be up for a while."

"Can I leave my light on?"

"Do you want me to turn it off once you're asleep?"

Lily nodded. He kissed her and left the room.

A moment later, he knocked hard on Devlin's bedroom door. The guttural rap continued unabated. Alec opened the door and walked in.

Lying on the bed, Dev had his hands cradling his head. "Dad!"

Alec went straight to the stereo and hit the power button. His ears rang in the ensuing silence.

Devlin sat up. "I was listening to that!"

"I could hear it outside," Alec said grimly. "You're lucky one of the neighbors didn't call the cops."

The teenager sneered. "It wasn't that loud. Can't I have *any* privacy around here? You didn't even knock!"

"I knocked. You didn't hear."

Face twisted with what looked frighteningly like hate, Devlin snapped, "Is that all?"

"No." Alec crossed his arms. "Your sister is huddled in bed crying because she watched a movie tonight that scared her. I expect better judgment from you than that."

"She *told* you?"

"She shouldn't have told me that she

watched *Signs* tonight? Did you pledge her to secrecy?"

"No! I thought she'd like it!"

"Uh-huh." He watched the boy closely. "Did you like it?"

"Yeah, I thought it was cool." Devlin shrugged. "I rented it because I saw it at a friend's house. It's not like a horror flick or anything."

He did, to his credit, sound puzzled. Maybe, Alec thought with a sigh, he was expecting too much of a fourteen-year-old. At eleven, Dev wouldn't have admitted being scared by a movie. He, too, might have thought his sister would like one just because he had.

"I seem to remember the mom in it is dead, and one of the kids gets taken by aliens. That hits close to home for Lily."

Devlin picked at a hole in his jeans and didn't say anything.

"Didn't you notice she was getting scared?"

"Kyle came over. We didn't watch." He raised his head, the same anger darkening his eyes. "You make me babysit, but I don't have to do *everything* with her."

"No, you don't. But it would be nice if you had paid enough attention to notice she was afraid to turn her light off."

159

Devlin flushed. "Why do I have to babysit anyway? None of my friends do! I can never go anywhere, because I'm stuck with my *sister.*"

The loathing in his voice rocked Alec back on his heels. Dev resented having the responsibility of staying with Lily that much? Or was this just part of the bigger problem: the fact that he wanted nothing to do with his father or home?

Quietly Alec said, "You know if you have something specific to do, I can get someone to stay with Lily. Or she can spend the night with a friend. I don't think it's unreasonable to ask you to stay home with her sometimes. Kyle doesn't have to do the same because he's the youngest in his family. Don't I remember his big sister taking care of him?" He didn't wait for an answer. "I'll be on the computer for a while. Please clean the kitchen before you go to bed."

Smoldering silence was the answer. His jaw clenched, Alec strode from the room. After glancing in at Lily, he headed downstairs and took refuge in his office.

He didn't turn on the computer, only sat frowning at the dark screen. He'd had such a good evening. Talking about Linda had hurt, but not as much as he'd expected. He was glad he and Helen were past that hurdle. She probably hadn't wanted Linda to become real to her any more than he had wanted to imagine Helen with her husband.

But the way they had talked had left Alec feeling at peace about their past marriages. They had both loved, lost and grieved. It sounded like Helen, too, had finally reached a stage where she could let somebody else into her life without any feeling of guilt.

He had been glad to see that he didn't bear any resemblance to Ben. That might have bothered him. He liked, too, the fact that Helen was very different from Linda, except that both loved their children fiercely. He didn't want a carbon copy of Linda. He wanted to love a different woman, to have her share his life as completely as Linda had.

Helen, he was becoming increasingly certain, was that woman. She was smart, compassionate, direct, kind to his kids. And, from the moment he first saw her, he had wanted her. Sitting here right now, his fingers curled into fists as he imagined the heavy silk of her hair, always sleek against her head because she confined it. There was a fragility about her, in part because of that porcelain skin. Slender ankles, delicate wrists — he'd swear they weren't any bigger around than Lily's, an intriguing, unnameable scent that clung to her whatever she wore, a mouth that smiled easily and tasted like . . . vanilla. Home. She was all contrast: pale face against the dark fire of her hair, vulnerability and strength, doubt and certainty.

He was fast falling in love with Helen Schaefer, and thought she might be reciprocating.

Hearing the thud of footsteps on the stairs, followed by cupboard doors banging in the kitchen, Alec grimaced.

Nothing like knowing that your much-loved firstborn child was likely to derail a new romance. Who in their right mind would *want* to take on stepparenting a sullen, rude, resentful teenage boy?

Helen was making some gutsy changes in her own life. Alec just hoped she was up to one more: taking the huge risk of loving him, encumbrances and all.

CHAPTER SEVEN

Helen saw Alec half a dozen times in the next two weeks, but always around other people. She and Kathleen had scheduled craft fairs that ran Friday through Sunday the last weekend in July and the first in August. Helen also tried to spend as much time with Ginny as she could to make up for her planned absence the following week.

Ginny insisted on doing every day of both fairs with Helen, despite invitations to do fun stuff with her friends.

On the way to Anacortes on Saturday morning, Helen asked, "Are you *sure* you wouldn't rather have gone to Hood Canal with Jennifer?"

Jennifer's parents owned a waterfront weekend "cabin," with four bedrooms, just south of the Hood Canal bridge. It apparently included a dock, several boats, a gigantic trampoline, and a fire pit.

"Making s'mores over a beach fire sounds

like fun to me," Helen continued.

Ginny shrugged. "I just didn't want to go."

It occurred to Helen suddenly, with amazement at her own denseness, that Ginny had never spent a night away from home. Sleepovers hadn't interested her.

Oh, dear, Helen thought.

She let a few miles pass before commenting, "I'm going to miss you next week."

Ginny fastened eager eyes on her mother's face. "I could go with you!"

Helen squeezed her daughter's small hand. "I did think about taking you. But it would be an awfully boring trip for you —"

"I don't care!"

"And," Helen continued, "it wouldn't look very professional to have a child with me when I go into stores."

"I could wait in the car." Ginny almost quivered as she pleaded. "Please? Please?"

Of course Helen wanted to succumb. How could she say no to that face?

Are you ever *going to be able to say no to her if you give in every time?* an inner voice asked tartly.

Ginny couldn't always go with her. They might as well get over the hurdle right away, rather than putting it off until the next business trip.

"Ginny . . ."

"Please?"

Helen sighed. "Let me think about it, okay? I suspect you'd have a better time staying home. We'd be driving miles and miles through dry, uninteresting country. You'll be bored while I'm talking to store owners. We wouldn't have time to do much that's fun for you."

Ginny began to protest again, but Helen raised her hand.

"Let me finish. I was going to say that, on the other hand, you *can't* go with me once school starts, whereas this time you could. And you're good company. But let me think about it. No," she said, before Ginny could get her mouth open. "No pleading. I'll say no right now if you keep arguing."

Ginny pretended to "zip" her lips.

Helen couldn't help laughing.

The Anacortes Arts and Crafts Fair was one of Helen's favorites. The town itself was charming, full of wonderful Victorian houses. The ferry to the San Juan Islands left from here, and the main drag, Commercial Street, ran directly down to the shore. A marina was only blocks away, seagulls soared and the scent of the Sound was everywhere. Antique stores, kitchen shops, B and Bs and boutiques attracted tourists. This year, like last, the closed street was jammed with shoppers by ten in the morning, and the stacks of soap kept having to be replenished during one of the busiest days Helen and Kathleen had ever had.

Late in the afternoon, Emma took Ginny off to look at other booths. The crowd on Commercial Street had thinned, leaving trash strewn on the pavement and exhausted exhibitors — Helen and Kathleen included — slumped in lawn chairs.

When Helen asked her about Ginny tagging along on the sales trip, Kathleen frowned thoughtfully. "Maybe you should take her," she said at last. "It might help when you *have* to leave her if she can picture what you're doing. And she'll know you're not exactly having fun."

Helen puffed out a breath. "Ginny doesn't care about fun. Haven't you noticed? She's less interested in playing than any kid I've ever met."

"Hmm." Kathleen weighed that. "You're right. She's awfully solemn."

"I don't know if she's actually scared about being left, or just afraid she'll miss me, or what." Helen gazed sightlessly at the booth across from them. "I'm sorry! If she's scared to sleep or really freaks out, you're the one who'll have to deal with her."

Kathleen patted her arm. "What are

'aunts' for?"

Helen gave a choked laugh. "What would I do without you guys?"

"Make an honest-to-goodness salary, instead of putting in ridiculous hours trying to start up a business?" Kathleen suggested.

This laugh felt more genuine. "Ah, but you're my road to obscene wealth."

Kathleen's face brightened. "We're doing really well again this weekend, aren't we?"

"Do you have any idea how many people have stopped by and said, 'Oh! I bought some of your soap here last summer and I *loved* it'? After which they loaded up."

"Isn't that amazing?" Kathleen smiled at a woman who wandered into their tent. Raising her voice, she said, "Hi. Ignore us. We're too tired to stand up."

The woman laughed. "Actually I have a booth down the way — jewelry." She took a card from her shorts pocket. "I swore I was going to find time to look at everyone else's stuff. And I've got to tell you, I love your soap! I've been buying it at Whole Foods in Seattle."

Helen met Kathleen's eyes and both burst out laughing. After Helen explained their recent conversation, the woman nodded. "Isn't that the best compliment you can get?"

Not long after, Ginny's hand tucked securely in Emma's, the two girls returned from their expedition. Helen was conscious of the way her daughter's gaze sought her out when the girls were still half a block away, as if Ginny had been afraid her mother would disappear while she was out of sight.

Maybe, Helen thought, she'd better find the money for Ginny to have some counseling.

Or was this fear something shared by all children who'd had a parent die? Ginny clung; Devlin Fraser, apparently, was testing his father constantly. *Are you really here to stay?* he seemed to be asking.

But why? Ginny's insecurity, Helen could understand. It might stem as much from Helen's emotional withdrawal during that last year of Ben's illness and the months following the funeral as it did from the loss of her father. Her mom's grief had scared Ginny. Now she had to be sure all the time that her mommy really was here.

Had Alec, too, withdrawn from his children? Was that what had scared his son? Or was something way more complicated going on inside the boy's head?

Well, *he* wasn't Helen's worry; Ginny was.

On the drive home, Helen said, "I've

decided you can come with me next week."

"Yeah!" Ginny bounced happily, restrained from hugging her mother only by the seat belt.

"We'll try to have a good time. Make the trip a little bit of a vacation, too. After all, you've never seen the Columbia River, or the apple orchards in Wenatchee, or the wheat fields near Walla Walla."

"Alec says lots of wine comes from eastern Washington. I guess they grow grapes there or something."

"So I understand." Helen grinned at her daughter. "I doubt we'll tour any wineries, though?"

Her daughter's nose wrinkled. "Wine is gross!"

Helen laughed. "It's an acquired taste."

Of course she had to explain "acquired." When Ginny concentrated, the mechanics of her mental storage were visible, as if a file drawer was pulled out, a new card dropped in, the drawer slid back in place.

"Oh," Ginny said, the process complete.

"You do understand that you can't come with me every time."

The delight on Ginny's face faded, reminding Helen painfully of the wraithlike child Ginny had been when they first moved into Kathleen's house.

169

"Uh-huh."

"Are you scared by the idea of me leaving?"

Ginny bent her head and nibbled on a fingernail. Her voice was small. "Not scared 'zactly."

"You can't get homesick, because you'll *be* home."

"But I won't know what you're doing."

Helen cast her a puzzled glance. "Sure you will. Especially after you go with me once."

Ginny was quiet.

Helen drove, sneaking sidelong looks at the curtain of pale brown hair veiling her daughter's face. Finally, gently, she said, "What do you think I'll be doing?"

Ginny's shoulders jerked.

Helen waited.

"What if something happens to you?" the eight-year-old burst out. "And we don't know? What if you just don't come home?"

"Oh, honey! Nothing will happen to me! I'm a careful driver. Besides, I'll have my cell phone and I'll call at least once a day so you know where I am."

Ginny stole one desperate look at her mother's face. "Do you promise?"

Cross my heart almost slipped out. Thankfully, Helen remembered the rest: . . . *and hope to die.*

"I swear. And I will keep my purse with me every minute so if I were to get in a car accident or faint gracefully on a sidewalk, anyone could look to see who I am and where I live."

"But you won't."

"Faint gracefully?" She gave Ginny's small hand a last squeeze. "Probably not. I'd probably topple over like that piano the Lanskys were moving. Remember?"

She was rewarded with a giggle. The neighbors had been sure they didn't need to hire a mover when they bought a used upright piano. Unfortunately, they'd gotten it halfway up the front steps of their house when it began falling back. The two men below had jumped out of the way and the piano had crashed to the concrete walk with a spectacular symphony of splintering wood and discordant notes. The neighbors who had gathered to watch had stared in horror.

"No," Ginny said, "you'd flop like Pirate does." She lurched to the side to mimic their orange tabby, who loved to have his tummy rubbed.

"Well, thanks," Helen said in mock annoyance.

Her daughter giggled again.

Helen hoped she'd done the right thing, giving in this time. But that night, when told about the trip, Jo wasn't so sure, shaking Helen's confidence. Logan, on the other hand, snorted when Helen told him that Jo thought Ginny needed to experience her mom going away — and coming back safely.

"Sounds sort of like the kind of swim lessons where you shove the kid in the deep end and see if he drowns."

"But eventually I'm going to have to shove her in!" Helen heard the desperation threading her voice. "Aren't I?"

Logan, who had been pouring a cup of coffee, joined her at the kitchen table. Built like a longshoreman, with shaggy dark hair, he had the kindest eyes she had ever seen.

"I don't know about that," he said, between sips. "Aren't you giving her lessons already? You've been working, dating. Here's my suggestion. After this trip, why don't you make the next one short? Just an overnighter. You could go over to the Peninsula, maybe, or up to Bellingham. Time after that, you can be gone a couple of nights. You don't want to be on the road all the time anyway, do you?"

"No," she said gratefully. "No, I don't. I'd miss Ginny. I'd miss all of you!" She flashed a brilliant smile at him. "I'd kiss you if I wasn't afraid of your wife."

His low, rough chuckle was almost as sexy

as Alec's.

Alec came up to Anacortes Sunday and dragged her away from the booth for some of what he called comparison shopping.

"I want to see what artists haven't applied to Queen Anne. And whether we want 'em."

Ginny materialized at her side. "Can I come, too, Mom?"

Much as she loved her daughter, Helen's heart sank just the tiniest bit. Visions of stolen kisses had danced in her head.

"Nope," Kathleen said from the depths of the tent. "Ginny, I need you. We can't spare more than one of us at a time."

Ginny shot Alec a resentful look, but turned dutifully. "Oh. Okay."

"I won't be gone long," Helen promised, then mouthed to Kathleen, *Thank you.*

Kathleen winked, provoking the very chuckle from Alec that Helen had been thinking about last night.

He fell silent so quickly, however, that Helen glanced at him in surprise. As they made their way through the crowd, a frown drew his brows together.

"Ginny doesn't like me much, does she?"

Surprised, Helen replied, "She hasn't actually said. And I haven't asked."

He looked down at her. "Afraid?"

"No-o."

173

"Uh-huh."

She punched his arm. "Come on. Have you asked Devlin how he feels about me?"

Somewhat grimly, Alec said, "I don't have to."

Nudged by the crowd, they were briefly separated. When they came together again, Helen said, "That bad, huh?"

"He hasn't exchanged ten words with you. But he doesn't like me, either."

Helen didn't know what to say. Alec must know his son loved him, whatever the boy's behavior suggested. She simply didn't know enough about their conflict to offer any ideas. She'd seen them together only the once, at Nordstrom. Maybe the problem wasn't all Devlin; maybe Alec was too stern, expected too much, felt a sense of competition and tried to assert dominance. She couldn't be sure that she was hearing the whole story from Alec.

"Where are your kids today?" she asked.

He had paused at a booth displaying wrought-iron garden stakes, trellises and arbors. "Both at friends' houses. I'd have brought Lily otherwise."

"Ginny liked her. She's spent so much time with Emma, she thinks kids her own age are silly."

"Lily seemed to like her, too."

They bought caramel apples and ate them as they walked. Alec kissed the tip of her nose and said it was sweet. And sticky.

Helen greeted exhibitors she knew and studied the displays of those she didn't. Traffic control in one booth was cleverly designed, she thought; the mood another created was somehow chic and upscale, making her think of shops in Belltown, Seattle's exclusive neighborhood. She grabbed a couple of particularly catchy business cards. The ones for Kathleen's Soaps had been cheap and needed a redo. Too bad they couldn't capture the scent of raspberry cream or cinnamon-oatmeal in heavy card stock.

Alec spoke with a few vendors, suggesting they apply to the Queen Anne arts and craft fair next year. Because it was a relatively new one, some of the well-established crafters hadn't yet tried it out. While Lucinda and Helen and Kathleen spent virtually every weekend all summer at fairs, other artists who depended more on retail sales or showed in galleries might only do a few. Helen was beginning to think Kathleen's Soaps might follow suit in a couple of years. These fairs were fun but exhausting.

A ripple of apprehension spread from her chest. Her business trips would determine the future. If she was a failure . . .

Helen pulled herself up short. She'd done just fine so far, hadn't she? She had been far braver than she'd ever dreamed she could be. Building sales was slow work. She wouldn't expect too much, and she wouldn't let herself get discouraged if the first trip or the second or even the third didn't yield instant success. Even a few new retail outlets would pay off and gain exposure for Kathleen's Soaps.

Alec did manage to give her a few brief but thorough kisses at intervals as they toured the fair, which spread out over what seemed a mile or more of street.

When he eventually left her back at the booth, it was after extracting a promise that she would have dinner with him Monday night. Tuesday morning she and Ginny would set out on their great expedition.

Helen made a vow to herself: tomorrow night, she would tell him that marriage wasn't in the cards for her. She had to. She wasn't being fair, letting him think she might be interested in more than she was.

And maybe, setting ground rules now would be smart for her, too. Drifting along the way she had been wasn't a good idea. Sometimes lately she'd begun to imagine that falling in love didn't *have* to be dangerous or selfish.

But she of all people knew better, so she'd get it out in the open. She owed both of them that much.

He couldn't leave the house these days without Devlin picking a fight. His son twirled on the bar stool to face him when Alec paused at the kitchen door to say he was leaving. Despite the lengthy showers, Dev's blond hair looked lank and greasy. In a black T-shirt, Alec's son looked older than fourteen, and somehow dangerous. He was the kind a store clerk would watch carefully.

The usual sneer curled his mouth. "You can't go a *day* without seeing her?"

Tension throbbed in Alec's temples. "Helen is leaving town tomorrow on a business trip. She'll be away for almost a week."

"You'd probably go with her, if you trusted me to babysit." He said the last as if it were a curse.

"That's mean!" his sister said, from in front of the refrigerator. She'd been peering inside, but now glared at Devlin. "Like you have to *do* anything!"

"I have to stay home, don't I?" he all but snarled. "I have to make sure you don't watch scary movies." His tone became viciously solicitous. "Or you might cry yourself to sleep."

Her lip trembled before she whirled to stare steadfastly into the refrigerator.

Not usually a violent man, Alec felt his hands ball into fists. His voice grated. "I didn't raise you to mock other people for their fears. Lashing out at your sister because you're mad at me is beneath you."

A mask closed over Devlin's face. His posture radiated cold indifference. "Who says I'm mad at you? I don't care if you want to spend every night with your girlfriend. As long as you don't marry her, what's the big deal?"

"And if I do decide to marry her?"

His son looked at him with those hate-filled eyes. "She's not taking Mom's place." He spun again, all the way around, then jumped from the stool and sauntered out, bumping Alec on the way hard enough to hurt.

"Oops," he said, and took the stairs two at a time. The slam of his bedroom door had barely quit vibrating the pictures on the walls before the monotonous bass of his music took over.

Stomach knotted, Alec stayed in the kitchen doorway, torn by indecision. How could he leave Lily alone with Devlin after that display? But he hated to cancel on

Helen when she'd be away for a week.

His daughter closed the fridge door and faced him. Her shoulders were squared, and he saw on her face that she had read his mind.

"It's okay, Daddy. Dev's actually not that bad when you aren't home. Anyway —" she shrugged "— if he stays up there I'll just watch a movie or something. You know, I'm old enough to babysit. Mrs. Byrd down at the corner asked me the other day. Only you weren't home, so I couldn't."

"Babysit?" he echoed.

"I'm almost twelve. She pays three dollars an hour, and Will is really sweet. She just wants me, like, when she goes to the grocery store or something. Usually when he naps, she said. Not for hours and hours."

"Oh." She was growing up. Look how calmly she was distracting him.

"Can I?"

"Babysit?"

Unlike Dev, she did not roll her eyes. "Just during the day?"

"Uh, I don't see why not."

She was responsible. Face it, she was more responsible than her brother. He wasn't altogether sure who was in charge of whom, but Alec knew which of his kids he trusted more.

"I won't be late," he promised, and held out his arms.

She catapulted into them, letting him know she'd been more upset by her brother's outburst than she had let on. She hugged him fiercely, then pulled back. "*I think Helen is nice, Daddy. Don't listen to him.*"

"Despite what I said, Helen and I haven't talked about getting married. It's not time for that yet."

"Is it?" Her expression was entirely too adult. "You really like her, don't you?"

"Yeah," he admitted. "I do."

"Before she died," Lily said unexpectedly, "Mommy told me she hoped you would marry again someday. So you wouldn't be lonely. And 'cuz she thought Dev and I needed a mom."

Linda had said the same to him, but he hadn't listened. He'd gripped her hand and fought tears. "I won't have to. You're not dying, Linda. *You're not.*"

He still remembered her steady gaze and his sudden realization that he was crushing her hand.

"I want you to," she'd whispered, before closing her eyes and drifting into sleep, effectively preventing him from further argument.

She had died just two days later, without saying any more. Since remarriage was the last thing on his mind then or anytime in the past two years, he hadn't thought more about what she'd said except as an example of how generous her love for him and the kids had been.

But he was grateful now that she had given him her blessing. He didn't want to have to agonize over how Linda would feel about a usurper. The troubled family she had left behind had enough worries.

"Did she say that to Dev?" Alec asked.

His daughter's brow knitted. "I don't remember if he was there. But I don't think so. I don't know if she talked to him."

He wished she had. He wished she could now. She wouldn't recognize her own son in the punk who'd shouldered past his father tonight.

He kissed Lily and promised again not to be late.

He and Helen had decided on pizza tonight. She was leaving early, had spent the day packing, and didn't want to have to dress up. As far as he was concerned, she looked just as good in shorts, sandals and a T-shirt as she did in her more elegant outfits. Her legs were long, slim and faintly golden, her feet charmingly sturdy in what

181

appeared to be Birkenstocks. Tonight her hair seemed to want to slip out of its habitual ponytail. She tugged irritably at it as they went down the front steps.

"Emma talked me into trying one of her scrunchies instead of a ponytail holder. They work fine, she said."

The weight of her auburn hair was definitely defying the black cloth circlet. He wondered if she had any idea how beautiful it was.

"Maybe it feels the way you would if you wore a corset most of the time. It's slumping in relief."

"You're a big help."

He laughed. "You about ready for the great adventure?"

"Oh, getting there." Helen sighed and cast a look at her aged car as they walked past it. "I wish the air-conditioning worked better. What do you bet it picks this week to give up the ghost?"

Alec frowned at her Escort. "I forgot the shape your car is in. That's a lot of miles to put on it. What if you break down somewhere between Yakima and the Tri-Cities?"

She patted her purse. "I have a cell phone. I'll call a tow truck. Besides, my car has always been reliable. I had the oil changed, the tires checked and rotated, and the window-washing fluid refilled. We're ready for anything."

He didn't like to think of her on a long trip in that heap of junk. He unlocked the Mercedes. "If you're going to be doing much of this kind of traveling, you'll need a new car."

"I'm hoping for a couple more years from this one."

"You won't get 'em if you're flitting off to Portland and Boise every other week." He held open the passenger door for her.

She crossed her arms and made no move to get in. "You're not lifting my spirits."

"Can't I worry about you?"

Her expression softened. "I suppose so."

Alec kissed her lightly. "I'll shut up. I promise."

They went to Pagliacci's on Broadway, sipped soda pops and talked. Mostly about her forthcoming trip, her decision to take Ginny, and her realization that she'd never been separated from her daughter overnight.

Halfway through dinner Alec excused himself, pulled out his cell phone and dialed home. He hoped Dev didn't answer. Lily wasn't allowed to.

He got the answering machine. "Hi, kids. Just checking in. Lily, can you pick up?"

She did. "Hi, Daddy."

Aware of Helen across the table, he asked, "You okay?"

"Sure." Lily's answer was light, as if she'd forgotten the earlier scene. "I'm reading."

"Dev?"

"He came down a while ago. I told him he was a jerk, and he said, yeah, he guessed he could be sometimes. That it's not *my* fault he has to stay home when his friends are all hanging out somewhere."

An apology, of sorts. "Good," Alec said. "All right. Just checking. I have my cell phone on."

"You always say that."

"Sorry. I worry."

When he clipped his phone back on his belt, Helen said, "Everything okay?"

"Yeah. Devlin and I had it out earlier." He gave a crooked smile. "For the ten thousandth time."

Her face creased with compassion. "I'm sorry."

"One of these days, I have to figure out what the real problem is." He managed a grin. "Besides hormones."

"And me?"

"The idea of anyone taking his mother's place upsets him," Alec conceded.

She looked more bothered than he had

expected. "But you've assured him I'm not?"

"I'm afraid tonight I got mad and said, 'So what if I do marry her?' That's when the you-know-what really hit the fan." He realized he was watching her carefully, wanting to know how she'd react to the word: *marry.* Him and her.

A shadow scudded across her face, a look he didn't understand. A second later her expression had become serene. She straightened in her chair, squared her shoulders and said firmly, "Then he'll be comforted to know that you're dating a widow who has no intention of remarrying. Feel free to tell him."

He felt as if she'd just bodychecked him more effectively than his son had. Stunned, he said, "You mean that?"

"Yes, I think so." She didn't quite want to meet his eyes. "People tell me someday I'll change my mind, but . . . I can't imagine. It hurt losing Ben. I don't want to go through that again. I learned things about myself, too. Things that . . ." For the first time she faltered. "That make me believe it wouldn't be fair of me to marry again."

Things? What was she talking about?

"You'd rather be alone?"

She laughed merrily. He didn't buy it.

185

"Alone? I'm never alone! You've heard me complain!"

"Ginny will grow up," Alec said brutally. "Leave home. You won't live with Kathleen and Logan forever."

Her gaze met his at last, her expression apologetic, as if she saw in his reaction that he *had* been thinking, at least distantly, of marriage. "No, but I hope I'll always have friends."

Things? He couldn't leave it. Had she been unfaithful? She seemed the soul of integrity.

He shook his head. "I can't believe you were anything but a wonderful wife. Would he tell me different, if Ben were here?"

Pain flared in her eyes. "I don't know. I . . ." She swallowed hard. "Please, can we talk about something else? No." She reached blindly beneath the table for her purse. "I really should get home and finish packing. If you don't mind."

He stood when she did, and they walked silently the two blocks to the car. Not until they were on Roosevelt Way heading north did she say, "I'm sorry if I took you by surprise. If you were thinking . . ."

"Thinking?" He raised his brows, hoping the expression didn't appear as affected as it was. "I hadn't gotten that far. We've never

186

discussed how either of us felt about remarriage. And with kids it's problematic."

"Yes," she said. "I thought it might be good if you could allay Devlin's fears."

He chuckled. "You mean, instead of threatening him?"

She smiled. He was more convincing than he'd thought. "Something like that."

In front of her house — Kathleen's house — Helen touched his arm. "You don't have to park. I'll just hop out."

They ended the evening with a peck on the lips and her promise to drive carefully next week and to call as soon as she got back.

She hesitated, gave him a last, curiously desperate look, and jumped out. Halfway up the steps to the house, she waved, and he drove away.

On the way home, he used his turn signals, checked the mirrors when appropriate and obeyed speed limits. He did it all as if he were having an out-of-body experience. He knew the sensation: it was shock. He'd felt as peculiar several times — when his wife was diagnosed, when she died and when he had his heart attack.

Funny, he hadn't known how serious he was becoming about Helen Schaefer until she dropped her bombshell. In the back of his mind had been the idea of her in his home. Of her making the kitchen a warm, loving room again. Guiding Lily through adolescence, softening Devlin's inexplicable anger. Giving Alec a solid center to his life again. Something — someone — to hold on to.

Safely in the garage at home with the door shut, Alec turned off the car, but sat unmoving for a long while.

CHAPTER EIGHT

The week alone with Ginny was a delight. Helen didn't regret taking her for one minute. Ginny chattered happily but not too much, and craned her neck to look at the dry ski hills and empty lifts as they drove over Snoqualmie Pass.

At the first couple of stores in Ellensburg, Ginny waited in the car. But the day was hot, Helen didn't like leaving the engine running, and at the third store, she said, "Come with me this time, but let me do the talking, okay?"

Ginny gave her a wounded look. Helen pretended not to notice.

The owner of the small gift shop thought it was wonderful that Helen had brought her daughter on a business trip. "Mine," she said, "is asleep in the playpen in the back. That's partly why I opened my own business. I didn't want my kids to be in day care from eight to six."

Helen had left samples with the previous two shop owners, but this store was one she really wanted to have sell Kathleen's Soaps. A wonderful conglomeration of antiques, local crafts, garden art and kitchen goods crowded shelves and walls and spilled onto the floor. Concrete cats sat beneath bins of aprons. Silk flowers leaned artlessly from ceramic crocks, and dried herb wreaths scented the air. A real cat crouched on the counter next to the cash register, his unblinking gaze fixed on Ginny.

The owner was a short, plump woman who admitted to being an ex-employee of H&R Block. Now long, thick hair was carelessly confined with a pencil stabbed through the bun, and she wore a fuchsia print apron over jeans and a T-shirt. She told Helen, "I love having my own business!"

She sniffed the soap samples, took a bar to the bathroom and worked up a lather, then discussed prices and discounts. "I'll give it a try," she decided.

"How wonderful! I have enough in the trunk to get you started. We keep adding new products and scents, and you can decide which are appropriate for your store."

The cat, a fat Russian Blue, decided to let

Ginny pet her, and the shop owner heard all about Ginny's cat, Pirate, and how they'd found him as a kitten with one eye hanging out.

"We don't know if he can see out of it," Ginny said, " 'cuz he won't read an eye chart, but it doesn't matter. We love him no matter what."

Helen and Ginny had decided to spend the afternoon in Ellensburg and then drive on to Yakima, where they'd booked a room in a B and B. Helen had used the internet and phone books at the library to research businesses she wanted to approach, but she asked her hostess to recommend others.

She struck pay dirt almost immediately. A fruit stand/antique and gift store right next to the freeway had been looking for a new line of soaps, and she unloaded more from the trunk of her car. Others in town promised to think about it.

Ginny was awed by the Columbia River and the bleak, volcanic landscape. Irrigated orchards and wineries turned vast stretches green against a brown backdrop. The wind turbines Alec had talked about whirled endlessly on high ridges. Helen wondered if his company had made any of these.

They spent an entire day in the Tri-Cities and a morning in Walla Walla, a college town

191

and county seat made famous by the massacre of the missionary Marcus Whitman and his wife. They visited nineteenth-century Fort Walla Walla and peeked into log cabins, a tiny one-room schoolhouse and a jail. Helen's pleasure was in watching Ginny tour the museum, carefully reading every placard, staring wide-eyed at corsets and old-fashioned children's clothes, wagons, a spinning wheel and a butter churn.

Ginny slept much of the way to Spokane, waking to gaze silently out the window at the hills of golden wheat. Helen spent two days in Spokane, finding only one sure taker and a dozen more shop owners who promised to get in touch.

This was the first time in two years that Helen had had Ginny to herself for more than a few hours at a time. Her pleasure in the days of conversation made her question again her decision to give up the security of a regular income and with it the chance to make a home just for the two of them. And yet, she was pleased with what she'd accomplished on this trip, walking in cold to meet shopkeepers, and was hopeful that orders would pour in. As she drove miles of long, straight, empty highway, Ginny asleep beside her, with nothing to look at but tumbleweeds piled on rusted, falling-down barbed-wire fences, she dreamed of making enough money to buy a house.

And she thought about Alec. She attributed the sting of tears to the grit blowing across the highway, leaving streaks of yellow sand on the pavement. Some must have come in through the vents and gotten into her eyes.

Oh, he'd profess to be glad when she called, Helen guessed, but she wouldn't be surprised if he was vague about getting together. Or perhaps they'd meet once or twice, then the intervals between phone calls would increase.

She shouldn't care so terribly much. She wished she'd told him how she felt in the beginning. It wasn't as if he'd said anything about the future or falling in love, but she had seen the shock on his face. He must have been thinking, at least in the back of his mind, of marriage and stepparenting and all those things that she wouldn't, couldn't, do.

But an ache under her breastbone told her that she didn't want to lose him. Why couldn't they go on the way they had been? They could date, and be friends. Wasn't that enough?

Half a dozen times she was tempted to call him on her cell phone, just to say hi, but she always stopped herself. She didn't want to spoil the time with Ginny by finding out that he'd lost interest, now that he knew she wasn't a candidate to become Wife Number Two. This week gave them both a chance to think. To miss each other — or not.

After Wenatchee, the highway climbed into the Cascades, the forest growing thicker and greener until they reached Stevens Pass and more empty ski lifts and lodges that looked odd without snow crowning their roofs. Then they were back in Western Washington, dropping in sweeping curves toward Monroe and Everett and I-5, which would take them back to Seattle.

"Are you glad to be almost home?" Helen asked Ginny as they passed the freeway exit to Edmonds.

"No, I had fun."

"Even if all we did was drive?"

"We did lots of other stuff. Besides, I like going with you."

"I'll take you when I can," Helen promised. "Maybe we'll have time for one more trip before school starts." Ginny would have to start staying home soon enough.

Ginny's face brightened. "Really?"

"Why not? At least a short one. Bellingham and Leavenworth, or maybe onto the

Peninsula to Poulsbo, Port Angeles and Port Townsend."

"That would be so-o-o fun!"

Helen laughed and ruffled her hair. "I think so, too."

Ginny was quiet for a few miles. They had reached north Seattle when she said, "Are you having dinner with Alec tonight?"

Helen glanced at her in surprise. "I haven't talked to him in a week! When would we have planned that?"

Ginny shrugged. "I just figured."

Helen bit her lip. "Don't you like him?"

"He's okay." Her head turned so fast she risked whiplash. She studied her mother in alarm. "Why? You're not marrying him or something, are you?"

"Don't be silly. You'd be the first to know, kiddo." Helen stole another look. "Would that be so bad?" The moment the question was out, she wished she could snatch it back. She had no intention of remarrying, Alec or anyone else!

Her daughter fidgeted with her seat belt. "It might be okay. 'Cuz he's probably got a nice house, and I liked Lily. Only . . ." Her words gained momentum. "We might never have time to do stuff together. Just us. And maybe I couldn't climb into bed with you if I got scared."

195

"I will *always* have time for us to do stuff together. No matter what. I promise."

"Really?" Ginny looked at her with such fear in her eyes, Helen's heart squeezed. This was a child who would never forget the year when her father was dying and her mother hadn't had time for her.

Helen would never forgive herself for neglecting her small daughter. No, she could never, ever go through that kind of loss again.

"Really," she swore, swallowing the lump in her throat.

"Okay." In an abrupt change of mood, Ginny bounced. "We're almost home, Mom!"

Painfully near to tears, Helen smiled. "So we are."

Alec had spent the week counting the days and then the hours until he could talk to her again. He went through a stretch of being angry at himself for not being able to dismiss Helen from his mind. He was falling in love with her, and she had gently let him know that the feeling wasn't mutual. He'd be an idiot to interpret her remarks, made out of the blue, any other way.

But, after a couple of days of bitter hurt, he had begun reexamining their conversations, their kisses, her expressions. And he didn't believe she wasn't attracted to him! She seemed to like spending time with him as much as he did with her. She had never been coy, had always been free when he asked her out, had never even hinted that she didn't have the same hopes most single adults shared.

She'd taken his daughter bra shopping! Did a woman afraid of commitment and family life do something like that?

So what had happened? Had their last kiss been too passionate? Had he said something to make her panic? Was it Devlin? Had she decided she couldn't deal with a problem teenager?

When he should have been working, Alec tried to remember every word Helen had ever said to him. Especially the last ones.

It hurt losing Ben. I don't want to go through that again.

Yeah, okay. It had hurt. But he'd read that the happier people's marriages had been, the more likely they were to remarry, and quickly. So why not Helen? Had her marriage really not been that great? If she and Ben had had unresolved problems, or she'd never felt secure in his love, then the pain of losing him in such a final way might have been worse.

Alec stared at the figures on his computer monitor, willing them to grip him. Expenses had been skyrocketing. Where could they cut? Numbers created patterns for him, when he let them. These wanted to; shapes almost formed, as if he saw mysterious movement from the corner of his eye. But when he looked directly they were gone. He couldn't concentrate.

Maybe Helen and Ben had been on the verge of divorce. Had he intended to leave her? What if she was grateful initially for his illness, because he stayed?

I learned things about myself, too. Things that make me believe it wouldn't be fair of me to marry again.

Didn't that suggest guilt? She believed she was unworthy in some way.

I can't believe you were anything but a wonderful wife, he'd said. *Would he tell me different, if Ben were here?*

He had glimpsed some inner torment that she had not intended to reveal.

What? he asked himself in frustration, for the hundredth time.

Alec's speculations got wilder. Had Ben suffered so terribly? Had she somehow engineered his death and now felt like the black widow, who might kill any mate?

Was there anything she might have done

198

that would make him agree that she shouldn't ever marry again?

If so, he couldn't think what that would be.

His obsession with learning her secret — if she *had* a secret — only grew as the week went on. The more ludicrous his conjectures — perhaps she never had been married, and "Ben" was a fiction — the worse his loneliness became.

He'd been kidding himself. He wasn't falling in love; he *was* in love. He had been living for their near-nightly phone calls, for the chance to see her every few days. He wasn't a mature man enjoying a relationship with an interesting woman; he was a lovesick teenager whose grades were plummeting because he couldn't think about anything but his sweetheart.

She hadn't been sure what day she'd return. Would she call him? Alec somehow doubted it. And he didn't want to seem too eager.

Grimacing, he remembered those high-school courtship rituals: *saunter by, pretend you don't see her, but glance back as if looking for a buddy and hope you catch her looking at you.*

What difference did it make if she knew he was eager?

But he kept his hand from the phone. Not tonight. He'd wait until tomorrow. He could hear himself, casual, vaguely surprised she was back, saying, *Good trip? Hey, when did you get in?*

Tuesday night he called her. Logan answered.

"Alec. No, Helen isn't in. She and Kathleen are off somewhere."

"Ah. Well, tell her I called. Did she have a good trip?"

His nonchalance was wasted.

"Sounds like she did," Logan said. "I'll give her your message."

Alec hit End and set down the phone. He'd been primed to hear her voice! His stomach was churning.

Now what? Wait to see if she returned his call? Try again tomorrow?

An hour later, the phone rang. Somewhere in the house, one of the kids pounced on it.

"Dad!" Devlin bellowed. "It's for you."

"Thanks!" Alec called back, and picked up. "Hello?"

"Hi." Helen was laughing. "His lung power is awesome. I can see why he's a great athlete."

He laughed, too. "We wouldn't need intercoms or that modern convenience called "hold" if everyone had Devlin's technique."

"It beats Ginny's. She listens gravely, then sets down the phone and walks off to look for the person. They have no idea if she heard them, they got cut off . . . ? Who knows?"

"Discourages those telemarketers, though."

She gave that delightful chuckle again. "How true."

They did the "How was your trip? Great" thing then. He'd thought she might have dreamed up some reason to be rushed, but she chatted just like she always had, telling him how much fun she'd had taking Ginny new places. "We went to the water slides in Moses Lake, which was great fun. Of course, I'm sunburned again. Oh, and your wind turbines!" Helen exclaimed. "They're fascinating. I see what you mean. They almost belong, but not quite. It's as if some alien culture left them behind, marching silently along the ridges."

"Yeah, that's it," he said, pleased.

"Only, you're one of the aliens who built them. I kept trying to reconcile you with those weird towers."

"So you thought about me." If that wasn't pathetic!

201

"Of course I did!" she said warmly. "I almost called you half a dozen times just to talk."

His fear eased. "You did?"

"Yes, but I told myself the week was just for Ginny."

"And business."

"And business," she agreed, and told him about her successes and failures and maybes. "I added four new outlets while I was on the road, and I've already heard positively from two more stores. So I'm feeling pretty good about it."

"Saleswoman extraordinaire!"

"That's me," she said smugly, then spoiled the effect with a belly laugh.

"I missed you." Alec heard the huskiness in his own voice.

She was silent for a moment. "I missed you, too."

"I want to see you."

"Okay."

"Lunch tomorrow?"

She agreed. They set a time and place, and ended the call. The lovesick teenager inside him tried to figure out what it meant. She loved him. She loved him not.

He hadn't sounded any different, Helen reassured herself a dozen times while she waited for Alec the next day at a Queen Anne bakery. Maybe they *could* go on as they had been. Maybe she'd been mistaken in thinking her announcement had dismayed if not shaken him. Maybe he was relieved!

She sat at a small wrought-iron table on the sidewalk, shaded by a canopy and screened from the street by greenery. When Alec stepped outside, he looked straight at her as if none of the other diners existed. He made his way through other tables to her, bent over and kissed her, his mouth lingering long enough to make her heart flip-flop, then he sat down.

"I forget how beautiful you are."

Blushing from the kiss and the expression in his eyes, she laughed and shook her head. "We've already had this argument, and I'm sure you lost."

As if he hadn't heard her, he said again, more deeply than he had on the phone, "I missed you."

She took a breath. "Alec . . ."

"I can enjoy your company even if you won't marry me, can't I?"

Helen told herself it was relief that swelled in her chest. "Yes, you can. I'm glad."

His expression suddenly arrogant, he said, "I'm going to change your mind, you know."

She gaped at him. "What?"

"Hi." A teenage waitress laid menus in front of them. "Can I start you with something to drink?"

Never looking away from Helen, Alec said, "Give us a minute."

"Oh. Sure." She wandered away.

Helen shook her head. "I can't believe you said that."

"That I'm going to change your mind?"

That he wanted to marry her. Wasn't that what he had just told her?

"We hardly know each other."

"I know you well enough, Helen Schaefer." His voice was low and rough. "I want you in my life."

"I *am* in your life." She was almost dizzy with exultation. How could she fight him, when she felt this way?

"But not beside me when I wake up in the morning. Not at the breakfast table, not curled next to me on the couch while we watch the news, not brushing your teeth in the bathroom while I hang up my suit."

"I . . . I haven't even seen your house." She was breathless.

"We'll fix that." His expression was intense but tender, and very determined.

"Alec . . ." She closed her eyes so she couldn't see him. "I did mean what I said. I can't . . . I just can't."

"Why?"

Her throat closed; she shook her head.

"If you won't tell me, I'll refuse to believe you."

She took a shaky breath. "Alec, I don't want to . . . to hurt you."

He shook his head and reached across the glass-topped table for her hand. "If I get hurt, on my own head be it. You've warned me. I'm refusing to be scared off."

Helen was shocked to find that she was *glad.* She didn't want an anemic relationship where they were good friends. She wanted to be loved, with exactly the fierce hunger she saw in his eyes now.

It's just that she was afraid, so afraid, to love him the same way.

"After watching Linda die, it doesn't scare you to know you might have to go through that again someday?"

To his credit, Alec took her seriously. "Yeah, it scares me. If you told me you had cancer . . ." His jaw muscles flexed. "I think it might even be worse the second time, because now I *know* . . ." He moved his shoulders as though to relieve tension. "But how can I protect myself from ever having to watch someone I love die? I can't. My parents are still alive. I'll probably go through it with them. I have kids. Do you know how many teenagers die in car accidents? The doctors don't think there is a hereditary component to Linda's kind of leukemia, but can we be sure?" He looked into her eyes. "People you love die, Helen. That's life."

She knew what he said was true. But he hadn't had the long, drawn-out battle with death that she had waged. He hadn't made his beloved wife suffer because he wouldn't wave the white flag of surrender.

"I do know that," Helen conceded.

"But that isn't all that's bothering you."

"I told you." She bit her lip. "I was left hating myself in the end. It's . . . not a comfortable feeling."

The waitress stopped at their table again. "Ready to order?"

"Yes." Helen flipped open the menu and seized on the first item she saw. "I'll have the crab sandwich."

"And you, sir?"

Frowning at Helen, he said, "I'll have the same. And a lemonade, please."

She went away, and Helen grasped for her composure. "I don't want to talk about it, Alec. Maybe sometime. I suppose . . . oh, I owe you that much. But . . . not now."

He searched her face, then nodded. "All

right. Another time."

Would she have the courage? Helen didn't know. Maybe. It seemed she felt braver all the time.

"Did you tell Devlin what I said?" she blurted.

He smiled faintly. "No. Remember, I intend to change your mind."

"Oh."

"He wouldn't be comforted anyway." Alec looked away. "He uses you to get to me. That's all."

"Will you put him in counseling again?"

The creases between his nose and mouth deepened. "And join him. Obviously, we have issues to discuss."

Helen touched his hand. "Good for you."

The sandwiches arrived, and she discovered she was hungry after all. Alec asked more about her trip, and her future plans.

"Thanks to you," she told him wryly, "I worried about my car the whole way."

"You talked once about buying a van."

"Kathleen and I did discuss it. But even if we did, the mileage would be lousy for long road trips."

This commonsense discussion laid a veneer over deeper emotions, although Helen felt her cheeks warm a few times when she saw the intent way he watched her.

He had to go back to work and expressed frustration with an afternoon meeting. "I'm soothing investors, my specialty." He grunted. "Income has far outpaced our original projections, but with the economy so chancy they're nervous."

Trying to lighten his mood, humorous, Helen said, "And with all my anxieties, I probably made your day worse."

"No." His eyes darkened. "Spending time with you improves any day."

She felt her smile tremble. "I'm glad."

"When can I see you again?"

"I have grand plans for the rest of the week. A bunch of soap has cured long enough and needs to be unmolded and packaged. I also have appointments to look at soap dishes, believe it or not. I'm trying to find a couple of different types — enamel or ceramic or wire. Kathleen had visions of us making the wire ones, but it's too time-consuming. I don't know how many we'd sell, but it would be great to offer some at fairs."

"Friday night?" he asked. "Dev is going to a concert at the Tacoma Dome with friends and spending the night with one. If Lily can wangle an invitation, too . . ."

A thrill of anticipation mixed with nerves shot through her. They could be alone. Truly alone, for the first time.

CHAPTER NINE

Ginny's bedroom was half little girl's room, half art studio. When Ginny called "Come in," Helen entered.

A few neglected Barbies flopped arms and legs over the rims of plastic storage boxes stored on shelves. Her bed was covered by a sunshine-yellow chenille spread — Ginny had curled her lip at any suggestion of *pink*. A square of vinyl flooring, spattered with paint, protected the wood floor beneath Ginny's easel, where a half-finished charcoal sketch hung. She liked modeling with clay, too, so her desk was topped with a piece of Plexiglas and she kept various types of artist's clay in plastic tubs.

Helen paused in front of the charcoal drawing. "Hey, this is really good."

Ginny was sketching their cat, Pirate, who had apparently been sleeping on her bed. She was deftly giving personality to the long-haired orange tabby with shadings and the mere suggestions of line.

"Do you think so?" From where she sat on the bed, Ginny cocked her head and frowned at her own drawing.

Helen shook her head and laughed. "Yes, I think so! No, I'm not just being motherly and encouraging."

"Well, but you would be," Ginny argued.

"Yes, but . . ." Amused and exasperated, Helen said, "I refuse to argue." She pirouetted. "How do I look?"

"You look pretty."

Slyly Helen asked, "Really? You're not just saying that?"

"No! You really do. . . ." Ginny caught on and crossed her arms with a harrumph.

"Because you are my daughter. You'd say that anyway."

The eight-year-old stuck out her tongue, then giggled.

Helen couldn't resist stealing a glance at herself in the full-length mirror hanging on the closet. She hadn't worn this dress in years, not since before Ben's illness. It was a simple slip with spaghetti straps and a plunging back, in shimmery bronze silk. The skirt hugged her body down to her ankles, where it flared above strappy, heeled sandals. With her hair up, she thought she did look . . . well, not pretty, but elegant.

Careful not to wrinkle the silk, Helen sat on the edge of Ginny's bed. "Don't try to wait up for me, okay? I'll be really late tonight."

Her daughter nodded glumly. "I wish *I* could go to a play."

Helen smiled. "We haven't been in a while, have we? Let's check to see what the Seattle Children's Theatre is doing. You wouldn't like this one anyway. Trust me. I'm not sure *I* will."

Ginny's forehead crinkled. "How come?"

"Well, Shakespeare can be hard to understand."

"Oh, will you tell me about it after?"

"I'll report on it tomorrow."

"Promise."

Helen laughed. "I will. I swear. But —" she looked stern "— *not* tonight. You can't wait up for me."

"Oh, all right."

"And quit scowling." Helen kissed her forehead. "Moms are entitled to have fun, too."

But how *much* fun? she wondered guiltily, when she heard the doorbell downstairs.

She had been delighted when Alec called Wednesday to say he'd bought tickets to the performance at the Fifth Avenue, the beautifully restored theater in downtown Seattle.

212

"I missed it the last time around," he said.

"I did, too." Helen didn't say that she missed most of the traveling shows and locally produced ones. Her budget only allowed for an occasional trip to the Seattle Children's Theatre.

She didn't feel guilty about the lovely dinner Alec was taking her to or the performance.

"The kids'll both be gone tonight," he had said quietly, at the end of the conversation.

If a heart could somersault, hers did. The idea of seeing his home tonight was both exhilarating and frightening.

Was she in love? If not, should she be contemplating going home with Alec? If she was in love, how could she be? After vowing she'd never do anything so foolish!

Descending the stairs, she pinned a smile to her lips, determined that he not see her nervousness.

At the sight of Alec, Helen's heart took another uncomfortable leap. The well-cut suit showed off his broad shoulders and the crisp white shirt was the perfect foil for his hair, silvering at the temples, and lean, tanned face. His eyes darkened as he watched her come, and she flushed with self-consciousness.

"I feel like Cinderella," she announced,

trying to make light of the moment.

"If you'd been at the ball, nobody would have looked at Cinderella."

Kathleen, whom Helen had vaguely noticed standing in the hallway, applauded. "Very nice! Logan, come take lessons."

Her husband appeared in the doorway of the living room, a smile in his eyes. "I have my poetic moments." He caught sight of Helen and said simply, "Wow."

Kathleen rolled her eyes at Helen. "See what I mean?"

"A sincere 'wow' is much appreciated." Helen detoured to kiss Logan's cheek before she laid her hand on Alec's arm. "Don't expect me until late."

Kathleen laughed. "I feel as if I should say, 'Have fun, children!' Or maybe I ought to issue a dire warning about your curfew."

"Maybe you should be jealous instead," Helen teased over her shoulder, as Alec gently urged her out the door. "I haven't seen *you* dressed up in a long time."

"You do have a point." Kathleen waved and shut the door behind them.

"You're always lovely," Alec murmured. "Tonight, you're sensational."

"Thank you."

During the drive, he took her hand. They didn't talk much. Even during dinner at

Palisade, where they ate by candlelight, watching the boats pass the soaring windows, conversation seemed . . . not strained, but *careful.* As if each word mattered.

Instead of feeling adult and sophisticated, Helen found herself remembering the night of her senior prom, when she had dressed like this for the first time. Proms could be awful disappointments, but hers wasn't. In a rented tux, her date had been far more handsome than he was in the halls of their high school, and riding in a limo was exciting, a glimpse into the lives of movie stars and business tycoons.

No limo tonight, but Alec's Mercedes was even better, she decided, as he pulled into the multistory parking garage half a block from the theater. She almost laughed. Alec *was* a business tycoon.

The Fifth Avenue Theatre was gorgeous, from the brightly lit marquee to the restored 1920s gilt Oriental decor. The crowd was well dressed and expectant.

Helen was more captivated than she'd expected to be by the show's gorgeous sets and the compelling performances by the actors.

After long and enthusiastic applause, the entire audience on its feet, Alec and Helen joined the slow exodus.

Alec's hand was warm, clasping her upper arm as they made their way past clumps of theatergoers rounding up members of their party or animatedly discussing the play. Words floated after them as they went through the double doors out into the warm night.

"Uninhibited . . ."

"Tragic . . ."

"Beautiful . . ."

As the light changed and Helen and Alec started crossing the street, he said, "Well? What did *you* think?"

"I thought it was marvelous. The actors were incredible. Did you read the bios? Most of them were local."

"There were some superb performances, weren't there?"

The Mercedes felt as if it had shrunk, becoming a tinted bubble that separated them from the world outside. Helen concentrated on her breathing.

Alec put the key in the ignition but didn't start the engine immediately. She felt his gaze on her face.

"Would you like to come to my place to talk about the show over coffee?"

"That would be nice," she said primly.

Alec cleared his throat. "Okay. Good." Under his breath, he muttered, "I hope Dev cleaned the kitchen before he left."

Helen laughed. "I've seen dirty dishes before."

"He and his friends can trash a kitchen."

"Growing boys have big appetites."

"You can say that again."

They had gotten — temporarily — past the awkwardness. They chatted about the kids. Another parent had driven a group of boys down to the Tacoma Dome and was picking them up after the concert, and Lily was spending the night at a girlfriend's.

"Difficult as he is, Devlin makes friends more easily than Lily does. She's more reserved — shyer, I suppose. Maybe it's harder for girls. I don't know. It seems like boys always move in a pack."

Helen nodded. "I know what you mean. Ginny's had a hard time, too. In her case, it doesn't help that she has never been interested in group activities. She played soccer one year, softball another, and didn't much like either. But she's got a couple of pretty close friends now."

"Lily's the same. Lately her circle is expanding. I'm getting the impression that teenage girls move in packs, too." His tone was humorous. "Safety in numbers, maybe."

"Could be." Helen congratulated herself on her light tone. In fact, she was very aware of how alone she and Alec were. They had dined in busy restaurants, strolled in the middle of fair crowds, shopped with their kids, kissed in parking lots and on her front porch. But, except for brief car rides, they had never been really *alone.*

Until tonight.

His house was on upper Queen Anne Hill, on the west side where the land fell sharply toward the Sound. In the dark she could see only that the houses in his neighborhood were good-sized and charming. Many were built of brick, with Tudor beams or fairy-tale peaks above leaded-glass entry doors. Yards were ample and beautifully landscaped, with flowers tumbling down stone retaining walls and wisteria and clematis twining over arbors built to echo the porch pillars.

His house was a large, white, Cape Cod–style home with black shutters framing small-paned windows. As at Kathleen's, the garage was at street level, but because of the slope of the hill, was also part of the basement. The door glided up and the Mercedes turned in. Alec touched the opener attached to the visor and the door began closing behind them.

Unlike Kathleen's garage, this was double-car width. A lawn mower was on one side, tools hung on hooks and Peg-Boards, and two tall cabinets with closed doors corralled any other clutter.

"Logan would approve," Helen blurted.

Alec shot her an odd look. "Of my garage?"

Blushing, she said, "Well, and Kathleen, too. They're both neat-freaks."

"Ah." He pulled the keys from the ignition. "Dare I admit that the garage is neat because I hardly ever touch anything in it?"

"You're not a gardener?" She felt compelled to make conversation.

"The yard is low-maintenance. I do what I have to." His mouth crooked. "What I can't make the kids do."

"Oh." Dead end.

"Let's go upstairs," he suggested.

"The house looks beautiful." She almost made a face at her own gushing.

Alec circled the car toward her, his eyes — well, she didn't quite meet them, so she wasn't sure what expression they held. But he said conversationally, "I've always liked it. The part that's now the living room and the kids' bedrooms was built in the twenties, and there was a major addition to accommodate a master suite and family room fifteen years ago. Fortunately, the architect stayed true to the spirit of the house."

He opened a door and gestured for her to climb up the steps. Skirt gathered in her hand, Helen was conscious of him right behind her.

She opened the door at the top of the stairs and stepped into the kitchen, a gorgeous room that — almost — made her forget why she was here. Rag rugs and polished wood floors, cherry cabinets and antiques created a dream kitchen.

"You must live in here," she said, slowly turning. "This room is perfect."

For a moment, Alec was silent. Then, in a reflective tone, he said, "Funny thing, but I realized not long ago that I avoid the kitchen."

Helen had a peculiar sinking sensation in her stomach. "Was this Linda's favorite room?"

He gazed past Helen toward the dining nook, something in his eyes making her guess he saw a ghost. "I told you she loved to cook."

She nodded but doubted he noticed.

"We remodeled the kitchen after we moved in. When we were done, Linda stood just about where you are now, looked around, and said, 'It's perfect.' "

Almost exactly what she'd just said, Helen realized. The slow sinking in her belly became a nauseating plummet.

"I'm sorry. I didn't mean . . ."

He shook himself and focused on her for the first time since they'd stepped into the kitchen. "No, I'm sorry. I should have known you'd love this room. I always did, too. Like I said, it only dawned on me recently how much I associate it with Linda."

"Are you sure staying in the house was a good idea?"

"No. I'm not sure. But I thought familiar surroundings would help the kids hold on to memories."

Helen nodded. Perhaps, in selling her house immediately, she'd robbed Ginny of the chance to cling to remembrances of her father: *here* he held me, *there* he stood on the stairs and laughed. But she had been sure that most of all, Ginny would remember the dying man lying in the hospital bed that filled the living room. They had become so accustomed to tiptoeing, to keeping their voices down, to shutting doors softly, she hadn't thought they could ever *live* there again.

Alec made an impatient sound. "Can I get you coffee?"

"Um . . . coffee sounds good." She needed the bracing effect of caffeine to think sensibly. Alec, she greatly feared, was still in love with his wife. Helen hated the idea that he sought a substitute.

He'd been running water and measuring coffee. "While it perks, let me show you around. If you're interested."

"Yes, I'd love to see the rest of the house."

Swinging doors led into a central hallway furnished with the same warm touch. A ceramic vase stood on an ivory crocheted runner protecting the gleaming surface of a cherry console with turned legs. The watercolors on the pale peach walls were all of lush gardens and fat blossoms. White woodwork and oak floors continued into the living room, where a model of a wind turbine stood like a sculpture on the brick surround of the fireplace. Chairs upholstered in cream, rose and green were teamed with a cream-colored leather sofa. Gently faded Persian rugs with ivory backgrounds tied the furnishings together. Built-in white painted bookcases flanked the fireplace, and a huge philodendron clambered over the front window.

"The monster plant," Alec said wryly.

His home office was more utilitarian and clearly masculine, with a big leather chair, a cherry-wood desk, and ranks of filing cabinets and bookcases. A laptop sat open on the desk, flanked by silver-framed photos of Linda and the children. On the wall hung black-and-white photos, which she noticed all featured the power of the wind. A grove of palm trees bent as if in obeisance; a cypress clinging to a cliff had been twisted by winter winds; on a city street, wind-whipped rain was driven sideways.

The photos she left reluctantly, because she knew they were *his* choices. The rest of the house had probably been decorated by Linda. Helen hadn't expected to feel such dismay at being surrounded by his wife's unseen presence.

The family room was done in earth tones, the brocade upholstery richly combining teal, rust and orange, the paintings on walls more exuberant, the woodwork stained with a walnut finish. A big-screen TV and stereo occupied an entertainment center that filled a wall. French doors led outside. When Alec flipped on the outside porch light, she saw a brick patio with cedar furniture and an arbor.

"You have a beautiful home," she said simply, facing him. "I can see why you didn't want to give it up."

"Does it bother you that she lived here?"

"Bother me?" She feigned surprise.

He stepped closer. "It's not Linda on my

mind tonight."

Breathless, Helen raised her chin. "When I said that in the kitchen, you were thinking about her. I almost had the feeling you *saw* her."

He reached for her hand, his thumb idly tracing the fine bones on the back of her hand. "Oddly enough," he said in a meditative voice, "it was the first time I've really studied the kitchen when I *wasn't* thinking of her. I was wondering why I've been shying at shadows."

Helen searched his face. "Really?"

"Really." He lifted his other hand and cupped her cheek. "I can't pretend I was never married, Helen. I hope you wouldn't want me to."

"No," she whispered. "I wouldn't want you to."

"I know you've loved before. I hoped that doesn't mean you can't again."

Tears stung her eyes, unexpected and unwelcome. She swallowed. "I . . . don't know."

A ghost of a smile flitted over his face. "That's better than 'I can't, I won't.' "

He was teasing her.

"Is that what I said?"

"You must have been talking about something else."

"I suppose —" her voice sounded not at all like her own "— that depends on what you mean by 'love.' "

"What if we start with affection?"

"I think," Helen whispered, "I can feel affection again."

He smiled. "You have the most glorious hair I've ever seen. Or touched. I've wanted to run my fingers through it since the first time I saw you."

"Mmm." Eyes half-closed, she bent her head to let him stroke beneath her heavy fall of hair.

Helen went still. "I didn't think to ask whether it bothers *you* to have me here."

He neither flinched nor hesitated. "I wouldn't have asked you if it did. I told you. I want you in my life. My home."

His home. Which he had once shared with his wife. The idea shouldn't bother her, but it did.

"Would she resent me? In her place?"

Alec's hands dropped to his side. "No. Linda told me before she died that I should remarry. She wanted me to be happy again."

He paused, studying her face. "I haven't asked you. How would Ben feel about me?"

She didn't have to think. "Oh, he's probably rooting for you, wherever he is. Ben was a gentle, kind man, incapable of being

225

mean or possessive."

Alec nodded but still didn't touch her again.

Voice rough, he asked, "Have we killed the mood here?"

"I don't know." It was the shy Helen who answered, the woman who reacted, never led. *What did* he *think?* she was asking herself. *Had he lost interest?*

Indignation at her own timidity gave her courage. "No," she said firmly, "I think what we've done is cleared the air."

In a deliberate tone, he said, "I've wanted you since I turned the corner at the fair and saw this beautiful redhead hefting boxes out of the back of a pickup. I couldn't think about anything else the rest of the day. I talked to other exhibitors, but the whole time I was calculating how long it would be until I could work my way back to your booth." At last, he lifted a hand, brushing his knuckles along her jaw. "Even after I was home, I could hear your laugh, see the sadness in your face. And I worried about the wedding ring." He reached for her hand and lifted it. When he saw that she had taken her rings off, he looked at her.

"I thought it was time," she said tremulously.

Alec's laugh was low and shaky. "Yeah. I

226

thought the same." He lifted his left hand
to show her that it too was bare, only a paler
circlet of skin left as a reminder.

She lifted hers and laid it against his, palm
to palm, in a sort of vow. *From this day
forward.* Whatever happened, she would not
put her rings back on. Symbols *did* matter.

Alec had made her feel things she had
almost forgotten, and she knew he could
make her feel more. So much more.

If she dared let herself love him, and trust
an uncertain future.

CHAPTER TEN

"Mommy! Watch out! You're going to fall down!"

Teetering on in-line skates, Helen flapped her arms like a crow, let her ankles turn and toppled over onto the grass beside the paved path.

Alec watched in amusement as her daughter helped her up and said sternly, "Mom, you've got to *balance*."

"No kidding," she grumbled. "I never guessed."

Lily and Ginny both giggled. They were taking great delight in being much better at something than an adult was. Especially a *mom.*

The day was sunny after a week of clouds and rain, too nice to waste indoors. Helen had called that morning and said, "Want to do something with the kids?"

"If you don't mind me dragging my sullen son along. This is our day for family outings, and I'm making him go."

"He may sulk to his heart's content," she had said cheerily.

They were not alone at Green Lake, one of the many lakes in the heart of the city. A paved trail for walkers, bikers, baby strollers and skaters circled it. A park at one end offered a swimming beach patrolled by lifeguards, tennis courts and an indoor swimming pool. Woodland Park Zoo was just up the hill. Shops, bakeries and cafés, including a second Spud's Fish & Chips, were within a block.

Today Alec could hardly see the grass, so many families had spread blankets on it to picnic and sunbathe. Even halfway around the lake, he could hear the shrieks of kids in the water. Joggers trotted past and cyclists whizzed by.

Helen, however, was making about a quarter of a mile an hour. Her daughter was right — she apparently lacked balance.

"I'm going to be covered with bruises," she muttered, wavering on her feet again.

"On your butt." Ginny exploded in gales of laughter.

Predictably, Devlin had skated well ahead. Now he came back and executed a perfect stop. Lip curling, he said, "She fell down *again?*"

Alec's jaw clenched. He was going to develop TMJ if his charming son didn't outgrow this nasty phase in a hurry. Before he could remonstrate, however, Helen gave Devlin a dirty look and snapped, "If you want me to go faster, why don't you offer some advice instead of telling me I don't have very good balance, like the rest of your family?"

Startled, he actually answered her directly. "Well, you don't . . ."

She cleared her throat meaningfully.

"Uh." He frowned and studied her. "Your ankles are the problem, I think. They're flopping."

"Flopping?" She looked down at her feet and almost went over.

Devlin grabbed her just in time.

She clutched his arm. "I don't know why I'm so terrible! I roller-skated when I was a kid! This isn't that different."

"Some people," Alec said kindly, "don't have strong ankles."

Helen and Devlin both gave him dirty looks this time.

"Girls," Alec suggested, "can you move to the edge of the path? We're in the way."

An elderly couple riding sedately on a bicycle built for two offered grateful smiles and a "Good day!" as they passed.

"Maybe you should all go ahead." Helen made a face. "I could totter back while you guys zip 'round the lake."

"We're not going to desert you," Alec said firmly.

"See," Devlin said, "just think about your ankles and nothing else. Can you make them stiff? Like, pretend you have casts on both feet?"

"Casts." Still holding his arm, she went stiff all over.

"Uh, you don't have to have a body cast. Just on your ankles."

She frowned in fierce concentration. "Just ankles."

A pair of twenty-somethings in peak physical condition swept by on in-line skates, arms pumping. Helen rocked as if their wake had struck her.

Astonishingly, Devlin didn't pull away.

"Stiff ankles," he repeated.

Helen's legs straightened, and she released her death grip on the teenager's arm. Resolutely she moved one foot, then the other, in a choppy stride that was only a distant cousin to the glide of a practiced blader.

"Hey, that's good!" Devlin said from behind her.

Ginny clapped.

Grinning in triumph, Helen picked up speed. Alec winced, knowing what was coming. Her legs began to bend like pretzels, her feet tangled — then Devlin grabbed her, holding her upright.

"Ankles. You forgot your ankles."

Gasping, Helen rearranged her feet and straightened. "Ankles."

What had gotten into his son? Devlin had started the day sullen — as usual. He didn't want to come. He had to mow Mrs. Gregorski's lawn. He'd promised Curt he'd hang out later. It wasn't a *family* outing if Dad's *girlfriend* — said in a snotty tone — was coming.

"Last week," Alec had said, "I let you choose what we did." They had gone to the Experimental Music Project, an unusual museum that celebrated contemporary music. "This weekend it's my turn."

That wasn't the end of it, of course. They'd had a staring contest, Alec striving for an expression of calm certainty. Devlin looked away first, and he grumbled all the way to the car. When they'd picked up Ginny and Helen, he mumbled something that might have been a hello and spent the remainder of the ride staring out the window. The minute he'd put on his skates, he'd struck off ahead. A couple of times

232

he'd come back to sneer at Helen's ineptitude, taunt his sister for being slow and generally make himself loved.

Maybe he was just impatient to get the circuit of the lake over with, so he could go home. Could be he'd decided they would never make it if he didn't intervene.

Or had he actually taken pity on Helen? Alec hid a grin, even though he was behind the two. If ever anyone deserved pity, it was Helen today.

Maybe she just offended Devlin's athletic sensibilities, and he felt compelled to "improve" her. He had coached youth basketball for a couple of seasons.

"Hey, girls!" Alec called. "Race ya?"

"Yeah!" Lily grinned. "Dad's not that good," she told Ginny, not quite sotto voce.

Helen stuck out her tongue at him when he stroked by her. "Leave me in the dust, why don't you?"

"Looks like you're getting the hang of it," he said over his shoulder.

"Yeah." She still wore that frown of concentration. "Yeah, I think I am!"

"Ankles," his son warned when she wobbled.

She made a frustrated sound. "Every time I think about anything else . . . !"

"Then don't," Dev said succinctly.

233

Alec didn't see how she responded to that. He was lengthening his stride to overtake the two girls, who were zipping in and out of other traffic, their skinny legs pumping.

Devlin didn't stay with Helen the entire way around the lake, but Alec did notice that he kept coming back to check on her.

It got so when she saw him approach, she'd smile impudently and shout, "Ankles!"

Unaware his father was watching, Devlin actually grinned at her.

"Don't take up ice-skating."

Clomping stiffly along, she said with a certain grim note, "I promise you, the thought never crossed my mind."

Noting Helen's exhaustion, Alec kept pace with her for about the last mile, where the trail followed the shoreline and only a scattering of shrubs separated it from the speeding cars on Aurora Avenue, one of Seattle's busiest roads.

The minute they reached their starting point, she flung herself to the grass and flopped onto her back, arms and legs outstretched.

"I made it." She moaned. "I didn't think I'd make it."

"We didn't, either," her daughter confessed.

"You did fine," Alec said stoutly.

She rolled her eyes toward him. Amusement lurked in them along with perfect knowledge of how inept she'd been.

"That's the end of my in-line skating career. Devlin," she turned her head to look at him, "thank you. You're a lifesaver."

His cheeks turned crimson and he cast a hasty glance at his father before mumbling, "It's okay."

"Girls." Helen fastened her gaze on them. "I will make you pay someday for all those giggles."

The threat was met with renewed hilarity. Alec shook his head and for a moment met his son's eyes in complete agreement.

"I need lunch," Helen announced, sitting up. "Once I get these off."

"Our shoes are in the car," Lily said.

"Don't care." It took Helen only a minute to strip to bare feet. She stood with her skates in one hand and her socks in the other.

The others took a paved path; she walked across grass with a blissful expression on her face. Every time Alec looked her way, she was wriggling her toes or bouncing on tiptoe.

"See?" she said when they met up at the

car. She stood on one foot. "I have balance. I do."

The kids all gave her pitying looks. Alec smiled in reassurance. "Of course you do."

She glared at him. "Hand me my sandals."

"Can we have fish and chips again?" Lily asked. "I love Spud's."

"Me, too," Ginny agreed, as if they ate there all the time.

"Dev?" Alec asked.

Standing a good ten feet away from the rest of them, he shrugged.

"Helen?"

"Why not?"

Instead of sitting at an outdoor table, they then carried their lunch back across the street to the park, finding a stretch of grass in the shade. There they spread out and ate in contented silence.

Passing cars, the shrieks from the beach and the murmur of conversation and distant laughter melded into the background. Alec noticed that Helen's nose was pink again, although her daughter had become quite brown over the summer.

The eight days since she'd first visited at his house had been good. But only twice had they managed enough privacy to kiss. Once, just yesterday, she'd called and said, "I talked my way out of the fair in Whatcom County. Everybody else has gone except Logan, who's doing a job on Vashon Island." In other words, a ferry ride away. "Want to come over?"

"On my way." He'd dropped the phone, called up the stairs, "Be back in a couple of hours," and hadn't waited for a reply.

After touring the whole house, they ended up at Helen's bedroom door. Her bedroom was airy and relatively spartan; none of the lace and clutter so many women seemed to like. She had a handsome, wide dresser, a small, unusual secretary desk with a dozen or more small drawers, and a simple full bed with no headboard. The wood floors upstairs hadn't yet been refinished and were scratched and scuffed, but she'd spread a kind of shag rug that looked sinfully deep and was made of . . . He peered down at it.

"Men's T-shirts," she said helpfully. "You know, those white ones our fathers wore. It's really soft."

Her closet door was decorated with Ginny's artwork, all labeled with dates. Some of it was really good. Above Helen's bed was a complex, embroidered wool wall hanging, South American he thought, that described a world: small figures carried burdens on their back, built houses, pushed boats with long poles, herded llamas. Two

Seattle Art Museum posters decorated other walls. A simple bookcase was filled to overflowing with a stereo, CDs in wicker baskets, and books.

After the tour took them back to the living room, they spent the next two hours talking. It was a wonderful way to spend the afternoon.

Now, replete with fish and chips, Alec lay back on the grass and watched her talking to the girls and Devlin, who did no more than grunt in return.

She would win him over. She was too nice for him to resist. Alec indulged in a brief fantasy in which his son, under her gentling influence, became again the laughing, curious, outgoing kid he'd once been.

A little sleepy, Alec let himself soak in euphoria as if it were a hot tub, bubbling and steaming around him.

It felt unbelievably good to be happy again. A grin tugged at his mouth at the inanity of the thought. Of course being happy felt good; that's what happiness was.

The last time he'd been happy, though, he hadn't fully appreciated it. He'd fallen in love in his early twenties, married a terrific woman, had great kids, a satisfying career with enough variety to keep him interested. Everything had come easily. Sometimes that had frightened him, but on the whole he took it all for granted.

In one way, Alec still believed you *ought* to be able to take a relationship for granted. That's what trust was all about, wasn't it? You shouldn't have to live day to day thinking, *This could end.*

But he guessed he never again would live without that awareness hovering, somewhere in the back of his mind. Maybe it sharpened happiness, made him more aware of it. Maybe he would appreciate the good things in life more, now that he knew how easily they could be snatched away.

But he'd like to think he could get to the point where he had some faith that life would continue on an even keel, that he could safely feel happy.

Maybe that's what today was about, he thought sleepily. He sensed Helen's wariness was collapsing like the Berlin Wall, and he was starting to believe she would marry him eventually. She'd overcome her own fears enough to let them be together.

Of course, she hadn't yet told him why she'd come to hate herself by the time Ben had died. Alec guessed it was some form of guilt, which so often became tangled with grief.

I could have made that one loving gesture.

I should have said . . .
I didn't tell him . . .

You could go on and on forever, regretting. Or you could forgive yourself as part of the healing and let it all go.

Helen, he hoped, was doing that now. She laughed more easily. She didn't shy away so much from his casual mentions of the future. She was more willing to get involved with his kids.

Wondering if anyone would notice if he closed his eyes, Alec had one last coherent thought.

Yeah, it'll be all right.

Helen kissed Alec goodbye right in front of all of their children with a reckless abandon that was foreign to her.

What are we hiding? she thought defiantly.

The girls looked disinterested. Devlin turned his head away so quickly she couldn't tell what he thought. He hadn't been so bad today. In a burst of optimism, she decided that Alec had been overreacting to typical teenage sullenness. She couldn't be sure, of course, until she spent more time with them, but the fourteen-year-old had been nice to her. Maybe he'd be okay with . . .

Well, Helen didn't know what she wanted him to be okay with, except in a hazy sense of future possibilities. But she didn't want him to actively dislike her, she knew that much.

"Call you later," Alec murmured in her ear, before hopping back into the car.

Helen took Ginny's hand and climbed the steps. "Wow, it was nice taking the whole weekend off. Although I do feel guilty." She'd done the setup on Friday for the craft fair in Lynden, but begged off first Saturday and now Sunday.

"Logan said it would be fun to go today."

"Logan was lying. He was being nice."

Ginny looked perplexed at the idea of kindness masquerading as deceit. "Was Raoul being nice, too?"

"No, I think Raoul really did want to go." Helen unlocked the front door. "He's never done it. He probably thought it sounded cool." They stepped into the empty house. "Logan, on the other hand, spent too many weekends working fairs last year. Remember?"

Ginny put her skates in the closet. "I don't think he's very good at selling stuff."

Helen laughed. "I don't think he is, either."

After Ginny was in bed that night, she thanked Logan again and told him what the eight-year-old had said.

He was having a rare cup of herbal tea, his feet up on a second chair in the kitchen. He gave a grunt of amusement. "She's right. I stink. Do you know what a dive I took to build the cabinets in here when Kathleen first called me?"

Smiling, Helen pulled up a chair. "No, did you lose a lot?"

"Big time." He shook his head. "I knew she couldn't afford what they really cost."

"And you were in love."

His eyes had a way of smiling even when his mouth didn't. "Something like that."

She poked his foot. "It better be love!"

"What about you?" he asked. "Ditching us this weekend. Is it love?"

Helen opened her mouth to say something like *Don't be silly.* What came out instead was, "I don't know."

His brows rose. "You don't know? Or you don't want to know?"

"I . . ." Panic wriggled in her stomach. "I think . . ." Her voice shrank to near a whisper. "I don't want to know."

Logan let it go when she made it plain she didn't want to answer any more questions.

But Helen found she couldn't let it go. Was she in love? If so, her vow had crumbled the minute she met a nice man.

242

Maybe, a small voice whispered, *the minute she met the* right *man.*

"My Monty," she thought, remembering the day she met Alec, when Lucinda told Helen about her tragic first marriage and the wonderful man she married later. How funny that she'd heard the story the very day she met a man she now suspected *was* her Monty.

She was almost glad to have planned a four-day trip to Portland that week. Clearly she needed to think.

The next morning, Kathleen and Ginny drove her to the airport and hugged her goodbye. As Helen went through security her last sight of Ginny was of a forlorn small figure waving.

With no companion on this trip, Helen had plenty of time for thinking. Days were full; she'd scheduled several appointments, and she dropped into as many shops as she could squeeze into business hours. But evenings in her hotel room were lonely despite brief conversations with Ginny and Alec. Ginny came first. Right after dinner every day, Helen called her daughter, who appeared to be doing fine. Still, her voice always trembled when she said, "Night, Mom. I wish you were coming home tomorrow."

Then it was TV or one of the several novels Helen had brought. More often than not, she found herself rereading the page over and over, or realizing she'd lost the thread of a *Friends* repeat or the movie of the week.

Maybe, Helen thought, she wasn't the same woman she'd been when Ben became ill. After his death, she'd decided her love had been selfish. Now, she suspected it had been fearful. She hadn't been able to envision a future without him, one in which she had to take care of herself and their small daughter. She wondered if he'd understood that. She almost hoped not. Knowing she was afraid, without job skills, their savings depleted, would have eaten at him as ruthlessly as the cancer did.

What if she told Alec why she felt so guilty? Would he understand, or be repulsed? Helen thought she owed him the chance to decide. She certainly couldn't marry him, assuming he asked, without baring her darkest secret.

Her resolve grew over the week. She had never admitted to anyone that she believed Ben had wanted to die long before she was willing to let him go. Grief disguised self-loathing, and nobody asked too many questions after the funeral.

But, thanks to Kathleen and Jo, she had survived, made a living, helped her daughter through the sadness. Once in a while lately, she'd see herself in a mirror and think, *Is that me?* She'd changed. She had confidence now. Once upon a time, she hadn't been able to believe that Ben Schaefer was in love with her, that he had actually asked her to marry him. She'd thought of herself as a mouse, ready to squeak and run. But years of happy marriage, the creation of Kathleen's Soaps and her own success as a business partner and saleswoman had had their effect.

She didn't think the idea of being left alone would scare her now.

Besides, how likely was it that lightning would strike twice? To refuse to love because the unlikely and unthinkable might happen again was ridiculous.

Wasn't it?

Emma, Raoul and Ginny were waiting at baggage claim when Helen landed in Seattle. Ginny raced to throw herself into her mother's arms.

Emma grinned. "Mom's making soap, and she didn't finish in time, so she deputized us."

"You're just as good," Helen assured her. "In fact," she decided, when Emma's tall

245

boyfriend heaved her suitcase from the conveyor belt and picked up her carry-on, too, "you might be better!"

Ginny clung to her the rest of the day, chattering at first and then quiet, as if she hoped her mom wouldn't notice how close she was sticking. At bedtime, when Helen tucked her in, her hand gripped her mother's fiercely.

"Don't go!"

Helen, who had been starting to stand, sat back on the edge of the bed. "I wasn't going far."

"I know, but . . ." Ginny still didn't let her go. "I missed you."

"I missed you, too, sweetie." She kissed her daughter again.

"Will you stay for a few minutes?" the eight-year-old begged.

"Of course I will! If," she added, "I can turn out the light."

"You won't go?"

"I promise."

After she turned off the lamp, Ginny snuggled under the covers and they talked quietly about the start of school and which friends would be in Ginny's class.

"I wish Mrs. Karol wasn't new," Ginny said sleepily. "I'd rather have someone I've seen."

"If she's awful, I'll go in swinging and demand you be moved to another class."

Ginny giggled, as if the idea was unimaginable, but Helen, filled with a new belief in herself, thought she could do just that. Well, not swinging, just forcefully demanding that her daughter get the best education. She could do that.

Helen sat even after Ginny had fallen asleep, watching her breathe, a small frown flickering then smoothing away. Her heart inexplicably ached as she wondered what worries filled her child's dreams. Were they echoes of her own?

At last she stood and eased from the room, leaving the door open a couple of inches, so that if Ginny woke up it wouldn't be completely dark.

Helen went downstairs and claimed the telephone, taking it up to her bedroom.

Alec answered on the first ring.

"I called earlier."

"Kathleen told me. I was saying goodnight to Ginny."

"This was the first time you've left her, wasn't it?"

"Yes, and she did just fine."

"But I'll bet she missed you." His voice roughened. "I know I did."

"Flattery will get you everywhere."

"Will it get me a date for dinner?" She heard his smile.

"Probably not," Helen agreed, wishing she could see him.

"Tomorrow?"

"I don't want to go out and leave Ginny. Any chance you'd like to bring the kids over here for dinner?" She'd lost track of whose turn it was to cook, but even if it wasn't hers, she'd offer.

"I doubt Dev would come. But, sure. Lily and I will."

"Tell him how cute Emma is."

Alec laughed. "Yeah. I'll do that."

Helen didn't really have any hope that the two of them would have enough privacy to talk, but she looked forward to his coming anyway.

It turned out that Emma wasn't there. She and Raoul had gone to a lecture at Seattle U. Kathleen and Logan were home for dinner, but were going to a movie afterward.

"Alec won't think we're rude, will he?" asked Kathleen.

Her husband snorted. "He isn't coming over here to see us."

Talk at the dinner table was lively as the adults discussed politics and recent education cuts made by the governor, then moved on to the new school year, Helen's trip to

Portland and Logan's colorful tales of his day spent selling soap.

"It was hot." He grinned. "I think customers thought *I* needed to use the soap. I kept seeing quivering nostrils as they backed away from me."

At last they left, Kathleen apologizing for not helping clean up. Ginny took Lily to her bedroom.

Helen rinsed dishes and put them in the dishwasher — a new addition the previous year — while Alec cleared the table.

Washing a pan, Helen blew a soap bubble at him. "What a romantic date."

He lifted a hand and let the bubble rest for a shimmering moment on the tip of his finger before it popped. "I enjoyed myself. I like Logan and Kathleen. And I got to see you."

The warmth in Alec's eyes made hers sting. She couldn't keep enjoying his company and not tell him. She had to do it now, before her quaking resolve failed.

Helen took a deep breath. "There's, um, something I want to talk to you about."

CHAPTER ELEVEN

At her words, Alec's gaze locked onto her face. He set a plate on the counter. "All right."

Helen concentrated for a moment on scrubbing the pan then rinsing it. This was harder than she'd thought it would be. Hundreds of miles away, safe in her lonely hotel room, she had rehearsed over and over in her mind. Now she couldn't remember the words.

But she had to start somewhere. Turning off the water, Helen said, "Do you remember when I told you once that I didn't like myself very much by the time Ben died?"

Alec hadn't moved. "I remember."

"We tried, oh, half a dozen treatments. The last was experimental. His oncologist tried to discourage us from that one." She couldn't look at Alec, so she concentrated on the soapy water. "And, I think, from the previous one. And . . . and maybe even from the one before that."

"Ben didn't want to give up."

"No." She made herself lift her head and look at him. "*I* didn't want to give up."

"Helen . . ."

She snatched her hands from the dishwater, dried them on a towel and flung it to the counter. Eyes dry and burning, she said relentlessly, "Don't you see? I was selfish. I couldn't let Ben go. I kept insisting we go for another treatment, and another. Everybody was trying to tell me it was hopeless, and I wouldn't listen. And he . . ." Her throat closed up completely. She breathed in and out, in and out, before she could get the last few words out. "He never said no. He kept suffering, for me."

Alec tried to take her in his arms.

She backed away. "You have to listen to me!"

His hands dropped to his sides. "I'm listening." His voice was deep and ragged. "But nothing you say will make me believe you were selfish. Do you think I wouldn't have tried anything to save Linda? I never really said goodbye to her, because I was still fighting, still trying to believe, until the bitter end. Does love mean gently letting go? Then it's not my kind of love."

Helen wrapped her arms around herself

and squeezed. "But everything happened so fast for you. It wasn't the same. Did you know she *wanted* to die?"

"Did Ben tell you he did?"

"No. But I knew. That last year . . ." She swiped at her eyes. "I have a few pictures of him bravely smiling, but you can see death around him like an aura."

Alec's expression was gentle. "How were you supposed to know what he wanted, if he didn't say?"

Helen gave a laugh that hurt. "I didn't give him the chance. I filled every silence. A couple of times especially haunt me. He tried to talk, but I was afraid. I wouldn't let him. I chattered, like . . . like some casual friend who had come to visit and was refusing to acknowledge his illness."

"Has it occurred to you that maybe he, too, kept hoping? That however much he was suffering, he was more afraid of leaving you?"

She grabbed a paper towel, mopped her eyes and blew her nose. "I don't think so. I did all the talking when he saw the doctors, too. Ben would weakly agree when I said, 'We want to go for it.' "

"Did you love him so much?" Alec asked quietly.

She looked at him through streaming eyes

and shook her head hard. "No. Yes, of course I loved him, but mostly I was scared to be left on my own. I knew our savings were gone, and I'd have to sell the house and get a job, but I had no idea where to start. I'd wake in the night with my heart pounding. I don't suppose you can imagine what it feels like to be thirty and have no job skills. I was a restaurant hostess when we first got married but hadn't worked since. And now I had a child and would have to pay for day care. I imagined being out on the street, losing Ginny. I could see her screaming as they wrenched her away from me." She shuddered. "Oh, I envisioned every horrible fate I'd ever read about in the newspaper. I *needed* Ben. If he'd just live, I wouldn't have to cope alone."

Helen closed her eyes. She saw Ben's face, the shadow of a smile that was the best he could do, and she knew: he had read her fear as if she had written a letter to him. A new kind of grief clawed at her. Ben had silently suffered, because that was what she needed from him.

She hadn't deserved his love.

Helen swallowed and forced swollen eyes open. "So now you know."

Alec was so close he was able to grasp her chin and lift it. "What are you so scared of,

Helen?"

Through the tears, she whispered, "Getting hurt." She squeezed her eyes shut again. "Hurting you."

The next instant, she found herself gathered into his arms. Even as she briefly struggled, he lifted her, carried her into the living room and sat on the sofa with her on his lap.

"And you think you're selfish," he murmured.

But I am! Helen wanted to cry. But she couldn't. She buried her face in his neck and wept. Alec held her and stroked her hair and kneaded her back and talked, saying nothing and everything.

"Get it out, love. It'll be all right. It will."

Would it? Over and over, he promised, and she had begun to believe him by the time she ran out of tears and lay exhausted in his arms.

He rubbed his cheek against the top of her head. "Sweetheart, I wish you'd told me sooner. You've kept this to yourself, haven't you?"

Feeling drugged, her voice slow and heavy, she whispered, "Who could I tell?"

"Kathleen, Jo?"

She shook her head. No. She loved them both. They were her best friends, the sisters she hadn't had. But they'd never watched someone they loved die. Not even Jo, whose mother had died when she was a child. No. They wouldn't understand.

His fingers continued to massage, probing for tension in her neck and shoulders and back, making her feel boneless, unable to move.

"If you'd joined a support group for widows, my guess is you'd find most of them harbor some kind of guilt. You didn't want Ben to die. What if instead you'd been praying he'd die sooner, so he *didn't* run through all the money? Or so you could go back to a job you love, and not spend your days in a sickroom?"

Helen's thoughts felt odd, as if a thick fog enveloped her brain. Still she listened as he kept talking, repeating a grief counselor's advice. She imagined each scenario, and the guilt that would be the aftermath.

What if she had persuaded Ben *not* to try the third treatment, or the fourth one? Would she have spent the rest of her life wondering if she'd given up too soon?

The clatter of footsteps on the stairs made her stiffen. "Oh, no! The girls! It'll scare Ginny if she sees my face."

Alec's arms tightened, and she burrowed into him.

"Girls," he said over her head, "can you give us a few minutes? Ginny, your mom and I were talking about your dad, and it made her sad. She's okay, but she doesn't want you to see her crying."

Helen heard Lily saying, "Let's go get a pop or something. Come on, Ginny."

A moment later, Alec said in a low voice, "They're off to the kitchen. Time for you to mop up."

She managed a laugh, something that would have been impossible a few minutes ago — and lifted her head. "I guess I can't escape without scaring you, can I?"

The tenderness in his eyes made her heart swell. "You can't scare me," he said huskily.

Her vision blurred. "You've made me cry again!"

He groaned. "I'm sorry! I didn't mean . . ."

"I don't know what I did to deserve you." She blinked hard, kissed his cheek and scrambled off his lap. "I'll be back."

Upstairs, Helen locked herself in the bathroom. She let the water run until it was steaming hot, then soaked a washcloth and laid it over her face. It felt so good, she repeated the process until the bathroom was filled with steam and her sinuses opened. Her face in the mirror was red and puffy, her eyes bloodshot. The sight was familiar. There had been a time when she'd cried so often, she scarcely recognized herself when her eyes *weren't* almost swollen shut.

But this time there was something different about her face. Brushing her hair, she kept sneaking peeks. Finally it came to her. She looked at peace. Her guilt had been like a deep infection, invisible but attacking her body's defenses nonetheless. Now, she thought, it had been lanced, the poison cleansed from her system. Just telling someone had helped.

But Alec had said things, too, that made sense. She and Ben had had to make dozens of decisions. If he'd recovered, she never would have questioned them. But with his death, she was bound to reexamine each and every one. There must be women with heavier burdens of guilt. Yes, she'd been a coward, but she *had* loved him. Surely, surely, she'd been as desperate to save him out of love as cowardice.

Helen took one last look at herself in the mirror, considered putting on makeup but decided it wouldn't do much good. Besides, Alec had already seen the worst.

As she came down the stairs, Ginny peeked out of the kitchen. "Mommy?" she said uncertainly.

Helen smiled and held out her arms. "Here, punkin."

Ginny clung to her tightly. "Are you all right?"

"I'm fine. It felt good to cry. But maybe —" she smoothed her daughter's fine, straight hair "— I'm done crying. I don't do it much anymore, you know."

Ginny's mouth trembled. "I hate it when you cry!"

Helen hugged her hard. "I know."

Sniffing, the eight-year-old let her go. "I guess I'd better tell Lily you're okay."

"And I'll tell Alec. Unless he's already fled to his car."

Alec hadn't. He was standing in front of the fireplace, studying a framed photo of Jo, Kathleen and Helen, taken two summers ago in front of the house. In the midst of one of their remodeling projects, they wore their most ragged clothing and were filthy, but the three stood with their arms around one another, grinning at the camera.

On that job, Helen remembered, they had made Kathleen rip out the plaster and wrench up rotten boards. "Helen and I are the skilled labor," Jo kept saying. Unlike on the first bathroom they had gutted, when Kathleen had somehow done almost none of the work, this time she had gotten down and dirty. After a tetanus shot, a dozen bandages and hair caked with plaster dust, she had laughed in triumph. Flexing her biceps, she declared, "I am woman!" Jo had just about fallen down laughing.

At Helen's soft "Hey," Alec turned.

"Hey yourself." His eyes searched her face, lingering on her puffy lids and red nose, and finally on her smile. "You're okay?"

"Yeah, I think so." *I really, really am,* she thought in amazement.

He reached for her hands when she got close enough, his grasp warm and strong. "Want to talk about it?"

She shook her head. "I said my piece. Unless you were lying and I *have* scared you."

Head bent, he said, "What do you think?" just before he kissed her. His mouth was tender, loving, soft, and her eyes closed as she let the balm of this kiss soothe her soul.

When he lifted his head, she leaned her forehead against Alec's chest. "I think," she said, in a small scratchy voice, "I'm falling in love with you."

He jerked in reaction. "Do you mind?"

"I did," she confessed softly. "But now I don't."

His fingers tightened around hers. "Good. Because I'm falling in love with you, too."

They simply stood there holding hands, Helen leaning against him, soaking in the quiet joy of obstacles overcome.

By the time they heard whispers from just outside the door, they were ready to step away from each other.

"You can come in," Alec called, and the girls appeared, clearly relieved at the sight of Helen looking composed again.

Alec made their excuses shortly thereafter. He had an early-morning meeting, he said, and besides he didn't like leaving Devlin on his own for too long.

When Alec looked into Helen's eyes and said "I'll call," she believed him. For tonight, her doubts and fears were gone.

They were falling in love. Maybe she did deserve a happy ending. She'd told Alec the very worst thing she knew about herself, and he still said he loved her.

Helen didn't kid herself that romance was a stroll in the park at their age, with three children to think about. It was probably more like their rollerblade outing. She'd stumbled and fallen again and again. Next time, they might try something that Alec wasn't very good at, although she couldn't think what that might be. But she wouldn't like him any less just because he wasn't a he-man.

She knew Alec was afraid Devlin wouldn't accept her, but after the way he'd grinned at her when she called "Ankles," she didn't believe it. He wouldn't go from that to telling his father he hated her, would he?

After tucking Ginny in, Helen went to work in the kitchen pantry. She cut long loaves of soap into bars, labeled then tied them with colored raffia.

She kept realizing she was smiling for no reason.

For every reason.

He'd lied to her. He wasn't falling in love. He was *in* love. Madly, passionately, deeply in love.

Alec wasn't, however, stupid enough to tell Devlin. *Give it time,* he told himself. *Let them get to know each other.*

She came to dinner at his house that week, bringing Ginny and Emma.

"To charm Devlin," Helen whispered in Alec's ear, as he kissed her cheek.

She wasn't stupid, either. Dev, prepared to be sulky, had flushed bright red at the sight of the delicate blond beauty.

"Wow! I mean . . . um, hi!" he blurted.

Emma gave him a delighted, conspiratorial smile, as if the two of them were teens against the world. "Hi. Aunt Helen said you probably had cool music."

"Yeah." His cheeks flushed even darker. "You want to look through my CDs?"

"Sure." She smiled at Lily. "Can I see your room later, too?" As Devlin led her away, her voice drifted back. "This house is *fabulous.*"

Without a word, Ginny and Lily raced off to Lily's bedroom like best friends. Alec drew Helen to him for another, more leisurely kiss.

"You, lady, are brilliant."

"Thank you." She curtsied. "Emma was at loose ends tonight, and I thought Dev'd like her."

"Like?" Alec laughed. "He won't get a coherent sentence out all evening. He'll feel young and gauche and be in love before the end of the evening."

He knew how his son felt. Helen looked especially pretty tonight, her hair bundled up but slipping out, a green tank top and shorts that weren't quite as abbreviated as Emma's.

Helen, however, was still thinking about Kathleen's daughter.

"Emma's pretty amazing, isn't she?" Helen's face was pensive. "Did I ever tell you she's anorexic?"

"In passing." He led her to the kitchen,

where he'd been cutting and dicing to make a stir-fry for dinner. "She's thin, but she looks fine."

"When I moved in, she was skeletal. It was scary. She'd reached the point where she was cold all the time, and she'd grown this weird fuzz on her cheeks. Her body was trying to keep her warm. The day Kathleen met Logan, Emma had collapsed in the bathroom." Helen shivered. "Ginny found her and screamed. I was at work already, but Jo told me later. Emma had been lying to the doctor and nutritionist about how much she was eating so that she could stay out of residential treatment. Kathleen signed the paperwork that day."

"And she got better?"

"She hasn't been back, but . . ." Sadness flickered. "Anorexia is a lifetime battle. Emma has her ups and downs. Mostly, she's doing really well. She and Kathleen worked out some of their problems, and she started making friends at school. Then —" she smiled "— she met Raoul."

"The young Heathcliff who is so often slouched on your living room couch."

"That's the one." She laughed. "Actually, he's very nice, and he has a delicious French accent. Plus, he loves food. Texture, taste, presentation. He's been good for her."

Alec was in a mood to think love was good for everyone.

"Can I do anything useful?" Helen asked.

"You could set the table. A good host would have done it already, I realize."

"Come on! You've eaten at our house! You're lucky if you get silverware there."

Thanks to Emma, even Devlin contributed to conversation at dinner, telling them about football practice and the basketball program at Queen Anne High School. He thought he'd be playing wide receiver on the JV football team.

"Devlin has great hands, and he's quick," Alec put in with a father's pride.

"Basketball is really my sport, though," he said, taking Alec's statement for granted.

"Wow." Emma gazed at him with her big blue eyes. "Maybe I'll come to a game sometime."

Crimson flared again in his cheeks. "That'd be great! I mean —" He cleared his throat and mumbled, "Cool."

Under Emma's eye, he was especially pleasant to Helen that evening, listening when she and Emma talked about craft fairs.

"I used to go to the one here," he admitted. "My mom and dad worked on getting it started. I haven't gone since . . ." His Adam's apple worked.

"Hey!" Emma's face brightened. "You should come work on our booth some weekend. Since you already know what you're doing. If you're not busy. We can always use help, and it would be fun."

Alec watched bemused as his son blushed and stammered, "Yeah, sure. If you need help . . . Especially if you're going," he was smart enough to add.

Emma's forehead creased. "Next we're doing . . . um . . ."

"How can you forget?" Helen asked. "We're doing the Puyallup."

"Oh, no!" Alec groaned. The Puyallup Fair was the state's biggest. It must go on for ten days or more. He'd be lucky to catch a passing glimpse of Helen. "Are you?"

"Yes, and I'm deeply regretting it." She scrunched up her face. "This is our first regular fair, but I'm betting people don't come to shop. They go on rides, they eat, they watch concerts. It's super-long hours, too. But maybe it'll be worth it. We'll see."

"The Puyallup Fair?" Devlin looked dazzled. "You mean, I'd get in free and stuff?"

"Yeah, but you wouldn't have much time to do rides or anything," Emma told him. "Well, maybe if you work during the day and then stay for the evening, or something like that."

His shoulders slumped. "I don't have my driver's license yet. I couldn't get there on my own." Clearly he was hoping she assumed he was at least sixteen.

"Raoul is flying home to see his family next week," she said. "He's my boyfriend," she added, as an aside. "He goes to Seattle U. Anyway, he won't be around that week." Her frown was severe. "I swear he planned it so we couldn't draft him."

Helen laughed. "I'd run away to Paris if I had an excuse, too."

A honeymoon would be an excuse. The thought popped into Alec's head the same instant Helen's gaze met his. Her chocolate-brown eyes were astonished then embarrassed, and he knew she'd thought the same thing.

Alec gave a devilish grin, then too late was aware his son was watching.

Who cares! he thought. Devlin would have to adjust to the idea sooner or later. Let him chew on it.

"How about if we all work the Puyallup?" he suggested. "Lily, you ready to sell soap?"

"Sure!" she exclaimed, wide-eyed.

"You mean, I have to go with *you*?" Devlin asked Alec, in that flattering way teenagers have.

Knowing his own kid hated his company didn't sting as much as it once had, but it didn't feel good, either.

After a pause, Alec said without emotion, "Not necessarily. You can hitch a ride with Helen or Emma another day. Or several days, if they can use you that often."

He saw the way Helen captured the boy's attention. "If you're really willing to work, and you won't want to take off constantly."

Devlin flushed for a different reason this time, but his eyes flicked to Emma, and he visibly swallowed whatever angry retort had risen to his tongue. "I can work," he said shortly.

"Good." She smiled. "Then you're signed on. Thank you, Devlin. We can really use you."

He was back to ducking his head, blushing and stammering, Alec saw with amusement. Clearly, women had a gift for handling Devlin that his father lacked. Maybe he could learn, if he watched Emma and Helen long enough. Then, seeing the way Emma batted her eyelashes, Alec thought, *Or maybe not.*

Later, when he and Helen were briefly out of earshot of the kids, Alec said, "Emma is lethal."

"She is, isn't she?" Laughing, Helen shook

her head. "I told her I had a feeling Devlin resented me, and asked if she'd mind coming along as a bodyguard. She got this look on her face and said, 'Watch me.' "

"She's good. The kid didn't have a chance."

Her forehead crinkled in worry. "He won't . . . oh, really fall for her, will he? Emma is always nice to everyone, and she'll be friendly to him, but . . ."

Alec shook his head. "Dev's not stupid. She's four years older, has a boyfriend, and is being sweet to him because of you. He may develop a crush — cancel that. He *has* a crush, but he won't expect anything to come of it. He'd be terrified if he really thought she was interested in him."

Her face cleared. "Oh, good. He was polite tonight, wasn't he? Do you think he likes me?"

"He hasn't said a word about you since his initial anger at the idea of me having a *girlfriend.*" Alec mimicked his son's tone. "How can he not like you?"

She grimaced. "Easily. You're prejudiced."

"You, honey, are a nice woman with a deft touch where kids are concerned. What's not to like?"

Half a dozen emotions skittered across her face. "I'm hardly perfect," she said finally in a constrained voice.

He let his voice drop. "You're perfect for me."

They were laughing when they joined the kids, saying goodbye at the door. Alec was feeling pretty good when Helen and the girls left.

Devlin stood in the entry staring at the closed door with his mouth gaping and his eyes soulful. "Is Emma really Helen's niece?" he asked in a faraway voice.

"No, Helen rents a room from Emma's mother, Kathleen. She's the one who makes the soap. Anyway, they all seem to be close. Ginny calls Kathleen 'Aunt,' too."

"Oh."

Knowing he shouldn't, Alec couldn't stop himself from asking, "So, is Helen growing on you?" He waited hopefully, lovesick, too.

As if he'd unbottled an evil genie, Devlin's face changed, became insolent. "She's hot, if that's what you're asking."

Stiffening, Alec said sharply, "It's not."

"Well, she is." Real anger darkened Devlin's eyes. "Actually, she's nice. Nicer than *you* deserve. I'll bet you haven't told her the truth, have you?"

As if feeling the waters begin to roil, Lily attached herself to her dad's side like a limpet.

"The truth?"

His son's mouth stretched into an ugly sneer. "You haven't. Like I had to ask. Duh," he seemed to mock himself.

"What are you talking about?" Alec snapped.

"Never mind." Contempt oozed from the teenager. "I'm going upstairs."

"Devlin!" Alex's voice rose to a roar as his son took the stairs two at a time. "Stop!"

The boy didn't. He disappeared into the hallway above, and a moment later his bedroom door slammed. Alec stared incredulously after him. How could he go from being a decent kid all evening to this kind of open defiance in the blink of an eye?

"What's he talking about, Daddy?" Lily's voice quavered. "What does he mean, the truth?"

"I have no idea," Alec said honestly, frustration squeezing his temples and tightening his neck muscles. "I suspect there is no truth. He's just being a snot."

"Oh." But she looked worried, and Alec could tell she didn't altogether believe him.

He didn't believe himself. There was something Devlin knew, or thought he knew, that might explain his long-simmering rage.

Question was, how did Alec get him to
spill "the truth?"

CHAPTER TWELVE

Alec decided to wait until tomorrow to confront Devlin. He felt too angry and bewildered now to have a calm conversation. Instead, he left Lily to her own devices and retreated to his office, where he picked up the photo of Linda and tried to consult her.

Of course, she didn't answer any more than she ever had.

When she died, he felt it. Blink. Light out. In the snap of a finger, she was utterly and completely gone. Since that moment, he had never had the slightest sense of her presence. Whatever his faith or lack thereof, he knew she wasn't hovering, anxiously watching over her family.

Maybe Linda had had complete confidence that he could cope on his own. Alec leaned back in the leather chair and closed his eyes, imagining her floating peacefully toward the light, her last thought, *Alec will do fine.*

He gave a gravelly laugh. Oh, yeah. He was just peachy keen.

"Linda," he murmured, "why didn't you talk to Dev before you left? Did you think he'd be strong enough to cope?"

Silence. He picked up the silver-framed photo again, studied it with a sadness that had softened lately. He'd found acceptance, and the ability to love again.

Lily, he sensed, was ready, too.

So why not his son?

Alec had to work the next day, leaving the kids on their own again. He was looking forward to school starting next week, and wished he had signed up Lily for some formal activity this summer. She hadn't seemed especially interested in any of the sports or classes he suggested, so he'd let it go — she didn't need day care — and he hadn't wanted to insist. But now he thought the summer had been too aimless. He suspected she spent ninety percent of her day either watching TV or hunched in front of the computer sending and receiving instant messages. She hadn't even developed a tan this year, like she usually did.

He hadn't slept well the night before, so when he came home he was relieved to find

Lily working on one of the few recipes in her limited repertoire of dinners.

"Corn chowder," she announced.

"It smells great," he said honestly. The bacon and onion were frying, and she was scraping corn from the cobs. His stomach rumbled. "Let me change, and then I'll help."

"It'll be ready in fifteen minutes."

"Where did you get the corn?" he asked, when the two of them sat down to dinner. He'd called for Devlin, who hadn't yet appeared.

Lily had set the pot on a hot pad in the middle of the table, so they could all ladle out seconds. She'd even heated garlic bread.

"Jennifer's mother stopped by. They have a vegetable garden in their backyard. She said too much was getting ripe at once, and would we like some."

"I hope you expressed undying gratitude."

Her nose wrinkled. "If you mean, did I remember to say thank you, of course I did!"

He grinned at her. "That's more or less what I was getting at."

Lily glanced past him. "Wow, look who's here."

"Don't be a smart mouth," her brother said.

Undaunted, she stuck her tongue out.

"Hurry up, it smells *really* good. I'm starving."

Dev sat, scraping the chair forward, and reached for garlic bread without another word. Whatever his mood, he rarely argued about appearing for dinner. His appetite would have frightened Alec, if he didn't remember his own mother grumbling when he was a kid about how hard it was to keep groceries in the house.

Tonight Dev ate half a loaf of garlic bread and inhaled three large bowls of his sister's corn chowder. He didn't once look at his father or speak to him. When he tipped the pot to peer in and saw that the chowder was finished, he asked, "We got any dessert?"

Lily made a face at him. "If you want apple pie, bake it yourself. You could at least say, 'Thank you, dinner was fabulous.' "

Devlin had one of his rare moments of civility. "It was good, Lil. Thanks."

Seizing his moment, Alec said, "Devlin, I'd like to talk to you. Lily, do you mind?"

Her gaze widened and flicked between them, but she stood quickly. "Do I have to clean the kitchen, too?"

"No, I'll do it." Alec waited until she had left the dining room before he looked at Devlin, who waited with his head bowed and his shaggy hair hanging over his eyes.

Feeling incredibly tired, Alec said, "Dev-lin, we've got to do better. I can make changes if you can. But you've got to talk to me. I don't know why you're so angry at me. Tell me. I can't fix what I don't under-stand."

His son shook his hair back and stared at Alec with eyes that seemed almost eerily blank. "There's *nothing* wrong."

"You just dislike my presence and object to everything I say because . . . ?" Alec spread his hands.

"I'm not a little kid." The boy's mouth, which so rarely smiled anymore, curled with disdain. "I don't need you to hold me up on my bike or throw the ball with me."

Alec had loved doing both. Summer eve-nings spent in the backyard tossing the ball with his son had been some of the best of his life. They'd shot baskets out front, in the hoop above the garage, or walked to the school to play one-on-one as Devlin grew older and grew in six-inch spurts to match his father's height.

Now, softly but intensely, Alec said, "I've outlived my usefulness? Is that what you're telling me? Now all you need is my money and an occasional ride somewhere, so you don't want to waste words talking to me?"

Dev looked away and mumbled, "It's not

like that."

"What is it like?"

The teenager said nothing.

"What," Alec asked with quiet emphasis, "is the 'truth' that I should tell Helen?"

"Nothing." Head hanging again, Dev muttered, "I was just, like, pushing your buttons. You know."

Alec could get nothing further out of the kid, no matter how many different ways he asked. Finally he said, "I give up. You can go."

Dev pushed back his chair, hesitated for a moment, then started out of the room.

"I love you," Alec said. Last-ditch. Words not said often enough.

Behind him, his son's footsteps faltered, then continued. A moment later, Dev was bounding up the stairs.

Wearily Alec stood up and began clearing the table.

Alec called nearly every evening. Helen counted on it, loved those few minutes of talking about their days, sharing frustrations, small moments good or bad, kids' accomplishments. The occasional evening when he didn't phone, like the one after the dinner at his house, found Helen restless, waiting, and finally mad at herself for needing him.

Here she was, proud of herself for her increasing self-reliance and success as a businesswoman, and she couldn't get through an evening without hearing from a man. Was she so desperate for advice, or the comfort of laying her worries on someone else?

But she knew that really she just needed to hear Alec's voice. She was as content listening to his grumbles or funny stories as she was sharing her own.

That evening she wandered into the kitchen after nine-thirty, knowing Alec wouldn't call any later than this. Kathleen was banging cupboard doors and slamming cans on the counter.

Helen winced as Kathleen grabbed a pile of dinner plates and whacked them down. "What are you doing?"

Hair disheveled, eyes wild, Kathleen barely spared her a glance. "I hate the way these cupboards are organized! Why are the dishes so far from the dishwasher? Why do I have to stand on tiptoe to find a can of tomato soup?"

"Um . . ." Wary, Helen edged closer. "Because we put things in places that seemed logical at the time?"

"Well, they're not!" A glass shattered in

Kathleen's hand and she shouted as blood blossomed on the pad of her thumb.

Helen grabbed Kathleen's hand and held it over the sink. She turned the cold water on and they both watched as blood ran down the drain.

"You stay here," she ordered. "I'll get ointment and a bandage."

Helen returned a minute later, tended to the cut, then steered her to the table. "Sit. I'll clean up the broken glass."

"No." Kathleen jumped back up. "I made the mess, I'll . . ."

Helen whirled. "Sit!"

Mouth tightening, Kathleen obeyed.

Helen carefully picked up the larger pieces of glass and dumped them in the trash can beneath the sink, then swept up the shards on the floor. Only then did she turn around and say, "Okay. What's wrong?"

Kathleen was a beautiful, controlled woman. When Helen first knew her, only Emma could bring her mother to despair and tears.

Tonight Kathleen's face crumpled. "Logan and I had a fight. He's . . . he left. Didn't you hear the garage door open?"

Helen sat down and took her friend's uninjured hand. "No. What did you fight about?"

"Nothing!" Furiously Kathleen scrubbed at her tears. "I don't know! I was talking about Ian, and he — Logan — said something snide, and I accused him of being jealous, and . . . We just replayed all our original problems." She lifted a bewildered face, drenched with tears. "It happened so fast. I don't understand."

"Everybody quarrels once in a while." Helen grabbed a paper napkin from the holder in the middle of the table and gave it to Kathleen.

Kathleen blew her nose. "But . . . but we haven't!" She sounded like a confused child.

"Didn't you fight with Ian sometimes?" Helen knew Kathleen's marriage had had an ugly end.

She shook her head. "No . . . well, yes, but it was different. We were just sharp. He'd say something edgy, I'd snap back, then fume for the rest of the day. Logan looked so angry."

"Or hurt?" Helen suggested gently.

"I don't know," Kathleen whispered. She reached for another napkin and wiped at her tears. "I love him so much."

Helen hugged her. "I know."

"Did you fight with Ben?"

Helen hesitated. "Squabbled, mainly. I think — I've come to realize — that he

always wanted to please me. I remember a few times being mad and *wanting* him to stand up for what he thought, but he didn't have a combative bone in his body. It was actually kind of frustrating."

It was that gentle part of Ben's nature, the desire to please, perhaps even the need to have a stronger personality make the decisions, that in the last months had kept him from saying, "No."

No, I won't go through chemotherapy again. No more radiation. I choose to accept that the end nears and die with dignity.

Kathleen sniffled. "Logan seems so . . . so *confident,* I forget that he has some insecurities. You know me. I probably said something horribly insensitive."

"You're not that bad!" Helen protested, then thought, *Oops.*

Tear-filled eyes lifted. "See? I am!"

Helen skirted the issue. "You really don't remember what upset him?"

Fresh tears overflowed and Kathleen shook her head vehemently. "What do I *say?* If he lets me say anything!"

Holding both her hands, Helen said simply, "I'm sorry. That's all he'll want to hear."

Kathleen went rigid. "Is that the garage door? Is he home?" She leaped to her feet and stared, wild-eyed, toward the hall.

Both of them heard the slow, heavy tread of steps coming up. Helen retreated toward the pantry when a door opened and a moment later Logan appeared, eyes red-rimmed.

"Kathleen?" He groaned. "You're crying. I'm a jerk. I don't know what got into me."

"I'm so sorry!" his wife wailed, and threw herself into his arms.

They held each other for a long moment, Logan's cheek against Kathleen's blond head.

Helen made the mistake of trying to ease the last few steps backward to take her out of sight into the pantry. Logan lifted his head and saw her. He gave a grimace that might have been intended to be a smile and said in a low voice to Kathleen, "Let's go upstairs."

"Okay." She grabbed a napkin from the table, blew her nose again and said in a teary voice, "I love you."

"I love you, too," he said, his voice raw with emotion.

Helen, standing forgotten in the kitchen, thought that she would give anything to have Alec say "I love you" to her just like that.

Helen helped preside for the first few hours

of Lily's birthday party. Lily had wanted to invite Ginny for the cake-and-ice cream part, even though she was younger than the other guests. Alec was grateful for Helen's easy way with the girls as she cut cake, led a rousing chorus of "Happy Birthday," and gently established a seating arrangement for the opening of presents.

Alec dreaded these things. It seemed as if one girl was always jealous because she wanted the birthday girl's attention while another had some personal crisis that meant tears and drama. Lily invariably had to spend her party smoothing feathers.

While Helen was there, everybody behaved. Bianca wanted to whimper about a broken heart, but Alec overheard Helen taking her aside and murmuring, "I'm so sorry you got hurt, but let's try to let Lily enjoy her party. I know you don't want to ruin her pleasure in turning twelve."

Actually, Bianca would have loved to spoil the party, Alec thought cynically, but once she'd been made to feel guilty she returned to the group looking noble. Her smile barely faltered at the edges.

With the cake devoured, ice cream drips wiped up and the wrapping paper in the recycling bin, the girls laid out sleeping bags in the family room, and argued about which

DVD to watch first. Helen and Ginny prepared to leave.

"Happy birthday, Lily!" Helen hugged her.

"Thanks for having me," Ginny said dutifully.

Lily thanked them nicely for their gift, a necklace with a sterling silver pendant that looked like an origami crane.

When his daughter hurried back to her other guests, Alec grabbed Helen's hand. "Don't abandon me!"

She laughed, her eyes merry, kissed his cheek and did just that.

Devlin came home late from a friend's house, cast one repulsed look at the half-dozen giggling girls, and shut himself in his bedroom. Eventually, Alec was able to do the same.

School started a few days later. With football practices filling Devlin's afternoons and leaving him exhausted, the teenager became easier to get along with.

Helen left for another trip down the I-5 corridor, stopping in Olympia, Chehalis, Longview and Vancouver. She went on to Portland to "visit their accounts," she said, and laughed.

"Accounts! Imagine. That sounds so businesslike!"

She was gone all of four days, and he

missed her terribly. Helen phoned once, but the connection crackled and she said, "I think my cell phone is dying. I'll call when I get home, okay?" He hung up feeling frustrated and lonely.

Alec decided dating wasn't enough. Phone calls every evening were a lot less satisfying than having Helen comfortably curled in a big chair in the living room reading, ready to go to bed when he went.

He wanted her to be his wife. He was in love with her, and he hoped she felt the same.

But Helen was no sooner home than the Puyallup Fair began, which meant early mornings and late nights for her and Kathleen. On the couple occasions Alec managed to talk to her, she was distracted and tired.

If he was ever going to see her, clearly he had to "do the Puyallup," to quote the jingle that was on every radio station.

He asked her to marry him while they swung above the fairgrounds on the Ferris wheel.

They had left the booth in the hands of Ginny, Emma, Lily and Devlin, and gone wandering among the maze of vendors in search of food. Peter, Paul and Mary were performing in the stadium, "Puff the Magic Dragon" soaring above the whistles and clangs and bloodcurdling screams from the midway. Night was falling, and the aroma of hamburgers and caramel apples and fries wafted through the crowd, mingling with the earthier scents of manure, shavings and hay from the barns. People ate as they strolled, carried neon pink stuffed panthers won at games, mock-dueled with light sabers, called to friends, gathered children.

Alec and Helen had cheeseburgers then caramel apples, which left Helen feeling sticky but contented. Alec's hand, when it found hers, was sticky, too, but who cared?

"Let's go on the Ferris wheel," he said suddenly, looking above her. "I haven't done that in years."

She looked up. "It's an awfully tall one."

"We'll be able to see the whole world," he coaxed. "Come on. The kids will be okay without us a little longer."

They would, of course. Business had been decent earlier in the day, but in the evening the teenagers came out for the rides, and they didn't buy soap.

"Okay," Helen said. "Just don't laugh if I scream."

He was already laughing. "You can't scream on the Ferris wheel!"

"I don't like heights."

"I'll hold you tight," Alec promised.

He bought two tickets, and in no time they were seated on the swinging bench, a bar lowered over their laps. With a lurch, the wheel started, then stopped for the next couple to be loaded.

Just as they were getting high enough to scare her, the Ferris wheel began to move smoothly. Helen squeaked as they neared the top, but the view was stupendous, the fairgrounds below a kaleidoscope of gaudy lights and crowds and rooftops. The sun was setting, a hazy orange over the Olympic Mountains. If Helen turned her head she could just see the dark bulk of Mount Rainier. Parking lots and city streets and countryside fell away as they were swept up, then down.

Alec's arm around her shoulders gave her courage to peek down and try to spot their booth. Helen laughed aloud with exhilaration.

"Oh, this is fun!"

"My little coward."

She elbowed him, just a little poke.

"Helen Schaefer," he said, "will you marry me?"

Her heart took a leap as dizzying as the Ferris wheel's upward surge. "What?"

He was looking at her tenderly. "You don't have to give me an answer, but I thought it was time I asked. I love you. I want you to marry me. I know I'm asking a lot. The kids and I come as a package, and you know Devlin is no prize right now."

"I . . ."

He covered her mouth with his hand, murmured, "Don't answer, unless you're going to shout 'Yes!' "

When she said nothing at all, his hand fell away and the lines seemed to deepen on his face. "I shouldn't have asked yet."

"No, it's not that." Joy and terror mingled, creating suffocating pressure in her chest. "I'm not saying no. I . . . I think . . ." She had to swallow. "I think I want to marry you. But I need some time."

His face changed again. Whoosh! They plummeted, swept by the operator and the line of waiting customers, rose toward the deep purple sky. Peter, Paul and Mary were singing "Lemon Tree," about bittersweet love. Helen hoped it wasn't an omen.

" 'Maybe,' " Alec said, "is plenty good enough for me right now."

He kissed her as they vaulted over the top of the world, bumped to a stop, swung. Lost in his kisses, Helen forgot to look down at the tangle of metal beneath them and the

288

ground so far below. And she forgot her vow.

Being in love was so sweet, how could it ever hurt?

She didn't surface until the carnie said in a gruff, amused tone, "End of the ride, folks."

"Oh!" Flushing, Helen let him lift the bar then scrambled to the platform, swaying as she tried to recover her equilibrium.

Alec gripped her arm and steadied her. Secure on the ground, she felt odd. The Ferris wheel continued loading and unloading behind them. She and Alec walked away in silence. She didn't know what to say. That same mix of panic and happiness made her a little queasy.

She wanted to marry him. More than anything in the world. She knew she did. The only thing stopping her was . . . what?

Hadn't she come to terms with the knowledge that she had clung selfishly to Ben when she should have let go? Helen thought she had, as much as she could. Until the day she died she would regret not having said, "The decision has to be yours. I'll support you, whatever you choose." Once, she had thought of herself as a sort of Typhoid Mary, believing she would bring pain to whomever she loved. She knew better now. She wasn't that woman anymore.

Was she afraid of being hurt? Of course she was. But wasn't she being paranoid, to shape her life around the possibility that Alec would get cancer or congestive heart failure or whatever, not in thirty or forty years, but *soon?* They both knew how quickly things could go wrong. She could just as easily be the one who got sick and *he* wasn't quailing at the possibility.

She stole a look at Alec, hoping she hadn't hurt him. He glanced down at the same moment, smiled and squeezed her hand.

"Just remember. I love you."

Helen sucked in a shaky breath, blinked against the threat of tears and forced her own smile for the kids as they turned into the booth.

"Make a million bucks while we were gone?"

"Yeah, right." Devlin's eyes narrowed as he looked from his father's face to Helen's and then back again.

Ginny hugged her mother. "You were gone *forever.*"

"Alec talked me into a ride on the Ferris wheel." She ruffled her daughter's hair. "It was very romantic and awfully high."

"Oh." Ginny's brown eyes were reproachful. "*I* like Ferris wheels."

"Then I'll take you for a ride on it tomorrow night." Helen looked around. "What say we shut the doors and go home?"

"Yeah!" Emma said, pushing herself out of the folding chair where she'd been slumped. "I am *so* tired."

Helen closed out the till while the others brought in the tables they'd set out front and lowered the plywood "awning," locking it securely.

Devlin, who had been unexpectedly cheerful that morning, walked several feet behind the rest in what appeared to be sullen silence. Or maybe she was misjudging. He might just be tired, like they all were.

She said quietly to Emma, "Do you know? Is something wrong?" She nodded just slightly to indicate the trailing teenager.

Emma glanced back. "No-o-o. I don't think so."

The walk to the exhibitors' parking lot seemed longer each day. Helen was glad to get there.

They'd brought two cars, and arrived at hers first. Pulling keys from her tote, she said, "Thank you all so much. Alec, Devlin and Lily, you were a huge help!"

"It was fun," Lily said.

"Yeah, it was." Alec squeezed the nape of Helen's neck. "You drive carefully."

"You, too." She rested her cheek on Alec's

hand, just for an instant. She would have liked to lean against him.

"You're worried about *him?*" his son said loudly. "That's a joke!"

As if in slow motion, they all turned. The teen's usually handsome face was twisted into an expression Helen could only think of as mean.

"Devlin!" his father snapped.

Shocked, Helen asked, "Why would you say something like that?"

In a tone suggesting they were all stupid not to know, the boy said, "Because he's going to die anyway." Turning an ugly look on his father, he added, "Or didn't he tell you?"

Beside her, Alec stared at his son as if he were a stranger.

A sickening sense of foreboding chilled Helen despite the warm night air. Her voice emerged just above a whisper. "Tell me what?"

"He had a heart attack! He tried to check out after Mom died." The boy's shrug was jerky, less indifferent than he was trying for. "So, he'll have another one. And then he'll croak."

From far away, Helen heard Lily crying. Emma had put her arm around Ginny, who shriveled against her and stared. Helen seemed incapable of responding to any of them. Instead, she turned and faced Alec.

"Is that true? Did you have a heart attack?"

Discomfort and something she read as guilt tightened his face. "I had a minor heart attack. There were . . . special circumstances. Even the cardiologist doesn't expect a repeat. I've gotten a clean bill of health ever since."

He said more, something in her face causing him to talk faster and faster, until they all heard the desperation underlying his explanation.

There was something about a kink in an artery that had created a bottleneck where a blockage occurred. A shunt. He had a shunt, to open up the bottleneck. He was in great shape. Ate right. The heart of a twenty-year-old, the cardiologist said. He ran four times a week. Damage was minimal. Meaningless. No reason to think . . .

She heard it all, and none of it.

A heart attack. All of this time, they'd talked about the pain of losing their spouses, and Alec had never said, "I had a scare myself." He knew how awful those two years had been for her, how afraid she was to love again, with the specter of that loss never leaving her side.

He had let her fall in love with him, and never warned her.

Her voice interrupting him was cold, harsh. "Please don't come tomorrow. Kids, get in."

She got in the car, closed her door and leaned over to unlock the passenger side. Emma and Ginny hurried 'round the car and scrambled in. Helen backed out and drove away, across the bumpy field, without once glancing at Alec or his children.

CHAPTER THIRTEEN

Alec stood motionless, staring after Helen's car. Two minutes ago, he'd believed she would marry him. Now, this fast, she was gone. Out of his life.

Agony gutted him. If he had been alone, he might have crumpled to his knees.

Lily's sobbing penetrated when nothing else might have. He turned, held out his arm to her and looked at his son. "Happy?"

Devlin's face was bleached white, his eyes shocked. "I . . ."

Unlocking his jaw, Alec laid down one rock-hard word at a time. "Don't . . . say . . . anything."

Guiding Lily, he turned and walked toward their car. He guessed Devlin was trailing behind; right this minute, he didn't care. He hadn't known he could come so close to hating his own child.

Lily cried the entire time. He unlocked her door, helped buckle her in, and walked 'round to the driver's side as Devlin climbed in the back. Then he drove home, without one of them saying a word the entire forty-five minutes.

Alec had barely pulled into the garage when Devlin wrenched open the car door, jumped out and raced upstairs. As the garage door closed behind them, Alec turned off the engine and sat wondering if he had the energy to follow.

And do what? Pretend to work or watch TV or read? Get on with life, as if he'd never met Helen? Cheer Devlin on in the next JV football game, as if he hadn't willfully, hatefully destroyed his father's chance at happiness?

Alec didn't know if he could do it. Any of it.

His eyes were dry and burning; his body ached as if he had the flu. He was tired to his bones, sad and angry.

If anything would keep him going, it was the anger.

"Daddy?"

He had been both aware and not aware of Lily, who hadn't moved to get out of the car either. Of her puffy face and wet eyes and shuddery breaths.

"Yeah, honey?"

"I'm scared."

Once again, she recalled him to obligations and the people who loved him. The thought hurt, because Helen wasn't one of them, but his daughter needed him.

He took her hand. "Why are you scared?"

Pained bewilderment gazed up at him. "Why did Dev say that?"

The blade in his chest twisted. "I don't know," Alec said thickly. "I guess I've got to find out."

"Will you —" her breath hitched "— forgive him?"

"He's my son. How can I not?" He knew it was the truth, but for now felt only anger and confusion. Why? *Why?* "I'll talk to him." But not now. "It's not your worry, Lily."

"I like Helen," she said in a small voice. "I thought . . . maybe . . ."

Pain crashed into him, a wall of it. He, too, had thought maybe.

I'm not saying no. I think I want to marry you.

Words to hug close to his heart. She loved him. She *had* to, or she couldn't have been so close to overcoming her fears.

"Devlin's right," he said to himself as much as to Lily. "I should have told her. It never occurred to me."

"*Are* you going to die?"

He turned his head to see Lily's eyes well-ing again with tears.

"No!" He bent to hug her fiercely. "You remember what I told you. I'm going to be fine. Your brother was just making trouble."

She nodded against his shoulder, sniffled. "Okay."

He gave one more squeeze, then released her. "Let's go up, shall we?"

Somehow he found the strength in him to trudge up the stairs to the kitchen, to ask if Lily was hungry, to be glad she wasn't.

"Can I watch TV?" she asked, and he nodded, his ability to give any more just about bottomed out.

Alec sat on a stool at the breakfast bar, propped his elbows on the counter and buried his face in his hands.

Would she listen to him? Would she believe he hadn't meant to lie, even by omission, that he had genuinely never considered his health an issue?

Was he in denial? he asked himself. Had he just not wanted to admit that if the artery had blocked once, it could again, that he might die, leave his children alone, put Helen through hell?

Alec didn't like to think of himself as stupid, but the last time Alec had seen his cardiologist, he'd said, "No need for you to come back in six months. Let's make it a year this time."

He was fine. Had never felt better.

That one scare had been a wake-up call. He'd grabbed fast food when he was in a hurry, never thought about the fat content of anything he put in his mouth, didn't worry about regular exercise because he thought he was reasonably fit.

He'd discovered when he started jogging that he wasn't fit. Too much time behind a desk or in the car had taken a toll. He'd started slowly, as Dr. Ritter advised, using the machines at the health club, doing a little bit of weight lifting, a mile jog four mornings a week. Now he did three miles before work, more on the weekends. He'd quit eating crap, read the list of ingredients before he bought anything and had lost ten pounds he didn't know he needed to lose.

Maybe he should have told Helen; he would have, eventually, when the subject came up. But he wasn't an invalid, he wasn't dying, he hadn't even come close to "checking out."

Lifting his head, he gazed unseeing through the window at the view over rooftops to the Sound. *Why?* he asked himself again. Why had Devlin said that?

With a jolt, he realized this was "the truth" Dev had mentioned a couple of weeks ago.

Was Devlin just making trouble? Or did he actually believe his father was going to die?

Frowning, Alec thought back. He'd started having chest pains even before Linda got sick. He just hadn't acknowledged it. He was too young, too healthy, to believe he could possibly have angina. Heartburn, he would tell himself, and pop an antacid.

He'd been slow to believe he was having a heart attack, too. Classic idiot, taking eight, ten antacids, adding some ibuprofen, because the shoulder and arm pain must have been a pulled muscle, the pressure in the chest more of that pesky heartburn. He drove himself to the hospital, thinking all the way, *They're going to pat me on the back and send me home.*

A neighbor had kept the kids for the night, and Alec's sister flew in from San Francisco to stay until he was on his feet again.

Yeah, he'd had a scare, all right, but he thought the kids had understood that a scare was all it was. He hadn't had a near-death experience. He remembered the fear in their eyes and the strain on their faces. These were kids whose mother had died only six weeks before. He wasn't sure now he'd realized how devastated they must have been.

Because that would have meant accepting that he hadn't had a little medical glitch, he'd had a heart attack. Heart failure. Blood not pumping. He could have died.

Lily had nodded with enormous relief at his explanation, hugged him and said, "I love you, Daddy."

Devlin had . . . Alec frowned, trying to remember. Nodded and left the room, he thought. Or maybe he hadn't nodded.

Maybe twelve-year-old Devlin's instincts had all been screaming, *Dad's snowing us. He doesn't want us to know.*

Alec hadn't told them, for way too long, that their mother was dying. He hadn't believed it himself. He'd throw himself into bed at night and think, *Tomorrow she'll have more color in her cheeks. The doctor and nurses will be smiling, because the chemo has finally kicked in.*

Medicine could do amazing things. He hadn't wanted Lily and Devlin to be as scared as he was. They'd understood she was dreadfully sick, but when Lily asked early on if Mommy was going to die, Alec had exploded, "Of course not!"

She'd shrunk back, and he remembered closing his eyes for an instant, getting a grip on himself, then pulling her against him and telling her about leukemia and the ways doctors could make it better.

He hadn't told them until the last couple of days that Mommy might *not* get better. By then, they'd probably known; in her hospital room it felt as if death circled the bed like a hungry wolf.

Devlin, Alec thought now, might have reasoned that if Dad had lied about Mom, why believe him when he said he was going to be fine? He'd had a heart attack. People died after they had them. Dev might have heard talk, gone on the internet, done some research, read about damage to the heart muscle and the temporary nature of the success won by angioplasty or bypass surgery.

He might have concluded it was just a matter of time.

Devlin had never come to Alec and asked for the truth. He hadn't expressed curiosity about where he and Lily would live if his father did die. He'd just withdrawn.

Alec felt like an idiot for not realizing sooner that Devlin's sullenness had begun then. He suddenly wasn't as helpful, or as eager to spend time with his dad. The open door that had allowed them all to talk about anything that bothered them had slammed shut.

Which still begged the question, *Why?* Helen had talked about how Ginny had clung for years after her father died. Afraid of losing a second parent, she had held on for dear life. Wasn't that the logical reaction?

Alec scrubbed a hand over his face, felt the evening bristles on his chin. His face felt numb under his fingers.

Why? he asked himself again. If you're afraid you're going to lose someone you love, you hold on tight. You think, *She can't die if I'm sitting here, holding her hand, believing.* You don't shrug and saunter away.

Unless . . .

He stiffened.

Unless you're already hurting so bad, you can't take it again. Unless you think, *If I don't love him, I won't care when he dies.*

Alec swore under his breath. Was that what Devlin had decided, whether consciously or not? That he couldn't let himself love his father?

As terrified as he was that Helen might never be willing to listen to him, Alec knew that he had to deal with Devlin first. Now. While he was still shaken up.

No music pounded from Dev's bedroom. Alec stood in the hall outside the door, a niggling fear twisting its way amongst the pain knotting his stomach. Devlin *had* come up to his room, hadn't he?

The knock brought no answer. When Alec opened it and went in, he found Devlin's bedroom empty. The fear spread. He checked the bathroom, then every other room in the house.

"Have you seen your brother?" he asked Lily tersely, when he passed through the family room.

Eyes widening, she shook her head.

Back in the kitchen, he grabbed his address book. Thankfully he'd always insisted that both kids provide phone numbers of every friend. No exceptions, they didn't go to anyone's house unless the phone number was in this book.

He started with Nick Arneson.

"Hi, this is Alec Fraser, Devlin's father. I'm trying to track down Devlin. I don't suppose he's with Nick? No? If you hear from him, will you let me know? Thanks."

He kept dialing. He knew damn well every one of those parents heard the terror behind the casual, just-temporarily-misplaced-the-kid tone. He didn't care. He just wanted to find his son.

Kyle Teuber was toward the end, but one of Dev's best friends. By this time Alec's throat felt raw and he was cold, enveloped by the awareness of how much more he had to lose today.

Mary Lynn Teuber answered. "Why, no, Devlin hasn't been over today." But her voice seemed to trail off.

Alec stiffened.

"You know, I thought I heard the doorbell earlier, but when I asked, Kyle said no, it must have been the dryer. I do have a load in." Exasperation edged her voice. "Hold on, Alec. I'll find out."

He waited, rigid, ears straining. A minute ticked by, two.

"Alec? Devlin's here."

He sagged and breathed, "Oh, good."

"He looked like he wanted to bolt, so I just marched him down to the kitchen with me. I can drive him home."

"No. Thank you. I'll come for him. Will you make sure . . ." His throat clogged.

"He'll be here," she promised.

Alec detoured to the family room to tell Lily where he was going, then went back down to the garage. He had trouble getting the key in the ignition and realized his hands were shaking.

Kyle's house wasn't more than a mile away. Alec parked in the driveway and went up to the front door. He'd no sooner rung the bell than the door swung open. Kyle's mother and Devlin stood there, Kyle hovering in the background.

She smiled at Alec, sympathy in her eyes. "Here's the wandering child." She leveled a stern look on his son. "Next time, say hi when you come in, Devlin."

He ducked his head and stepped out, following his father to the car. Night had fallen, but lights on each side of the garage let Alec see his son's face.

"You scared me," he said quietly.

Devlin shrugged but didn't look at his father. He flung himself into the car and slammed the door.

Alec got in, but made no move to start the engine. "You know, I'm not going to die for thirty or forty years."

The boy mumbled, "I just said that because . . ." His tongue touched his lips. He apparently couldn't think of a good explanation.

"Because you really thought it was true," Alec finished. "Didn't you?"

Anger fired in Devlin's eyes. "I know it's true! You lied! Just like you did about Mom!"

"No." Alec rubbed his hands on his thighs. "I was lying about your mother, but I was lying to myself, too." His sinuses burned. "I couldn't believe she might really die. I refused to believe it."

He heard a sound, and saw that Devlin was crying. Alec reached for him, but the teenager hunched away.

Alec pinched the bridge of his nose. His voice sounded ragged. "I also suppose it's true that I didn't want to believe anything big was wrong with me. Who does? The thing is, the doctors *did* fix it. I wasn't lying. The last time I saw Ritter, he told me I didn't need to be checked every six months. He says my heart looks great. The shunt isn't plugging up. He says my problem was equivalent to having something backing up the plumbing. A routine job."

Devlin wiped his nose on his shirtsleeve and shouted, "I don't believe you!"

"What if he tells you the same thing?"

His son gaped. "What?"

Thinking it through, Alec said, "What if I call Dr. Ritter and ask if he'll meet with us, explain what went wrong, what the odds are of a repeat?"

"He . . . he might lie, too."

"Why would he?"

"Because I'm a teenager! Nobody tells us anything!"

Alec gripped the steering wheel, his hands aching. "Devlin, the only thing I have ever not told you was that your mother might die. The rest of your life I've been honest with you."

Trying for his usual sneer, Devlin said, "That's kind of a biggie, don't you think?"

"Yeah. It was a biggie. That's why . . ." Alec's face worked as he fought to keep from crying. "That's why I lied to myself."

Devlin drew a shuddery breath and said nothing for a long while. Finally, his voice sounding terribly young, he asked, "What difference does it make anyway? Whether I believe you?"

Alec looked at his son. "Doesn't it matter to you? Whether I'll be there to see you play your first varsity basketball game, make you go to bed early the night before you take your SATs? If I'll be in the audience when you graduate from high school, and then college? Whether I'll meet your fiancée some day?"

Devlin was openly crying now. "I don't . . . I don't want it . . ."

"To matter?" His own eyes wet, Alec pulled his son into his arms. "I know. It hurts to lose someone you love."

Face against his father's shoulder, the fourteen-year-old cried like the child he still was. Alec held him, and cried, too.

Kathleen, Helen, Ginny and Emma arrived home the next night, exhausted. Logan met them at the front door. He kissed his wife, hugged Emma and then looked at Helen.

"Alec called."

Feeling hollow inside, she said, "I hope you didn't promise I'd call him back."

He didn't say anything, just looked at her steadily. She was the one to shift her gaze away.

After an awkward moment, he asked, "Anybody hungry?"

"Not me," Helen said. "I'm going to take a bath and go to bed."

Leaning against her husband, Kathleen pleaded, "Let's not do the fair again, okay?"

"Never!"

"We still have a week to go," Kathleen moaned.

A small whimper escaped Helen. "Bedtime," she told Ginny, who nodded and trudged upstairs with her.

She let her daughter have the bathroom first, then tucked her in. Ginny's arms clung for a moment longer than usual.

"I love you, Mommy."

She tried to smile. "I love you, too."

"Maybe . . . maybe Alec won't die."

Helen flinched. "Honey . . ."

Her daughter's anxious eyes stayed fixed on her. "He said it's not true."

"That's not really the point." She

309

smoothed Ginny's hair back from her forehead. "He lied to me. That's what really bothers me."

"What if he does die, and you never know?"

She tried to hide her shudder. "Ginny, I was dating him. Now I've decided that it isn't a good idea. I'm only sorry if you got attached to Alec and Lily."

Ginny's voice wavered. "What would happen to Lily if her dad died?"

All the questions she'd asked herself a million times, uttered aloud in her daughter's high, young voice.

Swallowing hard, Helen said, "She has an aunt and uncle. She and Devlin would live with them." Before Ginny could say another word, Helen kissed her again and stood. "Now, go to sleep. You have school tomorrow."

Ginny let her get almost to the door. "I'm sorry you're so sad, Mommy."

Helen paused, nodded and escaped.

In the bathroom, with hot water running into the tub and steam filling the small space, there was no one to know she was crying. Ignoring her tears, she poured bubble bath under the stream of water, undressed and climbed into the tub. Blessed heat enveloped her and she slid low, the

310

sweet scent of raspberries mixing with the salt of her tears on her lips.

What if he does die, and you never know?

Her face convulsed. Inside, she cried, *I can't watch him die! I can't, I can't, I can't! Don't ask me to. Please don't ask me.*

What if he had a heart attack tonight? Tomorrow? Next week? Helen imagined his children having to cope, sitting in the hospital waiting room, their father lying, face gray, on a narrow bed in the cardiac care unit, oxygen hissing and the ragged line of his heartbeat hobbling across a monitor. What if they couldn't reach their aunt or uncle right away, and were alone?

She had grown fond of them. Of the tall, gawky girl who wanted to be a teenager but wasn't quite yet, who'd been kind to Ginny and welcoming to the woman her father brought home. Oddly, however, it was Devlin who twisted her heart. He was in such turmoil already. How could he possibly deal with losing his father, too? Especially if they never cleared the air, if he had to live with the memory of how hatefully he had shoved his dad away?

Or was she misreading him? What he'd done yesterday was cruel. He must have seen in their faces that something had changed after they rode the Ferris wheel.

He'd been afraid that Alec had asked her to marry him. Either he detested her, or he couldn't bear the thought of anyone replacing his mother.

But, with an intensity that burned through her, Helen was glad he had spoken up. What if she'd already *married* Alec when she found out he had a damaged heart? What would she have done then?

She knew. She would have hated him, just as she hated him now. He had let her care, knowing . . . knowing . . .

Helen couldn't even finish the thought. Tears spurted afresh, clogging her nose, blurring her vision.

How could he have done such a thing? She simply couldn't believe he hadn't once, in all the times they'd talked about hospitals and illness and death, thought, *Oh, I should mention my heart attack.* He'd let her believe he was a fit, athletic man without a thing wrong with him.

Bitterness and grief swelling her own heart until it felt it might burst, she remembered telling herself blithely that lightning wouldn't strike twice. She'd been a fool. Such a fool!

She had really believed he loved her, but he couldn't have, or he wouldn't have lied. Not about the one thing he knew mattered so much to her. How had he justified it to himself? Had he thought, *She'd ask if she really wanted to know?*

What if she had?

Her inner voice suggested, *You could have asked for a bill of health. As if he were a horse you were buying.*

Helen sat up so suddenly water splashed over the rim of the tub. Agitated, she pulled the drain, let a few inches out, then pushed the plug back in and turned on the hot water again.

It wasn't that! she argued. She wouldn't have cared if he had a gimpy knee or an ugly scar or . . . or asthma. She just couldn't watch him die.

Doctors do clear arteries, close holes in the heart, mend valves, her voice reminded her. *A heart attack* didn't *mean he was going to drop dead in the next five years. Any more than a diagnosis of cancer was a death sentence. Just because Ben died . . .*

But he did. He did. And Alec had had a heart attack. Not just chest pains. His heart must have been damaged, at least a little, however he denied it.

What hurt so dreadfully was that, with the way things had ended, she felt as if he *had* died. One minute they'd been spinning on the Ferris wheel, colored lights sparkling as other rides whirled, the night air cool, his voice husky.

Helen Schaefer, will you marry me? I love you.

Inside, she had been crying, *Yes! Yes!* Her caution had been hard-won. But still, she'd known that she *would* say yes, once she had . . . oh, convinced herself that she'd thought it through and made a sensible decision, that love weighed more heavily on the scales than risk.

Then, still dizzy from the ride and the kiss and the amazing, extraordinary knowledge that she had been wrong and she *could* love again, the wheel spun one more time and the dreams were torn away like lace from a wedding veil.

It couldn't have been any more stunning if he'd had a heart attack and been whisked off in an ambulance. If, between one heart-beat and the next, he'd died, exposing all her careful reasoning for the tower of justifications it had really been.

Love versus risk. When she stopped cheat-ing, the risk side sank as if it carried a lump of lead, the love nothing but a mound of airy feathers, pretty but insubstantial with-out lies to weigh them down.

Letting the water drain from the tub, Helen stood and toweled off, wrapping her wet hair.

She'd found out in time. It hurt, but not as much as it would have a few months from now.

Or so, mocked her inner voice, *you'd like to believe.*

Devlin claimed that he didn't need to hear Dr. Ritter's take on his dad's health, but Alec called anyway. The doctor agreed to meet them for a quick lunch in the Harborview Hospital cafeteria.

The teenager was subdued, skulking at his father's back as they made their way through the labyrinth. Alec saw him stealing glances into rooms as they passed, his expression one of horrified fascination. After all, Alec remembered, Dev's only experience of hospitals had been the six weeks of his mother's dying.

Dr. Ritter was a big, bluff man with the long-fingered hands of a surgeon and an open face. Squint lines fanned from the corners of his eyes, his nose crooked and bulbous. Highly respected, he was also a nice guy.

"Hey, Devlin." He clapped Alec's son on the back hard enough to make him stagger. "Good to see you. Let me grab some food, and then we can talk."

Alec took a tray and followed. He and the cardiologist both chose the vegetarian chili in a bread bowl. Devlin set a sandwich and a muffin on the tray.

They found an out-of-the-way table and Ritter began eating hungrily. Alec guessed that he was used to interruptions and knew enough to gobble when he had the chance.

"I hear you have questions," the doctor said finally.

Devlin flushed, a curse of the fair-haired. "Yeah. I mean, I just thought after a heart attack, Dad would probably have another one. And, um, he says he's fine."

Ritter nodded, expression serious, and said, "Cardiac care has come a long way, Devlin. Before we had angioplasty, your dad would have been in trouble. We'd have done a bypass, but those are more likely to plug up, or have a graft fail. But, see, we think we actually fixed the root problem for him. His cholesterol is good, the walls of his arteries aren't thickening."

Alec watched as Ritter continued to talk and eat, drawing sketches on his napkin to illustrate points.

Devlin nodded and peered at the napkin and asked questions that didn't have anything to do with his dad but everything to do with cardiac surgery. They talked about

316

what a beating heart looks like when the chest is cracked open, how plugged places were pinpointed, where cuts are made to remove a dying heart and replace it with a donated one.

Ritter talked with passion about new frontiers in medical care while making what he did understandable to a fourteen-year-old boy. When his pager went off and he excused himself, Devlin sat with mouth slightly agape watching him go.

"Wow!" he said finally.

"Quite a guy, huh?"

Devlin turned dazed blue eyes on his father. "Do you think I'm smart enough to do that kind of stuff?"

"Yeah. I think you're plenty smart. It just takes a lot of years of school. Four for college, four for med school, then years more of internships and residencies."

"Yeah, but . . . !"

Alec grinned. "Let's start with high school. Okay?"

"Yeah!" his son said. He bit enthusiastically into his sandwich. "That was *so* cool."

He chattered on, repeating half the things Ritter had said, as if Alec hadn't been there listening. Alec, peeling an orange, looked up when Devlin fell silent.

Sounding troubled, he said, "I wish I'd,

like, asked you. I've been a jerk, haven't I?"

"Yeah. You have."

Earnestly he said, "It would be okay if you marry Helen. If she's not too mad."

Alec pushed away his tray. "I don't think her being mad is the problem. She's afraid, like you were."

"But . . . but you're okay!" Dev stared in bewilderment. "Dr. Ritter said so."

"Helen's not going to believe it. She was barely working up the courage to think she might let herself love someone again." He smiled wryly. "Finding out that someone has already flirted with death pretty much sent her scurrying for cover."

"But you can make her listen to you." His voice cracked. "Can't you?"

"I don't know." Alec let out a slow breath. "I'll try. That's all I can do."

Devlin stared down at his sandwich as if it had sprouted mold, then slowly wrapped it. "I'm sorry, Dad."

The ache in Alec's chest was half pain, half joy. "You know, I'm not. I think maybe you and I cleared the air, and I'm not sure how else we could have done it. As far as Helen goes, I was an idiot. I should have told her."

"But maybe she wouldn't have dated you."

"Maybe not." His mouth twisted. "But

honesty is always better."

His son frowned. "If she really loves you, she'd want to be with you even if you did have another heart attack. Wouldn't she? And, like, if she doesn't, maybe she doesn't love you that much."

"The thought," Alec admitted, "has occurred to me. I guess this was one way to find out."

"Maybe," his son said, brightening, as they bused their trays, "by the time you have another heart attack *I'll* be able to, like, run my Roto-Rooter up there and ream out your arteries." The idea clearly held major appeal. "Or even crack your chest open."

Alec laid an arm across his son's shoulders for the first time in a long while and said, "Uh-huh. Sure. I'll, uh, try to hold out until you're qualified."

Devlin thought that was the funniest thing he'd heard in years.

CHAPTER FOURTEEN

Alec left several more phone messages but didn't go so far as to show up on the doorstep, for which Helen was grateful. She could be strong as long as he wasn't standing in front of her.

It was bad enough that she had to argue with Jo and Kathleen. Not with Logan — he expressed his opinion with just a glance or the lift of an eyebrow, every time he found out she was ignoring yet another message.

Kathleen and Jo were more verbal.

Kathleen had her say almost every night. Jo took the day shift.

"Don't you love him?" she demanded.

The Puyallup Fair over, the kids all in school, Jo had taken to dropping in on her days off, or in the morning before she went to work.

Helen, who was writing prices on tiny tags to put on boxes and baskets of soap, didn't look up. "You here again? I thought you didn't live with us anymore."

Jo ignored this piece of rudeness, dropping into a chair at the kitchen table. "Kathleen says you still haven't called Alec."

Helen studied her tidy handwriting — *25*. It was so darn neat, she wondered about her psychological health. Kathleen, the control freak, had a bold, nearly unreadable scrawl. Go figure.

"Helen."

She still didn't look up. "No. I haven't called him. I don't intend to."

"Why?"

The question sounded genuine, so she finally sighed and met Jo's dark, worried eyes. "Because he lied to me, and I find that unforgivable."

"Would you have dated him if you'd known?"

"No."

She pulled the next basket toward her. This one was larger, holding a selection of bath oil, soaps, shampoo and body scrub — *45*.

"Then he had no chance with you at all."

She shook her head.

"You won't let yourself love him because he isn't perfect." Jo sounded like the voice of Helen's conscience.

Helen closed her eyes. "You know it isn't that. I could accept anything but . . ."

"A fatal flaw."

She winced. "I can't go through that again. I can't, Jo. You saw me. You know what it did to me."

Jo laid a hand over hers. "I do know. But I also know from Emma that Alec claims the heart attack was minor and that his cardiologist doesn't expect a repeat."

Helen's nostrils flared. "Why should I believe him? He lied by not telling me in the first place! Now he's trying to soft-pedal it. Would *you* believe him?"

"I don't know." Jo squeezed her hand then let it go. "I just wish you'd talk to him. Give him a chance to explain. Maybe . . ."

"Maybe what?" She sounded so hard! Helen realized. So unlike herself. "Maybe it'll turn out he had amnesia and didn't remember that he'd had a heart attack?" Sarcasm wasn't her usual style, either.

"Maybe," Jo suggested quietly, "he was afraid, too."

Helen sagged. "Don't do this to me, Jo."

"Afraid he'd let things get too far. Afraid if he told you, you'd do exactly what you have done — reject him. Afraid to face his own mortality."

She hated to think of him afraid to die.

He'd told her how desperately he had fought his wife's fate. What had it been like, so soon after, to discover that his own body was betraying him, that his kids might be orphaned? Every time she imagined the moment when somebody said, "Mr. Fraser, you're having a heart attack," she drew a curtain across the thought and refused to empathize.

Protecting himself, he'd hurt her. How could she forgive that, even if she could face loving a man whose heart was already damaged?

But how could she go on without him? How could she go back to the modest dreams she'd once considered adequate, the ones in which she bought her own house, raised her daughter alone, celebrated milestones with friends instead of a mate? Slept alone, worried alone, cried alone?

"He can't love me." And here, Helen saw with stark surprise, was her greatest fear of all. "Not really. Or he couldn't have set me up this way."

"But he didn't love you at first," Jo argued. "He liked you, he was attracted. No man is going to say, 'By the way, I had a heart attack,' the first time he meets a woman or takes her out. Is he?"

Biting her lip, Helen looked down. No.

That probably wasn't the kind of thing anybody talked about on a first date. She and Alec had gotten unusually close early on, because of the connection forged by the knowledge that both had lost a spouse.

"But later? When we talked about hospitals, and how they smelled and the sounds and what it's like to sit for hours at someone's side and watch them sleep? Why not then?" Helen was dismayed to hear herself pleading, longing for a reasonable explanation.

Gently Jo said, "Why don't you ask him?"

Tears stinging her eyes, she shook her head. "I can't. I just can't."

"You don't miss him?"

Miss him? Not a minute went by that she didn't think *I have to tell Alec about that,* or wonder what he was doing, what he'd said to Devlin, how school was going for Lily. Not an hour went by when she didn't think of his kisses or the husky note in his voice when he said, "I love you."

She had survived this long — ten days — by erecting a kind of wall. She knew how to endure, how to count the days until grief eased enough to let her forget, first for a few minutes, then a few hours, and finally even days. She did not think, *I'll never see him again.*

Or, worse yet, *What if he has a heart attack, and there is no one at his bedside to hold his hand and believe, however foolishly, that he will get better?*

The question would begin to form, and she wouldn't let it.

"I miss him," she said, almost inaudibly.

Relentless, Jo asked, "Do *you* love him?"

Throat thick with tears now, Helen gazed not at her friend but into a future without him. She was nodding when the first tears fell.

Jo held her while she cried, got her paper towels to mop up, murmured reassuring but meaningless things like "It's okay," over and over.

It isn't okay! Helen thought with a violence foreign to her nature. Despite all her vows, she'd let herself love Alec, and he'd hurt her.

In some ways, it was almost worse than losing Ben. Ben hadn't wanted to go, had done anything, everything, to stay with her. But when he died, it was final. Horribly, painfully, wrenchingly final.

There was no possibility she would see his name in the newspaper someday, or come face-to-face with him at a craft fair or the grocery store.

Ben had not taken children with him

whom she'd always worry about, wonder about, even miss.

She couldn't have had Ben back if she could just forgive a small lie. And — oh, yes — accept that she would have to watch him die all over again.

Jo watched her mop her tears. "I'm sorry. I didn't say anything you haven't already thought a million times, did I?"

Helen looked at her from swollen eyes. "Am I a coward? Were you afraid, Jo?"

Her petite, dark-haired friend gave a twisted smile. "Are you kidding? I was terrified! Ryan represented my deepest fears. I knew — *knew* — everything that makes life exciting or meaningful ends the moment you say 'I do.' I was sure that's how my mother had felt, giving up a singing career to marry my father and have children. After she died, Dad made it plain that Boyce and I were nothing but a duty. It was like —" she hunched, remembering, her eyes dark with pain "— he felt not one moment of joy in us. *That's* what marriage and parenting were, to me. Sacrifice, duty, joylessness."

"And you had to fall in love with a man who already had children."

"Yeah." Jo grimaced. "I'd just about come to terms with falling in love, figuring we'd have the kids only during holidays, and then their mom ditched 'em."

"But you're not sorry?"

"That I married Ryan? Or that we have his kids?" This smile was everything the last hadn't been: brimming with joy. "Not for a second. I love him, and I love them."

Helen sighed. "I suppose this was meant to encourage me to overcome my fears, et cetera, et cetera."

"Something like that." Jo grinned, in her pixie way. "Did it work?"

Helen looked down, wrote *25* although she had no idea what she was stickering, and said, "Nope."

But Helen knew this wasn't the end of it. None of her friends or housemates gave up easily.

It wasn't them she had to convince, anyway; it was herself. She was the one who threatened her own determination to stand firm.

She was the one who thought, *If I really love him, can't I forgive him?* And, *If I love him, would I want to be anywhere but at his side if he did have another heart attack?*

She was the one who lay awake at night and thought, *I am grieving, but he hasn't died. I'm grieving because I'm afraid I might have to grieve someday.*

Did that make any sense?

■ ■ ■ ■

"Telephone." Logan held it out to Helen.

She gazed at it as if a snake might slither from the mouthpiece. "Who is it?"

He shrugged. "Don't know."

"Not Alec."

"Nah, it's a kid."

Reluctantly she took the phone. Was one of Ginny's friends calling? How odd.

"Hello?"

"Um . . . is this Helen?"

Her heart skipped a beat, the voice was so like his father's. "Devlin?"

"Yeah, it's me."

He sounded so grave, she groped behind her for a kitchen chair and sank into it, conscious of Logan taking a step forward.

"What is it? Did your dad . . ." Her throat closed and she couldn't finish. "Is he all right?"

"What? Oh, yeah. I mean, he's really bummed. Every time I see him, he's staring into space with this expression on his face like . . . like someone died." He took an audible breath. "He looks like he did after Mom died."

Helen closed her eyes.

"And I know it's my fault. Because of

328

what I said."

Waving off Logan, she summoned the composure, or perhaps the kindness, to say, "Not altogether. Your motives may not have been the best, but you asked that your father be honest. In one way, I'm glad you did."

"Yeah, but the thing is, I was wrong!" Devlin burst out. "Dad took me to talk to his cardiologist, and he explained everything! He was so cool! He told me about heart transplants and stuff like that."

She swallowed. "Because . . . because your dad needs one?"

"Huh?" he said, startled. "Oh. No. Just 'cuz I asked. It's like, they can do these incredible things! I'm thinking that's what I might do. Be a doctor. Not the kind who, you know, swabs your throat and gives you an antibiotic. A surgeon. Maybe a heart one."

If she weren't so close to crying, she would have laughed. Alec's son had discovered his vocation — or, at least, a temporary enthusiasm — in the unlikeliest of places.

"I'm glad it was interesting," she said with restraint.

"So, you see?"

"No, actually, I don't," Helen admitted.

"Dr. Ritter said Dad is right. They *did* fix what was wrong, and he should be okay. He says they can always, like, ream out the spot again. He said Dad's health is great. Heart attack, I mean, that sounds like he's going to die, right? That's what I thought, but I was wrong. And . . . and I wanted you to know. So maybe you'd talk to Dad. Because —" his voice cracked "— he really misses you."

Now she was crying. Through the mist, she saw Logan's worried face, and she gave him a tremulous smile even as she said, "I thought you didn't like me."

Sounding flustered, Devlin mumbled, "I, um, it wasn't that. You're . . . I mean, you're cool and everything. It was, like, me and Dad. But we're cool now, too."

She blinked and sorted out this muddled recitation. "You wouldn't mind if your father and I got married."

"Right!" Obviously pleased that she was as sharp as he'd hoped, he said, "So, you'll call Dad? Or go see him?"

Laughing through her tears, she said, "Yes. I will call your father."

With deep significance, he said, "I have football practice tomorrow. And Lily is going to the mall with a friend. We'll both be gone *all* afternoon."

"Devlin, thank you."

"It's okay. I mean, if you're okay."

330

She was still laughing and crying when she hung up.

Logan laid a hand on her shoulder. "Are you okay?"

He didn't seem to get it when she laughed even harder, until the tears were from happiness and not grief.

Alec had all but begged to go with Lily, her friend Yolanda and Yolanda's mother to the mall. With grim humor, he could just see it: Yolanda's puzzled mother and he getting chummy over lattes at Starbucks while the girls squealed over cute shirts in one of those teenage shops.

Hanging out at the mall with no purpose — and no Helen — was just about the only thing he could think of that sounded worse than slumping behind his desk pretending to work when he really felt like he'd been hit by a Burlington Northern freight train.

Or he could go watch football practice.

Slumping lower, he thought, *Uh-huh.* And embarrass his son, who was just now remembering how to smile in his father's presence.

The doorbell rang, and for a moment he didn't move. It would be one of the kids' friends. Or a neighbor wanting Devlin to mow their lawn, or Lily to babysit.

But they'd both be exasperated to miss a job because Dad was too depressed to answer the door.

Aching all over, Alec got to his feet and went to the front door. He opened it to find Helen on the other side.

She was . . . beautiful. Her incredible hair, shining in the sun, was slipping out of a loose topknot. She wore a green-and-white oxford cloth shirt loose over a white tank top and chinos. Soft pink toenails peeked out of sandals. He saw, because he gaped, looking her over from head to toe.

She was a mirage. A figment of his imagination. He'd blink, and Mrs. Peirson from two doors down would be standing there instead.

So he didn't blink.

"Uh . . . may I come in?"

Not Mrs. Peirson's voice.

"Helen?" His voice was ragged, disbelieving.

Looking distinctly uncomfortable, she nodded. "I was hoping to talk to you."

"Talk to me?" He sounded like an idiot. He'd only left ten messages on her answering machine, begging her to talk to him! Now he sounded like he didn't know what she meant. "Please." Still stunned, he stepped back. "Come in."

He led the way into the little-used living room. Neutral territory.

"I can't believe you're here."

She flushed. "It . . . took me a while."

He was afraid to ask what had taken her a while. To forgive him? To decide to hear his side? Or to march over here and tell him where to go?

"I'd about given up." He moved his shoulders to relieve tension. "Please. Sit down."

She nodded and sat at one end of the couch, perching on the edge of the cushion, her back straight, knees together, hands clasped on her lap. The image of a lady, or a woman ill at ease.

They glanced at each other; Helen was nibbling on her lower lip and he was trying not to hyperventilate. When the silence stretched too long, both rushed into speech at once.

"I came to say . . ." she began.

"Helen, I never meant . . ."

Laughing uncomfortably, they stopped.

"Will you let me say I'm sorry first?" he asked.

She gave a tiny nod.

"It . . . genuinely never crossed my mind that my heart attack was an issue between us, or was important enough to mention." Alec grimaced. "That sounds incredibly stupid, I realize now. I've spent a good deal of time trying to figure out what I was thinking, and all I can come up with is that I didn't want to admit even to myself that there was anything major wrong with me." He rubbed his hands on his thighs. "I seem to be good at denial. I didn't — wouldn't — believe Linda was dying. Despite the thunderclap of being proved wrong — or maybe because of it — I refused to think of what happened to me as anything but a wake-up call." He laughed with a certain grim humor. "That's what I called it in my own mind. A wake-up call. Gosh, middle age is looming. Better start eating better, exercising, taking those vitamins." He took a deep breath and met Helen's eyes, dead on. "I was scared, Helen. Mainly for the kids, I think. I soft-pedaled my heart attack to them, too. Nothing for them to worry about." He was sweating. He rubbed his palms on his jeans again. "Only thing is, Dev didn't believe me. And I didn't notice."

"That was it, then? He thought you were going to die?"

"In a nutshell. Why say goodbye later when you can do it now?"

Her cheeks reddened. In a low voice, Helen said, "I do understand. That's what I was doing, too, you know. I had to get over being mad before I realized I was as sad as if you *had* died. Only, you hadn't. I'd done it to myself."

Hope swelled in his chest. *As sad as if he had died.* She wouldn't have felt that way if she didn't love him, would she?

"I need you to know," Alec said, "that I wasn't deliberately lying to you. Devlin hit me up a couple of weeks before that scene with you, asking if I'd told you 'the truth' yet. I had no idea what 'truth' he was talking about."

"Why would you, if he'd never expressed concern about your health?"

"What I can't figure out is why I didn't notice right away that his attitude toward me had changed. We could have saved a lot of heartache — if you'll forgive the pun," he added, "if I hadn't taken a year to start asking what went wrong. By then, I didn't tie the two things together."

"He called me, you know."

"What?" *Devlin?*

She smiled crookedly. "Your son. He told me you took him to see your cardiologist. He expressed great enthusiasm for cracking open chests and doing heart transplants, which really scared me. I thought he was telling me you were going to have to have one. But, no. He apparently wants to do

335

them. It took a while to get him back to the point of the call, which was that Dad was bummed, it was his — Devlin's — fault, and Dr. Ritter had convinced him that you really are okay. He said — I quote — that him and you are cool now."

Alec winced at his son's grammar. "I had no idea he'd think of doing anything like that. I'm . . . amazed. Somehow, as bad as these past two years have been, Devlin is still turning out to be a great kid. I don't know how that happened."

"Maybe," Helen's voice softened, "he has a great dad."

"If incredibly dense." He drew a shaky breath. "Is that why you came? Because Devlin asked you to? Because he told you I was okay?"

Tears glittered in her brown eyes. "No. You may never believe me, but . . . no. I've already decided that I couldn't bear it if you had a heart attack and died and I wasn't here. I'm afraid —" she tried to laugh and failed "— I was being a martyr in my own mind. You know. 'I must rush to his side and nobly, whatever the cost to me, give him my loving support.' I'm embarrassed, but, uh . . ." She worried her lower lip some more, then met his eyes, her own open and vulnerable. "It's also the truth. I want to be with you, whatever happens. To either of us. If you'll forgive me for . . . for not listening. For being afraid."

The rush of relief was so intense, it weakened him for a moment. When it ebbed enough to let in other emotions, Alec rose to his feet and took the few steps to her. "Forgive you?" His throat felt raw. "You haven't done anything, *anything,* that needs forgiveness. I'm the idiot who almost cost myself the chance with the woman I love."

Her eyes never leaving his, Helen stood, too. With a soft sigh, she wrapped her arms around his waist and leaned against him, her face pressed into his chest. "I love you," she whispered. "I love you."

Alec's arms locked around her, and he pressed a kiss on the top of her head. Oh, no, he was crying! These last weeks had been awful. Knowing he'd hurt her in the way she dreaded most had torn at him as painfully as the awareness that his idiocy — no, his cruelty! — had driven her away. He was lucky beyond belief to have met her, to have been persuasive enough to make her think she might overcome her own terrors to take a chance on him.

Then he'd blown it.

And now . . . now, she was in his arms, crying on his shirtfront, holding him as if she'd never let go. He must have made a muffled sound, because she looked up, eyes wet and mouth tremulous.

Alec kissed her with all the desperation of a man who'd thought he would never be able to again. She tasted of tears and coffee and *Helen,* a mix that went to his head as no glass of wine ever had. Hands on each side of her face, fingertips in her hair, he kept kissing her until he was drunk on her taste and her textures and her tremors.

"I love you," he muttered against her mouth, and kissed her yet again.

She strained up on tiptoe to press herself nearer to him, her arms leaving his waist to snake around his neck. The next time they drew breath, it was Helen who whispered, "I missed you. Oh, I missed you so dreadfully!"

Swallowing, he asked, for the second time, "Will you marry me?"

This time, her gaze didn't glance away. Instead, tears welled again in her eyes. "Yes. Please."

Relief would have knocked him off his feet if he hadn't had Helen for a prop. In a guttural voice, he said, "I thought I'd lost you."

Smiling through her tears, Helen whispered, "No. Never. You . . . scared me, asking for a commitment. Devlin gave my panic an excuse to flare. But I was too miserable without you not to fight it."

"I was about ready to lay siege to your house," he admitted.

Her smile faded, leaving pure emotion brimming in her eyes. "I'm lucky you're such a stubborn man. If you hadn't pushed, from the very beginning, I would have spent a lifetime telling myself I was *content*." She said the word with loathing. "But I don't think, somewhere inside, I ever believed it."

"I felt only half alive without you." Alec shuddered. "I'm so grateful that I have my son back, too."

"When I told Ginny I was coming over here, she said, 'Yeah! Can we tear out the wallpaper in my bedroom?' "

He grinned. "The guest room? I never did like those flowers. No self-respecting artist wants her bedroom with anything but bare walls to allow room for her own vision."

Helen said dreamily, "I was thinking that your basement is unused."

"Soap storage?" His hand explored the curve at the small of her back. "We can't live in a house that doesn't smell like eucalyptus and vanilla and raspberries and sandalwood and . . ."

She took up the litany. "Tangerine and bay, comfrey and rosewater."

"All at the same time," Alec finished. "By all means, bring it on."

"Oh, good."

Hauntingly beautiful, she looked up at him. "I will love you forever."

"Till death do us part," he murmured, lifting his hands to meet hers, palm to palm. "And something tells me that won't be for, oh, say forty, forty-five years."

With a catch in her voice, Helen said, "I'm counting on it."

And then, in the most potent way possible, they embraced life and each other.

ABOUT THE AUTHOR

The author of more than sixty books for children and adults, **Janice Kay Johnson** writes Harlequin Superromance novels about love and family — about the way generations connect and the power our earliest experiences have on us throughout life. Her 2007 novel *Snowbound* won a RITA® Award from Romance Writers of America for Best Contemporary Series Romance. A former librarian, Janice raised two daughters in a small rural town north of Seattle, Washington. She loves to read and is an active volunteer and board member for Purrfect Pals, a no-kill cat shelter.

The employees of Thorndike Press hope you have enjoyed this Large Print book. All our Thorndike, Wheeler, and Kennebec Large Print titles are designed for easy reading, and all our books are made to last. Other Thorndike Press Large Print books are available at your library, through selected bookstores, or directly from us.

For information about titles, please call:
  (800) 223-1244

or visit our Web site at:
  http://gale.cengage.com/thorndike

To share your comments, please write:
  Publisher
  Thorndike Press
  10 Water St., Suite 310
  Waterville, ME 04901

MR. S